SHAY SAVAGE

Cover Design: Mayhem Cover Creations

Interior Formatting: Mayhem Cover Creations

Editing : Chayasara

DEDICATION

For Hunter and all the staff at Thirsty's Oasis: It's a blessing to have such an awesome place to hang out and unwind. I always feel like I'm coming home.

Special thanks to my street team, who helped me keep my sanity during this entire process. I don't know what I'd do without you all!

TABLE OF CONTENTS

PROLOGUE   1

ONE   3

TWO   16

THREE   26

FOUR   39

FIVE   49

SIX   68

SEVEN   85

EIGHT   96

NINE   108

TEN   120

ELEVEN   138

TWELVE   150

THIRTEEN   164

FOURTEEN   173

FIFTEEN   180

SIXTEEN   190

SEVENTEEN   205

EIGHTEEN   220

NINETEEN   230

TWENTY   246

EPILOGUE   258

OTHER TITLES | SHAY SAVAGE   265

ABOUT THE AUTHOR | SHAY SAVAGE   267

PROLOGUE

I'm not stupid.

Though I wasn't a straight A student, I got good grades in college and not only did well on tests, but I actually understood the material. I finished on time, didn't waste my parents' money, made some good friends, and ended up with a decent job that paid the bills.

I never considered myself a rash person. I was the exact opposite of spontaneous. I always thought things through before I did them. I rarely opened my mouth without thinking first. I thought about the impact of my actions on other people before I did anything.

Then I met *him*.

The alarm in my head went off immediately.

I ignored it.

"Stay here," Aiden commanded. His fingers tensed around the grip of his weapon. "Don't get out of this fucking car for any reason, you hear me?"

I couldn't answer. I still couldn't breathe, much less speak. I'd never so much as *seen* a gun in real life unless it was holstered on a police officer's belt, let alone been so close to one. I couldn't take my eyes off of the gleaming black metal.

Aiden opened the driver's side door and started to get out, the gun clasped tightly in his hand.

"Aiden?" I managed to croak as I tore my eyes away from his hand and back to his face.

He paused, halfway out the door.

"I'm so fucking sorry," he said again.

"What are you doing with a gun?" I whispered. I felt like my body was trying to shut down, and I wondered what going into shock felt like. For a second, the phone call from my mother informing me of Dad's heart attack filled my head. At this moment, the feeling of all my blood leaving my veins was similar to how I had felt when she had told me he was gone.

I focused on Aiden again and couldn't understand what I was seeing.

Everything my subconscious had been warning me about Aiden Hunter began to fill my head. All this time, I'd been telling myself not to judge him. All this time, I'd been convincing myself that everything was fine, that *he* was fine. Since the moment I had met him, I'd been trying to convince myself that the only danger was in my head.

But it wasn't.

The Aiden in front of me wasn't the man I had known the past week. His face was barely recognizable. His eyes were dark and full of hatred. His jaw was locked, and his teeth were clenched. He had gripped his hands into fists, one of which held a deadly weapon. This man was not the one who cooked breakfast for me. This was a man consumed with raw fury.

Echoed words from Lance's girlfriend flowed through my head: "I have never seen him mad, personally, but I hear it's not pretty."

No, it was not pretty. It was not pretty at all.

And with that, my life was forever changed.

ONE

The alarm went off. I fumbled around for the snooze button, smacked it multiple times until the noise stopped, and then dozed until it went off again.

I groaned, yawned, and stretched before shoving myself out of bed and starting my day. The normal routine began—pee, shower, wash my hair twice because that was what the bottle said to do, make coffee, eat oatmeal with blueberries in it, and drink a protein shake so I didn't have to lie to my mother if she called and asked if I had. There was absolutely nothing unusual about my morning.

There never was.

I gathered up everything I needed to take with me to work and quickly surveyed my condo. Nothing was out of place. The throw pillows were at the proper angle against each of the arms of my neutral-colored couch, the remote control was right at the edge of the coffee table, and each of the coasters was properly stacked in their tray. From the bookshelf, a conglomerate of heroines surveyed the room as if their twelve-inch forms could protect the place from intruders. Princess Leia and Queen Amidala from Star Wars were joined by Wonder Woman, X-Men's Storm, Spider Woman, and Buffy the Vampire Slayer.

"So, what's your plan for the day?" I asked Buffy. "Got some vampires to take out? Maybe a few demons?"

She didn't answer, not that I expected her to. Sometimes I liked to hear a voice in the empty room, even if it was my own.

"I'm heading off into the oh-so-exciting world of corporate project management," I informed the whole group. "I bet you wish your day was going to be as interesting as mine."

I had always had a thing for the superwomen of movies and comic books. They were the epitome of strength, valor, and living life on the edge. They protected the innocent with their cunning intelligence and dedication. They led exciting lives.

Unlike me.

I looked into their blank eyes and shook my head, wondering if I was losing my mind. It would just figure. Only I could drive myself into insanity just because I had nothing better to do.

Sighing, I left the figures to their enthralling lives on the shelf and carefully locked the door to my condo. It wasn't that I expected to be granted superpowers so I could go about ridding the world of nefarious criminals, but the whole idea was so far removed from project management, it was enough to leave me wondering if I was actually becoming clinically depressed. I'd refused all the usual anti-anxiety medications when Dad died, determined to cope with it all on my own though Dad's clinic partner and friend kept telling me I didn't need to do it by myself.

It had been two years since a heart attack took his life, and though I missed him dearly, I was now able to rejoice in memories of my father and his impact on my life. Using anecdotes from the lives of his patients, he had taught me to always watch my actions and my words. I was careful both with myself and with those around me.

Always.

I considered giving Mom a call this weekend to see how San Francisco was treating her. Moving from my childhood home in Ohio to start a new life had been her coping mechanism after Dad was gone. As a result, our relationship had dwindled to the point where we only saw each other on major holidays instead of multiple times a week. Having her most of the way across the country made me miss her, and my father, more.

I never told her that. I didn't want to upset her or make her think she should move back. It wouldn't be fair of me to put that kind of pressure on her. She needed to restart her life for her own sake, and I wasn't going to do or say anything to get in the way of her goals.

In my garage, my slightly-rusting Mazda was pretty far removed from an invisible plane, but it was the best form of transportation—the kind that was paid for and still ran pretty well as long as I remembered to get the oil changed on time. Instead of villains, I fought traffic on the highway and a co-worker for the last space in the parking garage.

Lost that battle.

I smiled and pleasantly greeted the security guard as I swiped my access badge and headed into the building, up the stairs, and to my cubicle space overlooking the parking area. I checked my calendar, grabbed my laptop, and hoped there wouldn't be donuts at the first meeting of the day.

I couldn't win a conflict with myself any more than I could rush to take a parking spot from someone whose eyes I might have to meet later on in the day. It wasn't that I had a problem standing up for myself—I didn't—but when it came to the little things, it seemed easier to just give in.

Some superheroine I would be.

Meetings went on, project plans were updated, and I worked through my lunch to make sure everyone who needed continuous information regarding the financial impact of this and that were all informed. The day, though typical, went just fine until the last hour.

The little hand on the clock overhead clicked toward the five. I blinked and took a deep breath. Under the table in the meeting room, I clenched my fists and tried not to visibly shake.

Across from me sat Kevin Stump, the rat-bastard who had been hired as my new boss just a few weeks ago. As if his inane smile and ridiculous, over-styled hair weren't enough to make me want to punch him, the crap that came out of his mouth was far, far worse.

"I realize you've only been with us a few weeks," I said through slightly gritted teeth, "but this upgrade is crucial. I know the business units aren't going to see immediate results, but if you look at the long-term capacity of the servers-"

"Miss Ellison," Kevin sat back in his chair and rolled his eyes,

"I'm well aware of how these things work. Everyone here seems to be under the impression that this company is somehow unique to others out there, but it's not. I know when an upgrade is needed and when it isn't. This one can wait."

"If you look at the data," I started to say as I pulled out some of my charts, but he interrupted me before I could explain.

"It's irrelevant," he stated. He ran his fingers over the top edge of his hair but not into the actual strands. One of them might get out of place if he did that. "I've seen it, and it doesn't show anything conclusively."

I blinked a few times as I imagined Buffy stepping out from the giant whiteboard behind Kevin's head and shoving a stake through his heart.

"But these spikes here..." I pointed to one of the charts, but he dismissed me with a wave.

"We're done here," he said. "Inform the team they can focus on projects that will actually earn this company some money."

I wanted to call him an idiot. I wanted to throw my laptop—or at least my pen—right at his Chia-head face. I wanted to invoke my most sarcastic side and spew forth commentary worthy of Scott Adams himself.

I didn't. I couldn't.

Aside from needing the job, I didn't want to actually hurt his feelings.

Kevin stood and left before I could say another word. I sat there for a few moments until I realized my mouth was open and I was sitting alone in a conference room. I slammed my laptop closed and headed out.

I was still fuming when I got back to my desk. It was going to take me at least another hour to inform everyone on the team that all the work they'd been doing for the past month was now completely worthless, and it was already almost time to leave for the day.

My phone rang, and I glanced down to see my best friend's face on the screen.

"I'm going to Thirsty's after work," Mare said in her usual chirpy tone. "Wanna join?"

I took a deep breath and drummed my fingers on my desk. It

had been a crap day in the corporate world, and Kevin was a big, fat jerk. Okay, so he wasn't fat, but he was an ass, and he'd been hauling me into pointless meetings since the day he arrived in the building. All he needed was the pointy hair to become a walking Dilbert cartoon character, but it just wasn't funny anymore. The last thing I wanted to do was work late in order to explain why the project was cut, and I wasn't even sure what to say about it. I just knew that as soon as I hit send, a bunch of people would show up at my desk and keep me here even longer.

A drink sounded pretty good.

"Yeah, okay," I said into the phone. "Anyone else going?"

"The usual crowd," Mare responded. "It is Friday after all."

"Count me in," I said.

"Cool! See you there about six, Clo."

I hung up and shook my head slightly at Mare's constant need for shortening everyone's name. She couldn't seem to actually call me Chloe any more than she would allow others to call her Mary. It was always just *Mare*, like a female horse. She would even introduce herself that way—"My name is Mare, you know—like the horse!"

I browsed through my email, decided there wasn't anything that couldn't wait until Monday, and gathered up my things to head home. Of course, I got stopped on my way out by three people in the hallway. News travels fast, apparently, and they all wanted to know why the project was being cut when it was an important upgrade and why I didn't make that clear to Kevin.

As tempting as it was to throw him under the bus, it just wasn't in my nature. Aside from that, and unlike a lot of my coworkers, I was single and had to rely on myself for everything. I couldn't risk pissing off the new executive without another job lined up, so I attempted to explain his faulty reasoning as best I could before escaping down the stairwell, out to the parking garage, and into rush-hour traffic.

I drove cautiously and courteously. I didn't cut anyone off. I paused to let others merge in front of me, even though it caused me to miss the light.

My empty condo greeted me with its earth tones, clean lines, and superheroines. Though I told people cleanliness was important to me, it really looked so spotless because I didn't have much else to do with myself in the evenings or on the weekends. I did have something that resembled a social life and often went to movies and dinner with friends, but ultimately I came back here to my solitary, sterile abode.

I popped in a DVD just to hear Princess Leia's voice as she confronted Darth Vader. Reciting the lines was better than talking to myself.

My closet was full of outfits for evening get-togethers, but I decided on a pair of jeans and a T-shirt I'd bought in San Francisco when I went to visit my mom last year. Thirsty's Oasis wasn't a dressy kind of place—just a nice sports bar with lots of big screens, plenty of beer on tap, and friendly bartenders. There would be a few people coming from work and still dressed up a bit, but the majority of the crowd was casual.

The television greeted me as I came back downstairs from the bedroom to the living room. The movie was nearly to my favorite part, and I was tempted to text Mare and tell her I wasn't going to make it after all. An evening with the *Original Trilogy* at home was sounding pretty good.

"Of course it does," I mumbled to myself.

Suddenly feeling overwhelmed, I sat down on the couch and put my head in my hands. I knew for a fact that I was just feeling sorry for myself, and that pissed me off. My mind wandered to Zach, my ex, but I refused to let myself dwell. It wasn't the lack of a man in my life—I could cope with that—but between thinking about my dad, dwelling over my mother's distance, and fuming over Kevin being a total ass, it seemed as if something in the universe was ganging up on me.

"I need a little action in my life," I informed Wonder Woman. "You need any help with some criminals? I bet your bracelets would fit me."

She stared down from her perch and didn't accept my offer.

I shoved myself off the couch with great mental effort and checked myself over in the mirror. Turning my head left, then right, I decided my curly brown hair wasn't going to get any better, given the humidity, applied a little more liner around my blue eyes, and decided I was good to go. Even if Wonder Woman had needed a little help, I would have come up with some excuse as to why I couldn't be of assistance. Maybe I'd consider it later when I had thought about all the ramifications of leaving my job and friends to go on some grand adventure, but not now, not when I hadn't prepared for it.

Thirsty's was packed, and at first, I couldn't find my group. I meandered through the crowd saying hello to a few people I recognized until I saw Mare frantically waving her arms from a high-top table near the back of the bar.

"I've had a shit day," I said as I approached.

Mare and Nate sat leaning closely against each other in that way people who haven't quite admitted they were interested in each other often do. I thought they would be the perfect couple if they would just get on with it already. He turned his lively dark eyes from Mare to me.

"Join the club!" Nate replied. He held up an empty shot glass with his meaty hand in salute. He was short with straight, blond hair and geeky black glasses that seemed to drive Mare absolutely wild.

"Shots already?" I said with a raise eyebrow.

"I'm pretty sure I'll be driving him home," Mare said with a wink. She tossed thick auburn hair off her shoulder and threw her arm around the back of Nate's stool.

"It's been that kind of week," Gabe said from the other side of the table where he sat. He was the ever-present bachelor of our group and seemed perfectly content to be so. He handed me his shot. He didn't drink anything but light beer.

"What the hell," I mumbled. I took the thankfully-sweet shot and dropped my glass to the table before ordering a vodka and orange juice, my standby drink.

"My boss is a jerk," I said.

"The new guy?" Nate asked. Though he wasn't on my team, we worked in the same office. I nodded, and he laughed, which made his hair shake around his ears. "Trying to make a name for himself already?"

"If he wants his name to be mud, then yeah," I mumbled. "He cancelled the server upgrade."

"Moron," Nate mumbled. He was a hardware guy and used to

getting the smelly end of the corporate budget. All of us worked in the information technology field except for Gabe, who Mare and I knew from high school. "I thought everyone was calling him Chia Head."

"Chia Head?" Mare echoed.

"He looks just like one," I informed her. "His hair is ridiculous. I think he's got about as much brains on the inside, too."

"That's why it pays to be your own boss," Gabe said.

"If you don't mind feeding dick to people," Nate said with a snicker.

Gabe smiled and balanced the bar stool on two legs, causing it to creak. He was a big guy with a smile that always made his eyes sparkle like he was about to do something mischievous. He often did, too. He was a pastry chef in his own bakery, and he specialized in one-of-a-kind cakes for various functions. He did your normal birthdays and weddings, but most of his business was titty cakes for bachelor parties and penis cakes for the bachelorettes and divorcees.

Apparently, it was quite a lucrative business.

"I've never fed dick to a woman who didn't appreciate it," he responded. His eyes twinkled as he winked at me.

I shook my head and rolled my eyes at him. I'd never had a thing with Gabe though we flirted with each other a lot. Many people thought we were going to eventually hook up, but it never happened. We had always kept things in the "just friends" realm.

"Hey, Chloe," Gabe said as he leaned across the table, "the shop said my car is officially kaput. You still up for helping me find a new one next week?"

"Sure," I replied. "I did some checking yesterday, and there are all kinds of sales going on starting Monday. Lease returns, mostly."

"Perfect!" Gabe gave me a big smile and his eyes lit up. "You're my hero!"

"Heroine," I corrected.

"Heroin," Gabe replied. "I'm totally addicted to your company!"

"Ha!"

And so the night progressed with talk of work-overload, lack of comp time, and overzealous bosses who didn't know what the hell they were talking about. Shots were brought around again, and I seemed unable to stop myself from joining with the rest of them. I even bought a round myself to keep the tabs even. It was the polite thing to do.

"Well, I gotta run," Gabe said as he ran his hand though his styled blond hair. He got up from his seat and threw some bills on the table. "If any of you guys need a ride that doesn't cost you an arm and a major organ, now is the time!"

I checked my phone to see the time. It was still pretty early, and the thought of returning to my empty condo did not sound appealing at the moment. If I left, my weekend would have started exactly how it had started last week and the week before. Probably the week before that, too. Drink, chat, back home to my couch and a movie, and grocery shopping in the morning.

No wonder I didn't bother to wear a watch; I could tell the time just from what I was doing next.

Mare and Nate weren't any less predictable, but at least they could end up going home together even if it turned out to be a casual hook up. I hadn't had a hook up in…well…ever. I didn't do that kind of thing. There had to be at least three dates first, then kissing, then maybe a little more, and after I was sure the relationship seemed to be going somewhere, only then was sex on the table.

While I wallowed, Gabe flicked his eyes from my face to my half empty vodka and row of shot glasses.

"Chloe, you need a ride?" he asked.

I should have gone. If I had just let Gabe drive me home right then and there, everything would have remained the same. I would have been at work on Monday morning. I wouldn't have found myself in a situation way beyond my control.

"Nah, I'm good," I said. "I'll hang a while longer."

"Suit yourself," Gabe replied. After a quick goodbye and promises of staying out later next week, he wandered through the crowd toward the door.

I turned back to Mare and Nate who were gazing into each other's eyes, practically oblivious to my presence.

Fabulous.

I tried to engage them in a little conversation, but the topic maneuvered its way back to a movie I hadn't seen yet. My mind wandered to other patrons of the bar for a bit, and then I realized I hadn't heard a word Mare had been saying.

What a lousy friend I am.

I tried to focus again on her words, nodding and agreeing that a second *Magic Mike* movie would be the bomb. Another screwdriver appeared in front of me, but I didn't recall ordering it. My head was definitely fuzzy, and I was starting to wonder how in the heck I was going to get home. All the shots were catching up with me, and I was starting to feel a little sick. Blinking made the table spin, and I quickly I excused myself to the restroom.

Walking proved more difficult than I thought it was going to be. As soon as I stood, I realized just how bad off I was. I held on to a couple of the stools as I made my way to the ladies' room, thankful that there wasn't a line. Once I got myself into a stall, I found I couldn't even hover over the seat like I normally would and plopped down on the cracked toilet with a grimace.

As wooziness overcame me, I steeled myself against the feeling, no longer caring about the cleanliness of the toilet seat. I swallowed hard, leaning over my thighs and telling myself I was *not* going to throw up. I just needed to focus a bit. Slow breaths. I hadn't had this much to drink in a while, and at five-foot four and a hundred and thirty pounds, I just couldn't hold my liquor like I could in college. Still, I had been considered a pro back in the day, and I wasn't about to lose it now.

I hoped.

With determination and some more meditative breathing, I finished up and fiddled with the lock on the stall. It outwitted me for a moment. The little sliding bolt just wouldn't move the right way to release the lock at first, but I eventually managed to get myself out. I stumbled forward as I approached the sink and tried to wash my hands, but the lack of soap in the dispenser only allowed me to rinse off. The towel dispenser was obviously in cahoots with the latch on the stall door and made it very difficult for me to get the couple of sheets of paper I needed to dry off my hands. Instead, a big pile of them fell out at my feet, which I found remarkably funny for some reason.

Still giggling, I used one of the fallen towels to open the door, balled it up, and tried to hold the door open with my backside while simultaneously tossing the paper into the trashcan near the sink. The force of the throw was apparently too much, and I stumbled out the door and into a brick wall.

It was pretty warm for brick and not nearly as painful on my back as I would have thought it would be. I leaned back against it some more and sighed. The dizziness returned, and I nearly fell forward. That's when the brick wall grew hands and arms, which wrapped around me and kept me from falling on my ass.

Still dizzy, I turned to find the brick wall was wearing a grey, cut-off muscle shirt, which did nothing to hide the graffiti-like tattoos all over the arms that held me steady as I tried to get my bearings.

Where am I?

Oh yes…Thirsty's, outside the bathroom.

I looked forward and focused my eyes on the chest in front of me. I had to tilt my head up to discover it was, in fact, not attached to a brick wall but an actual face that was way, way up in the air.

The guy was massive. Just massive. He was well over six feet tall with shoulders that took up nearly the whole width of the hallway.

"Hi there," the brick wall said in a deep, jocular voice. "You all right?"

Alarm!

It's not that Thirsty's was known for a lot of riff-raff or criminal activity of any kind. It wasn't. I never would have walked into the place if it were like that. It was a typical sports bar in the suburbs of southwestern Ohio, mostly catering to the pro football crowd whenever the Bengals played the Steelers. The usual clientele were locals blowing off steam from work or commiserating about their failed marriages. Occasionally, there were a few singles looking to hook up. Most of the people I saw there I had seen before, even if I didn't know them.

This guy did *not* belong here.

Wherever they keep the official entries for men your mother warned you about, this guy's picture would be at the top of the list.

His arms and chest bulged with muscles. He really did resemble a brick wall. I could see the outline of his abs through his shirt, stacked like the bricks around a fireplace. Every visible inch of his darkly tanned skin was completely covered by a myriad of tattoos. I couldn't focus on any one image without all of them blending together like the mosaic of a swiftly moving, graffiti-covered train car. His nearly black hair was the same length as the neatly trimmed beard covering his face, and dark eyebrows framed his greenish-brown eyes.

Maybe I was feeling a little of that southern haughtiness my grandmother was known for displaying whenever we walked through a Walmart when I was a child. Maybe I was going so far as to profile the guy for his height, insane number of tattoos, ripped jeans, muscle shirt, and assumption that he had a Harley parked somewhere outside. Maybe I was just in shock from the abrupt encounter itself.

Aside from all of that, he was absolutely gorgeous.

Maybe I'm just drunk.

"Yes," I finally said, hoping I sounded more convincing than I felt. "Sorry, I just lost my balance a bit."

"I see that," Brick Wall responded. He smiled, and his eyes lit up with amusement. He shifted his weight from one foot to the other, and his fingers tightened around my hips, causing a ripple up his arms.

Good lord, he had a lot of muscles—great big, bulging muscles that couldn't be hidden by his clothing.

"You need some help?" he asked.

"No, I'm good," I replied. I tried to wave my hand dismissively but realized it had a bit of a death-grip on Brick Wall's forearms. His hard, muscled forearms, which ran all the way up to ridiculously broad shoulders.

I stared into his eyes, which sparkled with amusement. My skin warmed, and I became acutely aware of his closeness despite my intoxicated state.

I cleared my throat.

"My friends are waiting for me."

I tried to pry my fingers off the muscled arms, but my hands seemed happy to hang onto him and made it difficult to release my grip. I finally talked my hands into releasing him enough for me to take a step back, and his arms dropped from my waist, leaving the voided space a little cooler than it had been when he was touching me.

I took another step back, and even from this new perspective, I still had to crane my neck to look into his eyes. They were deeply shadowed in the dim light, making them seem sinister enough that I shivered a little. His beard was short and looked more like a five o'clock shadow, but it didn't extend to his neck at all. Instead, it all flowed in a tightly groomed line from his sideburns and into his hair.

"Sorry," I said again.

"No worries," he replied.

I walked carefully around him to keep my footing, glancing back only once to see him watching me walk away with his dark eyes and amused grin. It ticked me off a little. The last thing I needed was some lowlife laughing at me, drunk or not. I turned my head away from him and tossed my hair back off my shoulder.

And with that, I marched back to my friends.

TWO

Though I was pretty sure my drink had been nearly empty, a full one was sitting in my spot. My head had cleared a little after the shock of running right into a complete stranger—a really big, brick wall of a stranger—and I sighed and wrapped my fingers around the glass. The bartender had made another strong one, and I could barely detect the tinge of orange from the juice in the glass.

"So what's the weekend plan?" I asked. I thought if I involve myself in more conversation, it might sober me up a bit.

"Helping my mom with her wedding plans," Mare said.

Mare's mother was about to try for husband number four. Mare was giving this one as much as a year, though the last had only survived about eight months. "We have to pick a photographer and a florist. You should totally come with me to pick the florist. I hate flowers."

"Maybe you could do something other than flowers," I suggested.

"Flowers are the norm," Mare replied. "If my mom doesn't get the norm, she'll throw a fit."

I pursed my lips, wondering why they didn't just go to a justice of the peace and have it done. It would seem she'd be tired of all the wedding planning stuff at this point. I know I would have been.

"I know that look," Mare said. "What are you trying not to say, Clo?"

I glanced at her, slightly pissed at myself for being so transparent, and shrugged.

"You never say what you're thinking," she told me. "Sometimes it drives me nuts. I know you have an opinion in there somewhere."

"It's not important," I said quietly, tensing under the scrutiny. "Just forget it."

"You're just too uptight," Nate said. He held up his glass and pointed at me with the one finger not wrapped around the drink. "Whatever you have to say is not going to hurt *my* feelings."

"That's her dad talking to her," Mare said as she gave me a playful shove in the shoulder. "Always think twice before you speak."

"Three times," I replied with a smile. "He was usually right, too. People are always saying and doing things they regret. I think most of his clients were suffering from regret-syndrome."

"Yeah, but he was a psychologist," Nate pointed out, "and his clients were there because they regretted what they said or did. I say what needs to be said, but I don't regret it."

"Well, I don't say or do anything out of line, so I don't have to worry about regrets."

Thankfully, that was the end of the topic. Well, at least outside my head. My own words seemed to be floating around in my brain even as the conversation turned back to flower hatred. "I don't say or do anything out of line." It was the truth, and a rule by which I'd lived my life. It kept me out of trouble, allowed me to advance fairly quickly in my career, and generally kept me safe.

And predictable.

As I pulled myself from my own thoughts, Mare and Nate had gone back to talking about the movie I hadn't seen. I tried to focus— I really did—but I had no frame of reference. I looked down at my glass and let my finger slide through the condensation. The patterns were far too interesting to my intoxicated mind, so I looked away and back over my shoulder to find something to distract me from my own thoughts.

I saw Brick Wall again.

He was sitting with two other guys in one of the booths against the wall. The one next to Brick Wall had light brown hair sticking out of a stocking cap and wore a black T-shirt with some band logo on it. The man sitting across from them looked to be wearing a blazer of some kind. He was definitely better dressed than the other two, but I couldn't see him very well with the back of the booth blocking my view. There far too much noise for me to hear their conversation, but Brick Wall definitely didn't look happy about whatever the guy across from him was saying.

Abruptly, Brick Wall stood up and lurched toward the guy in the blazer. The guy in the cap rose to his feet and grabbed Brick Wall's arm tightly, as if he could have held him back. Brick Wall had to have at least six inches on the guy and probably fifty pounds as well. However, he stilled his movements, curled his upper lip slightly, and then sat back down. His chest rose and fell with a deep breath as he looked away from his companions…

…and right into my eyes.

I jerked my head back around to my drink quickly as I felt my face warm, embarrassed to have been caught eavesdropping. Well, not exactly eavesdropping, but close enough. The hairs on the back of my neck stood on end, and I wondered if he was still looking at me. I wasn't about to turn around and find out. I was still horrified that I had been caught staring at the same guy I had rammed into a few minutes before.

"Clo?"

"Hmm?" I glanced back at Mare's face as she raised her eyebrows.

"A little lost in thought there?"

"Yeah, sorry."

"I was asking if you were busy Tuesday after work." She leaned an elbow on the table. "We could hit a couple florists then."

"Sure," I replied.

The server returned, and I asked for a glass of water.

"I need to get moving if I'm going to make it to Mom's in the morning," Mare said as she handed her credit card to the server. She turned to Nate. "I assume you need a ride."

"I sure as hell ain't driving," Nate responded. "I just hope you aren't planning on taking advantage of my drunken state."

Mare chuckled.

"You good, Clo?"

"I'm going to drink my water," I told her. "I'll be fine in a bit."

"You sure? I can take you now."

"No, I'm good." I waved my hand around dismissively. "I need to hit the grocery store tomorrow, and I don't want you to have to bring me back to my car. I'll just hang a bit."

"You've had a lot," Mare stated. "Be careful and call a cab if you have to."

"I will."

Mare and Nate walked out, arm in arm. I finished the water but still wasn't in great shape, so I asked for another one when the server brought over my bill. I didn't even look at how many drinks were on it, just handed him my card.

As I sat at the now empty table, I felt life crashing all around me. It was probably just the alcohol talking, but it seemed like everyone around me had things to do and people to be with, while I sat on my own. I missed my dad and our long conversations. When Mom moved so soon after his death, it seemed as if I had lost her, too.

I felt tears in the corner of my eyes.

Oh, hell no. I was not going to be the crying drunk girl at the bar. I needed to get myself outside for some fresh air.

I stood abruptly and pushed back my stool, striking the person walking behind me.

"Damn, girl!"

I spun around to see whom I had hit, got my foot caught on the bottom of the leg of the stool, and fell forward—into Brick Wall's arms.

Again.

He lifted me into the air with no effort whatsoever and placed me on my feet. My shirt had ridden up in the process, and when he placed his hands on my sides to hold me steady, they ended up on my skin just above my jeans. He laughed.

"We have to stop meeting like this."

"I'm so sorry!" I cried.

"Then again, I'm starting to like it." His eyes twinkled as he looked down at me.

I was beyond flustered. Aside from the embarrassment of falling into the guy again, I was horribly distracted by the feeling of his hands on my sides. I could feel the grip of each of his long, warm fingers on my skin. He tightened his hold, and it sent a rush of sensation through my body, which focused right between my legs.

What the hell?

That little alarm in my head went off again, and I pushed away from him, barely stopping myself from falling backwards. I quickly straightened my shirt and steadied my footing. My heart was pounding, and my hands shook a little as I tried to regain some of my composure, failing miserably.

"It was just an accident." My voice sounded mousy and was was barely audible with the bar music blasting.

"Some accidents are good," he said.

I narrowed my eyes as he took a fast glance down my body. My drunken embarrassment was quickly turning into something else as my heart continued to beat frantically, and my palms got a little sweaty.

"Well, this was just your normal, everyday, bad accident." I swallowed hard and tried to figure out if what I had said made any sense at all.

"Well, I've specialized in train wrecks before," Brick Wall informed me, "so it's still all good from my perspective."

He took a half step closer to me, and I backed up and into the stool.

"I am not a train wreck!" I heard myself say. "I'm just a little…"

My words trailed into nothing as I contemplated what the rest of my sentence should contain. Again, I failed.

"You're a little cute," Brick Wall said.

I glared at him as my face warmed. I was in no shape for this sort of nonsense, certainly not with a guy like this.

A guy like what?

Alarm!

I needed to get the heck out of there.

"I'm a little out of here," I said haughtily. I turned slowly so I wouldn't lose my balance again and headed for the door.

Brick Wall followed me.

"Hey," he called out, "I wasn't trying to insult you or anything! Where are you going?"

I didn't turn around or respond even though I knew I was being rude by ignoring him. I still needed that fresh air—now more than ever. I shoved at the handle of the door, and inertia nearly slammed me into it. Realizing I was pushing the wrong side, I moved my hands over and tried again with much better success.

"Hey, babe," Brick Wall said as the door slammed shut behind him. "Really, where are you going?"

I concentrated on navigating the steps to the parking area and continued to ignore him. From behind me, I could hear him laughing, and I didn't like the sound of it at all. Angry and confused, I fished around in my purse until I came up with my car keys.

"Whoa!" Brick Wall exclaimed. "What do you think you're doing?"

"I'm going home!" I snapped back.

"Babe, you can hardly walk," he said. "There is no way you can drive."

My head swam again, and just to prove his point, I stumbled into the side of my car. A moment later, he was next to me, gently but insistently pulling the keys from my hands.

I turned, intending to get my keys back, but found my hands pressed against his massive chest instead. I didn't realize how close he was. With one hand right next to my head, he leaned against the car door. With the other arm extended behind him, he held my keys far from my reach.

"Give me those," I said. I wanted to sound strong and unafraid, like Princess Leia as she confronted Governor Tarkin, but the words came out as barely a whisper. I wanted to grab my keys from him, but his muscled and decorated arm was too intimidating.

"No can do." He shook his head slowly. "I can't let you go like this. Seriously, babe—you can't drive. Let me call you a cab or something."

I knew he was right. I just didn't want to be having this discussion with *this guy*. He didn't belong here. He belonged at the biker bar over by the Harley store or maybe in one of those gang-banger clubs downtown.

Did our downtown even have gang-banger clubs?

What the hell is a gang-banger, anyway?

Whatever it was, I was becoming increasingly sure he was one. I glanced around the parking lot, wondering if I should scream for help, but knew that would just cause a scene. He hadn't actually done anything wrong, and hadn't I embarrassed myself enough for one night? There wasn't anyone else in the parking lot anyway. Most of the cars were already gone, and I wondered just how long it had been since Mare and Nate left.

Why didn't I get a ride with them?

His body pressed closer to mine, and I looked up into his face again. His rough cheeks shadowed the rest of his features, and I wondered what they would feel like on my thighs.

Good lord, Chloe! What are you thinking?

Part of me was definitely thinking that he was really, really attractive, despite being nowhere near my type. My type was the same kind of guy Mare was attracted to—guys with glasses and degrees in engineering, like Zach had been. I didn't go for bad boys because they were…well, they were bad.

"I don't want a cab," I said. I needed to get my head back on straight and wondered if a screwdriver was going to be necessary. Then I remembered that screwdrivers were what got me here in the first place. "I just want to go home."

"Let me drive you, then?"

Images of me climbing onto the back of a souped-up Harley ran through my head. I'd never been on a motorcycle before, and the idea of holding on to someone and relying on my own grip to keep me from falling off the back was enough to make me shudder.

"I'm not riding on the back of a Harley!"

His brow furrowed.

"Harley?" He tilted his head to one side. "I'm in a Honda."

A Honda? No, that didn't fit at all.

"You are not," I said.

"I'm not?" His grin returned, and his eyes sparkled in the light from the streetlamp.

"No way."

"That's what it says on the trunk," he replied. "It's got that little stylized 'H' and the word 'Civic.'"

"You? In a Civic?" It was my turn to laugh. There was just no way a guy that size could possibly fit through the door of such a small car.

"Yeah, me in a Civic. What's wrong with that?"

"You wouldn't fit in a Civic."

He tilted his head down and to the side as he chuckled.

"Well, it's not easy, I'll admit." He looked back to my face again. "It beats sleeping in the parking lot, though."

I didn't know if I should believe him or not. I still couldn't imagine him with any vehicle other than a Harley, and the image was so stuck in my head, anything else seemed ridiculous. I took a deep breath and straightened my shoulders.

"Give me my keys. I need to get home."

"You know I can't do that." Brick Wall moved his hand behind his back, and my keys disappeared into his pocket. He placed his now empty hand on the other side of my head. "Now what's it going to be —call a cab or drive you home?"

He was very close to me now, and the heat from his body warmed the night air between us. If he moved any closer, his body would be pressed against mine. The thought made my ears—and other parts of me—tingle with anticipation.

I really need to sober up.

I glanced around at the little cage he had made with his body and wondered if I could duck under him fast enough to get away. The warning in my head was getting louder, contrary to the reaction of my body. I was trapped, and I should have been afraid. I wanted to be afraid, but I wasn't.

That's the alcohol talking again.

I looked into his face and realized he was still waiting for my answer. Instead of giving him one, I found myself focusing on his lips at the same time I wetted my own.

His eyes darkened slightly as they narrowed. He shifted closer, and I swallowed as the idea of his body pressed against mine became reality. He paused, watching my face closely.

This was it. I knew exactly what he intended to do, and this was my opportunity to say no. This was my chance to just insist on going back inside and having the bartender—a guy I'd known for years—call me a cab instead being driven home by someone whose name I didn't even know. Brick Wall might agree to give the bartender my keys while I waited for a ride.

I didn't move. I didn't protest. I licked my lips again and stared up at him as he slowly lowered his head to my level. I could have pressed against his chest with my hands, but I didn't. My elbows bent as his chest came closer to mine, pressing the backs of my hands into my breasts. As he leaned closer, I moved my palms up to his shoulders and around his neck.

He tilted his head to the side, and his full lips met mine. All I could do was press the back of my head against the car door and let him as the feeling of being trapped by his body magnified. Again, I knew I should be frightened, but the gentle touch of his mouth on mine electrified me. Even as my chin quivered, I gripped the back of his head with my fingers to pull him closer.

I didn't want a gentle kiss from him. It didn't fit any more than the idea of him driving around in a Civic. A kiss from him should be hard, fast, passionate, and rough.

I opened my mouth slightly, and he immediately took the invitation with his tongue. I could taste beer along with mint, as if he'd been chewing gum recently. I gripped the back of his head harder, and he took the hint. The kiss deepened, quickened. His tongue went from exploring my mouth to invading it. He pushed my body against the car as he moved one of his thighs between mine, and I could feel something hard and straight through the jeans encasing my hip. My whole body throbbed but especially that spot between my legs where his thigh was pressed.

Inside my head, a voice joined the alarm and screamed at me to stop what I was doing. I didn't listen to it. Instead, I moved my hips forward, increasing the pressure as he moved his hand down my side and returned the favor. My God, he felt huge. All those stupid "Is that a rabbit in your pocket?" jokes flooded through my head as he pulled back for a moment, taking my lower lip between his teeth and then turned his head the other way to kiss me again.

It was probably due to closing my eyes—maybe I should have gone with the ultimate in first-kiss faux pas and left them open—but every single drink I had consumed throughout the evening suddenly hit me at once. As his tongue entered my mouth again, I couldn't hold back any more. I pulled my arms from around his neck and pushed his chest as hard as I could.

He stepped back, thank God, just in time for me to turn to the side and puke on the pavement. My stomached heaved, and I gripped the handle of the car door for balance with one hand and held my hair away from my face with the other.

Searching desperately for some object on the ground to allow me to focus and get control back, my vision blurred in the broken white lines between parking spaces. I started to fall forward, but a strong arm stopped me from hitting the pavement just as everything went dark.

And with that, my boring existence came to an end.

THREE

My head felt as if there were a troupe of dancing elephants practicing their next circus routine just behind my eyes. I wanted to groan, but I was sure the sound would pierce my eardrums, so I held it in. I ached everywhere, and I was in a horribly uncomfortable position. My pillow felt like a rock against my cheek. Even when I tightened my arm around it, it didn't give way.

My pillow also seemed to have a distinctly musky scent to it, which I had never noticed before. In my groggy state, I wasn't making much sense of it. The throbbing in my head urged me to go back to sleep, and I didn't want to argue. I settled in and rubbed my cheek against the warm pillow, but something still wasn't right.

The scent, the feeling of the pillow on my face—it just wasn't right. My body ached along with my head, making lucid thoughts fleeting at best. I tightened my arms around the pillow, but it didn't give way like it normally did.

I opened my eyes a crack and discovered my pillow was covered in tattoos.

What the hell?

I swallowed hard against the lump in my throat as I tried to regain enough consciousness to survey my surroundings.

I was on a bed with the sheets drawn most of the way up my body. The bed wasn't mine. It wasn't even a proper bed—just a pull-out mattress from a faded couch. I was wearing nothing but my bra and panties.

My arms and one leg were wrapped around a shirtless Brick Wall.

Oh my God, no…

What had I done?

With a little shriek, I pushed myself away from Brick Wall and tried to climb off the mattress. I was tangled up in the sheet, which was tucked under the far side of Brick Wall's decorated torso, and for a moment, my legs were trapped under it, sending a wave of panic through me.

"Shit!"

Flailing my arms and legs until I could disengage from the fabric, I fell on my ass next to the makeshift bed.

"Ooof!" Shaking my pounding head to clear it, I crawled backwards a few feet on the floor as Brick Wall opened his eyes, propped himself up with one elbow, and looked down at me. The sheet covered up his lower half, so I couldn't tell what he was wearing, if anything.

Holding himself up with one arm made the muscles in his arm bulge. His biceps were enormous and decorated with…well, I wasn't even sure what. I could make out words, a face, some stars, and maybe a few flowers. There was hardly any skin showing anywhere on his upper body. He was covered from his neck all the way to where the sheet was pulled up around his hips. Even the backs of his hands were covered.

He had enough words and pictures on his body to open both an art gallery and a library.

Tattoos weren't my thing. I wasn't into guys like that. I liked nice, straight-edged guys who had office jobs and drove Toyotas. Regardless, I still thought he was kind of beautiful. Though I couldn't make out the details of the designs on his flesh, they still left the impression of telling a story—an intricate and beautiful story.

I shook my head again to clear it. I'd had my leg wrapped around him, asleep in his bed, and I didn't remember a damn thing after leaving the bar.

I felt my face heating up. This was definitely at the top of the list of situations my mother always told me to avoid. I didn't know where I was, how I got here, or even the name of the man I was sleeping with.

Oh, God, I slept with him!

Brick Wall smirked as I backed away on my hands and feet until I hit something on the floor—my own jacket. I grabbed it and wrapped it around my chest as I tried to catch my breath.

"You okay?" Brick Wall asked.

"No!" I shook my head vehemently. "No, I am not okay! This is not okay! Holy shit—I don't do this! I never do this!"

"Do what?" he asked with narrowed eyes.

"This!" I yelled as I waved one hand in the air between us. The other hand kept a firm grip on the jacket against my skin.

He wiggled his eyebrows at me as the panic I felt in my chest increased. I covered my mouth with my hand to keep myself from actually screaming.

"Relax," he said softly. "We didn't do anything. You passed out thirty seconds after we got here."

I processed his words, felt a moment of relief and then doubt.

"Why was I in bed with you then?" I demanded.

Brick Wall sat up and looked pointedly around the living space, which I hadn't actually done yet. As I did, I realized the whole place consisted of one room—a combination of a living room and bedroom area along with an eat-in kitchen. There was a small, closed door off to one side, which was presumably a bathroom.

"Where else would you fit?" he asked.

Aside from the pull-out couch, there was only one other chair, and it wasn't nearly big enough to sleep on. There was a card table with two chairs closer to the kitchen and a small stand with a television on top of it but no other furniture—only a suitcase with a pile of clothing in it.

"Why am I here at all?" Somehow, I still felt wronged and needed to prove that he had done something inappropriate. Anything that would keep this from being entirely my fault would have been a blessing, but I wasn't coming up with much. I tightened my hands into tiny fists against my chest even as I asked myself exactly what I thought I might do with them. It wasn't as if he'd feel it if I tried to hit him.

"Because you were trying to drive yourself home," Brick Wall said. "I was going to call you a cab or just drive you home myself, but you couldn't seem to remember where you lived. So, here we are."

I glared, trying to decide if I believed him or not. I did remember him taking my keys from me, so that part fit. Everything after that was a blur. Still, his explanation sounded reasonable, and I didn't see any motive for him to be lying to me.

You don't know this guy! You have no idea if he's telling the truth!

"Would you have preferred it if I had left you in the parking lot to fend for yourself?"

So much for blaming him.

"You're quite the cuddler," Brick Wall said with a lopsided grin. He reached up to put his hand behind his head and leaned back. "I kept pushing you off but finally gave up."

Though my face heated at his words, I couldn't deny what he was saying. I hadn't been with anyone for nearly a year, but Zach, my ex, often accused me of trying to smother him in his sleep. Nowadays, my giant, overstuffed pillow got the same treatment.

"Crap," I muttered.

"I'm just glad you didn't puke in the apartment," Brick Wall remarked. "I'm out in a few days, and I don't want to forfeit the deposit, you know?"

"Did I puke?"

"In the parking lot."

"Crap," I said again. The evening's events were starting to come back to me.

"Not the best first kiss reaction I ever got," he said with another half-grin, "but at least you didn't hit me."

"We kissed?" A shiver ran through me as vague memories of his body pressing mine against the driver's side door of my car and the taste of his tongue in my mouth ran through my head.

"You don't remember?" He raised an eyebrow.

"Kind of," I admitted.

"Definitely not the best reaction, then," he said.

Crap. After all of this, I'd hurt his pride too.

"I'm sorry," I whispered.

"Why?" His eyes narrowed again. "You don't have anything to apologize for."

"For not remembering?" The statement sounded like a question, and my organs felt as if they were dropping into the lower half of my body. "I mean, I remember a little…some of it."

There was a long pause as he stared into my eyes.

"Well, hopefully it's a good memory." He sat up and swung his legs over the side of the mattress, and I sighed in relief to see that he was actually wearing shorts. I focused for a moment on the additional tattoos covering his legs and even the tops of his feet. I couldn't quite read the lettering around his calves, but his feet seemed to be decorated with faces surrounded by flowers or clouds—I wasn't sure which. The images looked religious. Then I realized I was staring and quickly looked away.

The facts of the matter began to overwhelm me again. Yes, I'd desired a little more action in my life, but not like this, not with some tattooed stranger who was as far from my type as he could possibly be. This was a dangerous situation and one to be avoided.

"I need to go home," I stated.

"Will you at least let me make you some breakfast before I take you back to your car?" Brick Wall asked. "You've got to have a hell of a headache."

"I need to go home," I repeated quietly.

"You still ought to eat," he said. "I'm a great cook—I swear."

Great, I was hurting his pride again. I swallowed hard before answering him.

"I appreciate it. I really do, but I need to get home. I don't do stuff like this."

"Like what?" he asked.

"Like being half naked in a stranger's apartment on a Saturday morning," I replied. "I should be at the grocery store now."

"The store?" He laughed, and I felt my blood rise into my cheeks. "Sounds exciting."

"I always shop on Saturday morning."

"Then what?"

"Then laundry and maybe a movie."

"Yeah, that's some weekend life you lead."

I looked up at him and tried not to glare. I didn't need some guy I didn't know commenting on my lifestyle or habits, but I'd already offended him by not accepting breakfast and bemoaning the whole kissing thing.

I licked my lips, and clearer memories of his mouth on mine surfaced.

"I'm just...not a spontaneous person," I finally admitted.

"You mean like letting me kiss you last night?"

"That was...that was..." What the hell was that? My heart began to pound. I had no words for it. I couldn't even imagine myself in that situation though clearly I had allowed it. "I don't even know your name."

He smiled, lighting up his eyes.

"Hunter," he said. "Aiden Hunter."

"I'm Chloe," I said.

"You told me last night." Aiden grinned again as he stood up and offered me his hand. It was also covered in tattoos. There were stars around his wrist, a flower covering the back of his hand, and tribal markings all the way down his fingers. I hesitated, but good manners got the better of me, and I let him haul me to my feet with my other hand still clasping my jacket to my chest. I looked around on the floor.

"Um...where are my clothes?"

"In the bathroom," Aiden said. "They're probably still wet. I washed the puke off them in the sink, but I don't have a dryer."

I quickly excused myself to the bathroom to locate my clothes. Aiden had been right—my jeans and T-shirt were hanging over the shower door, and though the shirt was only slightly damp, my jeans were still soaked. I pulled the shirt on just as Aiden's head popped in the doorway.

"Want to try these?" Aiden held a pair of grey sweatpants out to me. "They're going to be big, but there's a drawstring. Should be enough to get you home."

The idea of wet denim was unappealing enough for me to agree.

"Feel free to take a shower or whatever," Aiden said. "There's also an extra toothbrush in the cabinet."

He walked out, and I pulled the ill-fitting sweats up over my legs, tied the drawstring, and rolled up the hem so I could walk. My sandals were on the floor of the bathroom near the shower, so I slipped them on too. I hated taking showers in strange places but did open the medicine cabinet to find an unopened, green toothbrush and made good use of that.

I caught my reflection in the bathroom mirror and stared at the smudged, mascara-darkened area around my eyes. I saw dull blue eyes, hair all over the place, and I still smelled a little like a bar. I looked like hell and wondered just how much worse I must have appeared last night when Aiden brought me here. No wonder he didn't touch me.

I rolled my eyes at my reflection. Was I seriously disappointed that he hadn't taken advantage of the situation? That would have been date rape, wouldn't it? If you can't give consent, it's the same as not giving consent—I'd heard that from all the sexual harassment training I had to complete at work every year.

We hadn't been on a date, of course.

Placing my hands over my face, I groaned in the back of my throat. I had to get out of this place, get home, and take half a bottle of painkillers. I obviously couldn't think rationally here. I wasn't even sure what to do with the toothbrush I had used, so I placed it next to the blue one that was already there in the little cup on the vanity.

After rubbing some of the makeup off my face with my fingers and cold water from the bathroom sink, I went back into the main room of the tiny apartment. Aiden was dressed in a white T-shirt with the sleeves cut out of it, tan cargo shorts, and a red baseball cap perched backward on his head. The shirt showed off a lot of his tattoos, but there were so many, my head swam whenever I tried to make sense of them. He was sitting in the single chair, flipping through channels on the television. He turned it off as I walked in.

"You sure you don't want to eat first?" he asked.

"I'm sure." I tried not to stare at his arm muscles, but they were just so *big*. And decorated. Very, very decorated.

"Give me a minute, and we'll get you back, then." He disappeared into the bathroom while I stood in the middle of the room, not knowing what to do.

Glancing around the room, I saw my purse sitting on the card table and retrieved it. I checked my wallet nervously and then sighed when I saw all the cash and credit cards were still there. I silently scolded myself for being so distrustful of a man who really hadn't done anything other than help me out, but the whole thing was so far out of my comfort zone, I didn't know how to react.

There was definitely the desire to examine my surroundings up close, but I didn't want to appear rude. Aiden was only gone for a few minutes anyway, and I would have died of embarrassment if I had been caught snooping around. As soon as he came out of the bathroom, I retrieved my wet jeans, and we left.

Outside, Aiden opened the passenger door of a small, silver Civic and then walked around to shove his huge form into the driver's seat. I buckled up and looked around. I knew the apartment complex from when I had been hunting for one myself, but I'd given it a miss. The neighborhood was a little run-down for my tastes, and the closest shopping was a strip mall with nothing more than a convenience store and take-out Chinese. It was a cheap place to live, but I could afford much better.

"What do you do for a living?" I asked Aiden.

"Sales," he replied.

"What do you sell?"

"I've sold a lot of different things," he said. He glanced at me out of the corner of his eye.

Alarm!

He didn't seem interested in elaborating, and the more I thought about it, the more I didn't want to know. Sure, he'd been a gentleman so far, but that didn't mean he wasn't dangerous. I watched him stare at the road through the windshield and noticed his fingers gripping the steering wheel tightly.

Nope. I did *not* want to know.

"What do you do?" Aiden asked.

"I'm a project manager," I said. "I work in the banking industry, managing teams for various initiatives. I work with the computer groups a lot, mostly on hardware and software upgrades."

"Fun."

I snorted out a laugh.

"Yeah, it's a blast."

"So why do it?" Aiden relaxed his grip on the wheel and turned the corner.

"It pays the bills," I said. "I love books, and I used to work in a library, but moving to project management made me a lot more money."

"I guess that's something."

"It might not be too exciting," I said, "but I like the people I work with. Well, most of them."

"Most?"

"My boss is an ass."

Aiden laughed as he looked at me with those twinkling green-brown eyes.

"He hasn't been there long," I continued, "and he seems to be doing his best to drive me insane."

"So quit," Aiden suggested with a shrug.

"It's not that easy." I looked down at my hands as I fiddled with the strap of my purse.

"Why not?"

"Because it's good money, and the drive isn't bad. There's no guarantee what I'd find would be any better than what I have, and looking for a new job takes a lot of time."

"Might cut into that grocery shopping, huh?"

I glared at him, but he just smiled back and adjusted the cap on his head. I noticed he had a small tattoo right on the upper part of his ear.

I wasn't sure why I felt the need to defend myself to this man. He probably didn't even have a real job. Sales people in my company made a lot of money, drove fancy cars, and lived in high-class neighborhoods, not the dump he was in.

"At least I can afford to eat what I want and live where I want." I looked back to my hands, realizing how my words probably sounded.

"Judging me by that apartment, are you?"

I didn't answer.

"It's not mine," he said. "I'm just borrowing it for the week. I'll be heading back home tomorrow."

"Where's home?"

"Miami, Florida."

"Ah." It didn't surprise me. Half the people in Ohio seemed to live in Florida for part of the year, which meant almost everyone I knew had family down there. "Are you visiting family or something?"

"Not exactly." Aiden pulled into the parking lot of Thirsty's and parked next to my car. The place was completely empty save for the handful of mist-covered cars left over from the night before.

As tempting as it was to ask him to elaborate, my inner alarms told me to let it be. My car and freedom from this crazy situation were right beside me, and I was eager to get back to a normal, comfortable routine. We both climbed out of his car and walked over to mine.

"Your keys," Aiden said as he held out his hand.

"Thanks," I said as I took them from his grasp, "for everything, I mean. Sorry I sort of went nuts this morning. It was just a little… shocking, I guess. Please don't take it personally."

"No worries," he said. "You were just a little disoriented."

"Yeah, I was. I don't do things like that."

"So I gathered." He looked at me sideways. "I get the idea you don't stray much from the norm."

I blinked a couple of times as I looked up at him. He was grinning again.

"Are you laughing at me?" I asked.

"Maybe a little," he replied, then shook his head. "Not really *at* you, it's just—you're making me think about my friends back in Miami."

"Why is that?"

"We're all big into living life to the fullest, you know? Live in the now, and deal with the consequences later."

"Sounds like you get into a lot of trouble," I remarked.

"Sometimes." Aiden reached out and took my hand in his. "Most of the time we just have a lot of fun."

"Doing what?"

"Mostly drinking," Aiden said with a laugh. He pulled at my hand until we were standing close together, forcing me to look up into his face. "A couple of them are big guys, and they can drink a *lot*."

"Big guys compared to you?"

"Depends on what you mean." Aiden raised his eyebrows and released my hand only to place his on my waist. I gripped his forearm, not sure if I wanted to push him away or bring him closer.

This was a bad idea. Playing games with a man like this wasn't safe. This was what I had always avoided. Still, I'd already hurt his pride once, and I'd practically insulted him, assuming he didn't make enough money for a nice apartment. Pushing him away would be rude.

His closeness was also having quite an effect on my body.

Aiden's eyes twinkled as he raised his hand and brushed my cheek with his fingers. His smile made him look boyish and much less threatening than the way his muscles and tattoos portrayed him.

I bit down on my lip as he moved his head closer to mine, just staring into his eyes and completely unable to move. I was sure he could hear my heart beating as I wondered if this was what a mouse felt like as it saw the shadow of an owl overhead. My mind told me this was dangerous, but I was unable to either fly or fight.

His mouth covered mine as he wrapped his arm around my back and pulled me against him. I gripped the edge of his shirt tightly as he kissed me, stealing what breath I had from my lungs. His full lips were warm and gentle on mine, and just as the tip of his tongue touched mine, he stopped.

Aiden pulled back, and I slowly looked at him. His eyes were hooded and dark, and his mouth was slightly open. I felt his breath against my lips as he spoke.

"It was nice meeting you, Chloe."

I licked my bottom lip, still tasting him there.

"You too," I whispered.

He released my waist and let his hand rest on my hip.

"Do I get to see you again?" he asked suddenly, and my heart began to pound intensely.

"I thought you were leaving tomorrow." My hand slid down his arm as he took a half step back.

"Yeah, I guess I am." His chest rose and fell as he took in a deep breath. "Maybe the next time I'm in town?"

"When will that be?" Was I seriously considering this? No, no I wasn't. I was just being polite.

"Not sure," he said. "A few weeks maybe."

It sounded like plenty of time for both of us to forget the whole night, which was fine by me. I was pretty sure he would find someone more like him in the meantime, and it wasn't like I was going to offer him my phone number. I'd likely never see him again.

Then I remembered something.

"I need to give you your pants back," I reminded him.

"Well, I have an appointment at noon I really shouldn't miss," Aiden said, "but how about I stop by and pick them up later?"

"What? Come by my condo?"

"Yeah," he said with a shrug. "Why not?"

"You don't know where I live." I didn't add that I wanted to keep it that way, but he must have sensed it.

"Do you remember where I live?"

"Yes."

"Bring them by after four this afternoon," he suggested. "I have to pack up a few things, and I have an early flight tomorrow."

"I have..." I hesitated and took a deep breath. "I have things to do."

"What?" Aiden laughed. "Groceries?"

I scowled at him but didn't have any kind of snappy comeback. The fact was he had me pegged. I didn't have any plans other than a movie at home—predictable and alone.

But going back to his place? Again? Intentionally? I had no idea what he expected, let alone what I might expect from another encounter. Yes, he had apparently been nothing but gentlemanly toward me thus far, but would that continue? Was this some kind of trap?

Why would he feel the need to trap me? If he was going to hurt me, he'd already had plenty of opportunity. Was I still judging him just because of the tattoos? How wrong was that?

Besides, I couldn't deny my attraction to him. He was so different from those I'd dated in the past, and the excitement of seeing him again tingled through my fingers where they still touched his arm.

"All right," I finally said. "I'll drop them by later."

"Yeah? Cool!" Aiden beamed. "I'll see you later, then."

He folded himself into his tiny car and drove off as I stood there with my keys in my hands and watched him disappear.

And with that, I wondered if I should just forget the whole encounter.

FOUR

I stood at the door to Aiden's apartment, holding his sweatpants —freshly washed—in a plastic bag on my arm. I had been there for at least four minutes but hadn't knocked yet.

I had spent all morning telling myself to leave his pants on his doorstep, ring the bell, and run away. I had spent the entire afternoon arguing with myself.

Everything about my encounter with Aiden Hunter was wrong. I didn't know him. None of my friends knew him. And I had made out with him both in a drunken stupor out in the parking lot and also while stone-cold sober the next day.

I had gone through all the known pros and cons.

The pros were easy: he was really, really attractive and a great kisser. Just being close to him seemed to make my body react in ways I hadn't felt in a long time, maybe ever. Yes, I'd been physically attracted to Zach and other past boyfriends, but the draw to Aiden was different—more tangible. It was also completely inexplicable.

The cons were also easy. There was no denying that I didn't really know anything about Aiden Hunter. That should have been enough to keep me away. He was sketchy about his work, which set off alarms in my head. Sales could mean anything. He was also scary-looking with all the tattoos and huge muscles. He was not my type.

However, I couldn't get over the idea that I was being totally unfair to him. If I had been a police officer, I would have definitely been accused of profiling. It wouldn't have been any different if he had been wearing a turban, and I had assumed he was a terrorist. I wasn't like that. I didn't discriminate against people because of how they looked.

Did I?

Maybe everyone does to some extent, but that didn't mean I had to act on it. Deciding to avoid him would be exactly that. Would I think differently if he had been in a suit, covering up the artwork all over his body? Probably. How screwed up was that?

The fact was he hadn't done anything wrong. He'd helped me out when I was too drunk to make any kind of rational decision, didn't take advantage of me, and didn't seem to be expecting any sort of repayment for his good deed. I, on the other hand, had spent most of my time judging him based on his appearance.

Who was the bad guy here?

Yes, he'd been a little dodgy on what he did for a living, but he might also just be a private person who didn't want to divulge too much to someone he just met. I hadn't told him much about what I did for a living, either. I wouldn't even tell him where I lived.

Deciding I was just being silly, I took a deep breath, raised my hand, and knocked. The door opened immediately.

"I was wondering how long you were going to stand there." Aiden's boyish smile beamed down at me as he waved me into the apartment.

My heart fluttered when I looked at him.

"You knew I was out there?" I asked as my face heated up.

"I saw you drive up." He pointed to the small window overlooking the parking lot. "Have a seat. I'm just finishing up my packing."

He stepped to the side of the door, but his shoulders were so wide I still brushed up against him when I walked in. The brief encounter sent shivers down my arm where our skin touched.

I scuttled past, ignoring the way my skin tingled where we met, and sat on the single chair in the living area and looked around. The suitcase that had been open that morning was now closed and upright near the card table. Aiden disappeared into the bathroom and came back out with a black toiletry bag, which he shoved into the front pocket of the luggage. The sleeper sofa was folded back, and the apartment looked even emptier than it had before.

"I thought you were leaving tomorrow."

"I am," he said. "I just like to have everything together the day before."

"You are very organized," I commented. He grinned at me.

"Want something to drink?" Aiden asked. "I've got beer and some Sprite, I think."

"No," I replied, "thank you. I just wanted to return these."

As I held the bag out to him, I tried not to meet his eyes as. Every time I seemed to look at them my brain turned to mush.

He laughed.

"In a grocery bag, huh? I guess you managed to get your shopping done."

"I did." I smiled sheepishly.

Aiden took the bag and crammed it into the top of the suitcase. He tossed in a few more items from the card table and zipped up the bag before sitting down on the couch and facing me.

"So, I was thinking," Aiden said as he leaned forward with his elbows on his knees, "maybe we don't have to wait until I get back. Maybe you could just come with me."

I stared at him a minute, trying to figure out if there was some joke I was missing. I was probably distracted by the movement of the muscles in his forearms when he leaned on his legs, and I didn't quite understand what he was trying to say.

"Come with you where?" I asked.

"To Miami," he replied. "I still have another week off from work, and I think maybe a nice little vacation would be good for you."

"Vacation?"

"Yeah—sunny Florida and all that. Have you been?"

"Of course I have," I said. "We went to Disney when I was a kid."

"Well, adult vacations have their own magic," he said with a wink. "What do you think?"

I blinked a few times. Was he really suggesting I go to Florida with him? The very notion was ridiculous.

"I think you're crazy," I replied.

"Maybe a little." He shrugged and looked down at his hands. "I just thought maybe…well, with what you were saying this morning…"

His voice trailed off and he looked out toward the window as I tried to figure out what I might have said that gave him the idea that I wanted to take a vacation at all, let alone with someone I had just met. I drew a complete blank.

"What did I say?"

"You said you never did anything spontaneously." He looked into my eyes again. "I figured maybe you'd like to give it a try."

I rubbed my hands on my jeans, annoyed with myself for whatever I had done to put such an insane idea in his head. At the same time, I envisioned myself lying on a beach with him at my side, half naked in the sand.

I shook my head to clear it.

"I don't do that for a reason," I said as I sat back in the chair and folded my arms. I needed to get a handle on my thoughts. "I have responsibilities here. I'm kind of expected at work on Monday."

"Don't you have vacation time?"

"Of course I do."

"So use it!"

"To go to Florida? Now? With you?"

"Why not?"

I still couldn't quite believe he was serious, but everything about him said he was. He was smiling but not in a joking manner. He was looking at me intently, waiting for my answer.

"Because I barely know you!"

"Perfect opportunity to get to know me better."

I didn't like the way he was using logic against me. I definitely didn't like the part of me that was actually listening to it.

"That seems a little extreme for a first date," I replied with a bit of a huff.

"Is that how you see it?" he asked. He raised one eyebrow and tilted his head to the side.

"Well, I…um…" His bluntness had caught me off guard, and I had no idea how to respond. Had I been presumptuous? I had just assumed he would see it as an intimate trip, but now I wasn't so sure. "It's just that, well, we kissed, and um…"

Aiden's smile grew.

"I'd love for it to be an extended date," he said, "but it wouldn't have to be if that made you uncomfortable. I just don't have anyone else traveling with me, and it gets kind of boring. It seems like you could benefit from a little excitement in your life."

"You think I'm boring?" I asked.

"I think you're *bored*," Aiden corrected.

"And that's a good reason to pack up and head to Florida?" I shook my head. Normal, rational people didn't do these kinds of things.

"It's not a bad reason," he replied.

I realized I was staring at him again and quickly looked away. I had no idea how to handle this. I couldn't possibly go on a trip with him on such short notice. He had to realize that, didn't he?

"I haven't budgeted for a trip," I said.

"My treat."

I glared at him, wondering if he was just teasing me, but again, he seemed absolutely serious.

"I couldn't let you do that."

"Why not?"

"It's just not…not proper." I glanced around at the sparse surroundings, wondering how he could afford a trip for one, let alone a trip for two. "I don't even know you."

He laughed.

"Fuck that," he said with a wide grin. "I don't care if it's proper or not. You're just making excuses. Come on, Chloe, why not take a chance?"

What was the worst that could happen? Did I really think he was going to kidnap me and sell me into slavery or something? That's the sort of thing that only happened on television. Besides, he was obviously stronger than I, and if he wanted to haul me off somewhere, I wouldn't have been able to stop him.

This was ridiculous. I had work. I had to help Mare pick out wedding flowers. I had told Gabe I'd go car shopping with him this week. People were counting on me to be here. I couldn't just pack up and leave with some strange, tattooed man, irrespective of how gorgeous he may be.

"No," I said, this time with more conviction. "I'm not going to Florida with you."

Aiden looked at me for a long moment, smiled slightly, and nodded. I noticed right away that his eyes didn't light up this time, and I immediately felt bad for rejecting him.

"All right," he said. "You can't blame me for trying."

"I don't," I said quietly as I stood up to leave. "I'm just not sure doing something like that on such short notice is in me."

"Oh, I don't know," Aiden replied. He stood up in front of me and placed his hand on the side of my face. "I think it's in there somewhere."

"Unlikely," I said as I tried to smile. I was keenly aware of how close he was to me, and again my body reacted. My skin tingled as he bent slightly to place his lips on the side of my neck. I closed my eyes and held my breath as he moved his hand to the back of my head.

"You can still change your mind," he whispered as his nose dragged along my cheek, making me shiver. "My fight was delayed, so I won't be leaving until almost noon tomorrow. You have some time to think about it."

Aiden pulled away abruptly and headed over to the kitchen area. He scribbled in a small notepad that had been sitting on the counter, tore off the page, and handed it to me. It had flight information and a phone number on it.

"Text me if you change your mind," he said.

"I'm not going to change my mind." I glanced at the paper as I headed for the door. My heart was pounding again, and I needed to get out of there before I said or did something crazy. I didn't seem to think clearly in his presence. All those muscles and his intense eyes kept me off guard. I needed to get out of there and back to the safety of my condo.

"Text me anyway."

I nodded, thinking it was better to let him believe I would contact him later even when I was pretty sure that was not in the cards. He took my hands in his and pulled me in close, brushed his lips against the corner of my mouth, and then opened the door.

I drove home slowly, replaying the entire conversation in my head. Go to Florida with him? He had to be nuts.

Monday morning I would have to explain the project cancellation to the team though they'd likely all heard about it by now anyway. I had to reassign resources, meet with accounting, and figure out where the budget for the server upgrade would land, now that it wasn't going to happen. I had to change contractor assignments, reallocate technical resources, and update the project plans. Mare needed a florist. Gabe needed a new car. The very idea of jaunting off with some stranger with no notice was ridiculous.

And exciting.

I pulled into my parking space and went inside my condo. I could have sworn Buffy was glaring at me.

"For all I know, he's a vampire," I told her.

As I looked away from Buffy, I caught sight of my father's picture on the other side of the bookshelf. His smiling eyes looked into the camera, and I reached out to stroke the frame.

"I have a pretty good idea what you would think of all this," I said to the picture. "Stay away from dangerous situations. The unknown is often dangerous."

After blowing Dad a quick kiss, I picked up the stack of papers on the desk and opened up all the bills. I sat down and logged into my bank account to pay the electric and cable bills that were due. Once I had all that paperwork cleared up, I began to file the papers. As I placed the last one in the appropriate folder, a piece of lined paper dropped to the floor.

Aiden's phone number and flight information.

I sighed and picked it up. He had seemed very disappointed at my refusal, and I supposed I should at least text him and wish him a safe flight. Maybe we could make plans to have coffee or something when he returned. That was safe enough, wasn't it?

Pulling my phone from my purse, I added Aiden Hunter into my contact list and hit the "send message" button to create a text. I stared at the blank screen for a moment before typing "Have a good flight!"

I didn't hit send.

Instead, I deleted the text and stared at the blank message screen again. Maybe I shouldn't send him anything. Maybe I should keep our brief encounter just that—brief. Sending him a message would give him my phone number, and doing that wasn't the safe way to go. I still didn't know much of anything about him.

He's probably a drug dealer.

I shook my head. The thought wasn't fair, and I knew it.

Fair or not, the logical and safe thing to do was to forget all about my weekend with the handsome, tall, and muscled stranger. I wasn't a love-struck child, and I wasn't a character in a romance novel. Real life just didn't work that way.

I woke early the next morning, and my very first thought was of Aiden. There were fleeting images of him in my head, walking along a sandy beach with waves crashing around his tattooed feet.

Had I been dreaming about him?

Unable to go back to sleep, I gave up and made coffee. It was still dark outside, and I wasn't hungry yet. I flipped on the television, which was tuned to one of those home and garden channels and showing one of those house-hunting programs. Coincidentally enough, the couple on the show was looking for a house in Miami.

"Figures," I mumbled as I stared at the screen. The realtor was discussing all the wonderful sights in the area, the beautiful beaches and fantastic restaurants within a ten-minute walk of the million-dollar condo in question.

Did Aiden live in a pricey complex like that?

"Not going to happen," I mumbled out loud. I tossed my phone onto the coffee table and hauled out my laptop to check my work emails. There were usually a few I could get out of my inbox before Monday morning, and I liked to have those taken care of before getting into work the next day. Along with a few notices about a weekend upgrade that had apparently gone horribly wrong, there was a meeting request from my boss to discuss project initiatives for the next year.

The meeting was set to last for three hours.

Not only did it double-book me for two of the hours, it also ran through lunchtime. There was no mention of bringing lunch in, and my schedule for the rest of the afternoon wouldn't even leave me time to run to the refrigerator to grab a packed lunch.

"Bastard."

It would be the sixth time he'd done the same thing to me since he'd started working there. He would schedule half-day meetings with no break and then expect everyone to just deal with missing lunch. Word at the water cooler was that he was watching for people who left early, too. It pissed me off, but of course I hadn't said anything. I'd fantasized about rubbing tar into his perfectly ridiculous hairstyle, but I hadn't said anything.

"You know what? Fuck him." The harsh word felt strange coming out of my mouth, but I didn't care. I opened up a new email and quickly typed up a message to Chia Head saying I was taking the week off. I clenched my teeth as I hovered the cursor over the send button.

I couldn't do it. I just couldn't.

Why not take the chance?

It was Aiden's voice, not my own, in my head. I looked at the clock and then again checked the piece of paper Aiden had given me. He said his flight didn't leave until noon, and it was only a little after nine o'clock now.

Up on the shelf, Wonder Woman seemed to be leaning forward, urging me to do it. If I squinted my eyes, I might have imagined Princess Leia nodding. Buffy could have been thinking about sharpening some new stakes, just in case.

"I could get fired," I said to the girls, then rolled my eyes at myself before they had the chance. I wouldn't get fired for such a thing. It seemed to take a major act of God to fire the idiots who didn't get any work done at all, and I always had great reviews.

I picked up my phone and stared at it for a moment before I typed another message.

I've decided to go with you.

Again, I did not hit the send button. It didn't matter if I wanted to go; I couldn't. The very thought was insane.

Wasn't it?

I did have vacation time to use. Though I'd gone to visit my mom and usually took off a few days around the holidays, I hadn't been on a real vacation in years. The project team had plenty of work to keep them busy for the next week, and the idea of having yet another marathon meeting with my asshole boss was stomach-churning.

I gripped the phone in my hand, hard enough to make my knuckles go white. My finger shook slightly over the send button on the display as I bit into my lower lip and felt my chest tighten.

Even if the trip was a disaster, it couldn't be worse than a week of meetings with Kevin. Nothing was worse than that.

I hit the send key.

"Oh, crap. What did I just do?"

A response came immediately.

Awesome! Can you be here in 30 min? I'll meet you at the Delta ticket counter.

The airport was twenty minutes away. I'd have ten minutes to pack.

Sure. See you then.

I hit send again. There was no turning back now. I sent Kevin my email notice of vacation and jumped up to pack a bag.

And with that, I decided I had lost my mind.

FIVE

"I'm really glad you decided to come," Aiden said as he handed me a boarding pass. "Do you want to check your bag?"

"No, it's okay," I replied. "It should fit in the bins. I didn't have a lot of time to pack."

"Decided at the last minute, didn't you?"

"Yeah, pretty much." I was sure my face reddened as I glanced at him. He was dressed in a grey T-shirt and camo shorts that reached his knees, showing off the tattoos on his calves. I was starting to wonder if there was any part of him unmarked. The same red cap was on his head—backward, of course.

"If you end up missing something, we can get it there," he said. He took my hand, grinned down at me with that incredible smile, and pulled me toward the escalators.

People kept looking over at us and then quickly looking away when I met their eyes. The first time it happened, I could only wonder if they knew I was doing something completely rash and borderline insane. Suddenly self-conscious, I looked down to see what I was wearing. There was nothing unusual about my outfit and my shoes matched, so I didn't think they were looking at me.

As it continued to happen, I realized they were actually staring at Aiden and his tattoos. I began to pay more attention to the passersby. Most people just gave him a subtle sideways glance, but several stared outright.

I had been in the midst of a near panic attack since I sent the text message, and being in the airport with him as people stared wasn't making it any better. I was excited to be going, but all my focus was on the feeling of his fingers interlaced with mine and the looks other passengers were giving us. I couldn't concentrate on the actual trip ahead.

"You're going to love it," Aiden said. "I live right on the beach. It's not overly fancy or anything, but the view is incredible."

"Do you have roommates?" I asked.

"Nope. Just me."

My heart began to pound again. I had to have lost my mind to be doing this. Yes, it was exciting, but it was also terrifying. I was going to spend a week alone with this man. What if his beach house only had one bed in it, like the apartment he stayed in here? I hadn't even considered what the sleeping arrangements might be, and now I was too embarrassed to ask.

I wasn't even sure how Aiden was viewing this little adventure. He said he'd like it to be a date, but we hadn't said for sure one way or the other. This was completely uncharted territory for me, and I had no idea what he was expecting. I'd let him pay for the plane ticket, and I was going to be staying at his house. What was he going to want in return?

"So, is this a date?" I asked. "I mean, a long date?"

"Do you want it to be?" His fingers tightened around mine.

"I…I'm not sure."

"How about we just play it by ear, then?"

"All right." I had to move fast to keep up with his long strides as we headed toward the gate.

"Are you nervous?" he asked as he gripped my fingers.

"No," I lied.

"You're shaking."

"Um…well, maybe a little," I admitted. "I've never done anything like this."

"Spontaneity suits you," he said. He reached his arm up to place it over my shoulders and brushed my cheek with his finger. "It puts color in your cheeks."

He pulled me next to him and pressed his lips to the top of my head.

"I'm a little nervous, too," he said quietly. "I just want you to have a good time. I want both of us to have a good time."

I still wasn't sure what he meant by that, but I didn't ask. Instead, I leaned into his body. My mind focused on the feeling of his arm around my shoulders. It was warm and comfortable, but it was something else too. I felt…protected.

Maybe that was the reason women were drawn to muscled guys. I'd never thought about it before, but despite his appearance, I felt safe with him next to me.

Getting through security took forever. Though we didn't have any of the forbidden items, Aiden was pulled aside and searched thoroughly before we could get past the checkpoint to find our gate. By the time we got there, we only had about twenty minutes before our flight would begin to board. That gave us just enough time to stop at a kiosk to grab some snacks for the flight. I picked out some trail mix and a bottle of water, and Aiden grabbed a bag of Swedish Fish.

"Really?" I asked as I nodded toward the candy.

"I love these things," Aiden admitted. He looked away from me. At first I thought he was embarrassed, but there was something off about his expression. He looked almost sad, and I wondered if I had offended him.

"I didn't mean anything by it," I said as I touched his arm.

"It's all good." He took the bag of trail mix from my hand and walked swiftly to the counter. The curve of his biceps increased in definition, and I noticed his hands were clenched around the bags of food. Despite what he said, it obviously wasn't all good. I wasn't sure how, but I had definitely pissed him off, and we hadn't even gotten on the plane yet.

My former boyfriend, Zach, had been a mild-mannered guy. There wasn't a whole lot that upset him, but over the eighteen months we'd dated, I learned what kinds of things set him off. You couldn't talk bad about the Catholic Church, even though he no longer attended mass, or you would definitely get an earful. I'd also learned to avoid conversations about Microsoft products because they would send him into a tirade about good software versus popular software.

This was why this trip was such a bad idea. I didn't know enough about Aiden Hunter to know what his triggers were. I had no idea what I'd said about Swedish Fish that upset him and didn't know him well enough to be comfortable asking about it. Anything I said might end up being a taboo subject for him, and it would be like walking through a minefield. Then again, he had said the trip was a good opportunity to get to know him better, so maybe I just needed to ask.

Another traveler walked past us and eyed Aiden up and down.

"Does that happen to you a lot?"

"What?"

"The whole security check thing," I clarified. "I've never been searched."

"Yeah, pretty much every time I fly," he confirmed. "I guess I'm used to it."

"Like the people who…well, who stare when you walk by?"

"It happens," Aiden said with a shrug. "People make their assumptions about you as a person, based on your looks. It happens to everyone, I suppose."

I thought about it but wasn't so sure I agreed with him. I never thought people were judging me by how I looked. Of course, there wasn't anything particularly unique about how I looked, either. Aiden, on the other hand, had gone out of his way to make himself look different from everyone else. That was bound to get people's attention.

As we sat down to wait for the flight, Aiden's phone rang before I had a chance to inquire any more about him. He looked at the number, glanced at me darkly, and then stood up and walked a few feet away before answering. He spoke in a low tone, and I couldn't hear any of the conversation though the desire to eavesdrop was great. He held the phone tightly against his ear and gripped his other hand into a fist as he spoke. He paced a few feet farther away then turned and glanced at me for a moment before looking back to the floor.

A voice over the announcement system called for first-class passengers to begin boarding, and several people around me stood up and grabbed their bags. Aiden continued to pace, and his voice rose in pitch as he started yelling.

"Listen here, motherfucker! You need to get off your ass and do something about it before I show up there and explain to you just how I feel about all this shit!"

I tensed and gripped the arms of the chair as a few other passengers looked up at him. He lowered his voice again, but I could still see the tightness in his jaw as he spoke into the phone for a few more seconds then ended the call.

He took in a long breath and huffed it out before returning to where I sat.

"Everything all right?" I asked quietly.

Aiden didn't look at me. He continued to glare at his phone for a moment before he shoved it back into his pocket and dropped his butt down in the seat beside me.

"It's fine," he said curtly.

Whatever it was, he clearly didn't want to discuss it. All ideas of asking about Swedish Fish left my head, so I went with a subject change instead.

"So, what do you do for a living?"

"I'm in sales," Aiden said.

"Right." I nodded and fiddled with my hands in my lap. "You said that, but you didn't say what kind of sales."

"Pharmaceuticals."

My heart skipped a beat, and my palms began to sweat. I was right! He *was* a drug dealer! And here I was, about to get on a plane and head to Florida with him.

What the hell was I going to do?

Our zone was called, and Aiden stood and picked up our carry-on bags.

"Ready?" he asked.

I wanted to say no, I was not ready. I wanted to turn around and run as fast as I could back to my car in long-term parking. I wanted to tell him it was all a mistake and whatever desire I had for a week of beach-life had vanished.

I didn't.

Aiden had paid for a plane ticket for me. We were here, and the plane was boarding. People were probably still watching him after his outburst on the phone. How would it look if I ran off now?

Instead of running, I simply nodded and joined him in line to get on the plane. I remained silent as the ticket agent checked our boarding passes, and the flight attendant led us to our seats. Aiden tucked our luggage into an overhead bin and handed me my trail mix before he sat down and buckled his seatbelt.

"Do you fly a lot?" I asked. I really wanted to return to normal conversation and forget his harsh words on the phone.

"Some," he said.

"Do you travel to Ohio a lot?" I asked.

"Pretty often," Aiden said. "I'm from the area, and I go back to visit friends and do a little business from time to time."

"Is your family there?"

"My mom is around somewhere." He turned toward me. "How about you? Have you always lived in the area?"

"Most of the time," I said. "I went to school out of state, and my mom moved away to San Francisco last year after my father passed the year before."

"Sorry to hear that."

"It's all right," I replied quietly. "I've gotten used to the idea of him being gone. It was hard at first, but I'm coping with it."

"Do you have siblings?" he asked.

"No, it's just me. How about you?"

"None," Aiden said.

"But your parents live in Cincinnati?"

"My mother does," Aiden confirmed. "My father died when I was in high school."

"Oh, wow. I'm sorry."

"It's all right," he said. "It was a long time ago."

I had been twenty-five when my father died. It had been so hard on me—I couldn't imagine losing him when I was still a teenager. I knew through my father's stories how difficult it was on a child when a parent was lost, and the child was still young.

That brought me to another question.

"So, um…how old are you?" I asked.

"Twenty-seven," Aiden replied. "You?"

"The same," I said with a smile. "I'll be twenty-eight in November."

"What date?"

"November fourth."

"Hmm." Aiden raised his eyebrows and smiled wickedly. "An older woman. I have to wait until the twenty-seventh."

"You make me sound dirty," I said with a laugh.

"Well, I've never dated an older woman before," Aiden said. "This is a whole new territory for me. I'm a little intimidated."

"You?" I crossed my arms in front of me. "Intimidated?"

"Oh, yes," he said with a serious nod. "Women are scary anyway, but an older one?"

"I'm sure I'm just terrifying."

"You are." He shuddered, and we both laughed.

I was glad his mood had lightened although I couldn't help but wonder what the phone call had been about. Was it one of his drug dealer associates? Was there some big deal about to go down, and something wasn't right about it?

Was I really thinking this way?

I never should have gotten on this plane, but I was stuck with it now, so I pressed my luck.

"Were you visiting those guys I saw you with at the bar?"

Aiden glanced over at me and then tore open his bag of Swedish Fish. He ate three of them before answering.

"Basically."

"Who were they?" I pressed. "Friends?"

"Associates," he said bluntly. "Do you want one of these?"

I took the offered sweet, as well as the hint, and stopped asking questions.

The rest of the plane ride went smoothly. I talked about losing my dad and how I felt about mom moving to the other side of the country shortly after. Aiden ate the remaining Swedish Fish with the exception of the yellow ones, and shoved the rest of the bag into his pocket. We talked about my job but not his. I did ask him more about his family.

"My dad was great," Aiden said. "We didn't have a whole lot, but he was one of those fathers who always made time for me. We did a lot of backyard sports stuff—throwing a football around, playing catch—all that shit. Then he died when I was fourteen. Mom pretty much lost it then, and I ended up raising myself at that point."

"Oh, Aiden, I'm so sorry. That had to be rough on you."

"I managed."

"What about your mother?"

"She was already a mess before he died, but afterward, she was a disaster. Dad didn't have any life insurance to speak of, and Mom couldn't hold down a job. I almost didn't finish high school because we were going to lose our apartment if we didn't get bills paid. I started working at the grocery store, bagging, and then later running the cash register. I had to put in a lot of hours just to keep the lights on. As soon as I finished high school, I moved out. I just couldn't take it anymore. My mother is still in Cincinnati and living off disability, but we haven't talked in years."

"That sounds really rough," I said. "You were so young, too."

"I grew up fast," Aiden said with a humorless smile.

I still had questions, but the plane began its descent into Miami. Aiden retrieved our bags from the overhead bin, and we headed off the plane and out of the airport.

"Do you have another Civic parked around here somewhere?" I asked.

Aiden laughed.

"Nah, I leave that for Ohio. Actually, I hadn't thought about transportation. We're going to have to improvise a bit."

"Improvise?"

"Yeah, not a big deal. I just hope it all fits."

Across the lines of taxis, I followed him out of the airport and to the parking garage. We took the elevator up to the next floor, and he led me over to a line of motorcycles. He stepped up next to a sleek, black machine.

"I have an extra helmet at home," Aiden said. "You get to wear this one in the meantime. I'm just not sure if your luggage is going to fit in the side bags."

"So you *do* have a Harley." I eyed him as he removed the helmet from the back of the bike and placed it on my head.

"It's a Yamaha R1," he said with a grin. He crammed our

luggage into the large, black bags hanging across the back of the bike. They fit, but just barely. "Have you ridden on a motorcycle before?"

Holy crap, he was actually expecting me to ride on the back of a motorcycle. It looked like one of those super-fast, super-dangerous ones, too. What if I fell off? What if another car didn't see us and ran into us? I couldn't do this—it was far too dangerous.

But what choice did I have? It was the only vehicle he had. I glanced back toward the row of taxis near the terminal exit, thinking I might just grab one of those and have the driver follow Aiden, but I knew I couldn't do that. Aiden was bound to be offended if I didn't ride with him.

"Never," I admitted, half hoping he would suggest a cab himself.

"Then you are in for a treat. Just hold on tight, and lean with me when we turn. I'll take it slow."

Aiden tightened the chin strap and made a couple more adjustments to the side straps before nodding and straddling the bike. He shoved the red cap into one of the side bags and strapped a pair of goggles around his head. I noticed the word "blessed" written across the back of his neck, right below his hairline, and a star beneath the lettering. Shaking my head slightly, I awkwardly climbed on behind him, painfully aware that I had no idea what I was doing.

"Where do I put my feet?" My voice sounded strange through the helmet.

"See the little bars down at the sides? Place them there, and then hold on to me."

With my feet firmly planted on the footrests, I leaned forward and placed my hands lightly against his sides.

"You'll have to hold on tighter than that," Aiden said as he turned his head to look over his shoulder. "Wrap your arms around my waist. Lean against me, and when I turn, lean with me."

I nodded and wrapped my arms around him. I had to turn my head to the side because of the helmet. It wasn't exactly comfortable, but the only thing I was really feeling was the pressure of his ass between my legs. Even in the Miami heat, my entire body warmed.

"You want the scenic route?" Aiden asked.

"Sure."

The bike roared to life, and I held on tighter as he put it in gear and moved forward with a slight jerk. It scared me, and I flexed my arms to hold myself on.

"You good?" he asked.

"Yes!" I called over the hum of the engine.

"Here we go!"

We zipped down the lane of cars, around other travelers hauling their luggage, and out of the parking garage. Aiden picked up speed as we merged onto the highway but stayed in the far right lane. I had the feeling he was going slower than he might have without me behind him, and I was glad for it. The ride was terrifying. Every time he shifted his weight, I moved with him awkwardly. I was sure I was going to cause us to fall.

We rode across a long bridge over the bay, and then turned north into slower traffic. I was glad we weren't moving so fast and was also distracted by the sheer number of people and glimpses of the ocean to my right. I pressed the side of my helmet to Aiden's back and held tightly to his torso, still keenly aware of his body where it pressed between my thighs.

We rode up Ocean Boulevard, passing towering condo high-rises and then smaller, single-family homes. We crossed another bridge, and an oceanside park appeared where I could see the sandy beach and crashing waves of the Atlantic. We passed another set of condos and then a few more homes before we pulled into a stone-lined driveway. Aiden pulled to a stop and put his feet down on the ground before killing the engine.

"Welcome to Golden Beach," Aiden said.

The place was beautiful. In fact, the whole neighborhood was beautiful. There were tall green shrubs surrounding the palms around the stone-paved driveway where Aiden had parked the motorcycle. Pink flowering bushes bloomed in the bright sunlight and accented the white stucco house beyond.

"It's not a huge place," Aiden said, "but it is right on the beach, as promised."

"It's beautiful!" I exclaimed. "This must have cost a fortune!"

I was immediately embarrassed by my comment, but Aiden didn't seem to mind.

"Not as bad as you might think," he said. "I got a good deal on it. There isn't a pool like most of the houses have around here, but I prefer the beach anyway."

I wondered if all drug dealers lived in such nice places and figured they probably did. Why else do something illegal if you didn't make a ton of money?

Am I really trying to rationalize this?

I shuddered a little at the thought as I dismounted the motorcycle and stretched my legs. Aiden dropped the kickstand and joined me in stretching.

"What did you think of the ride?" he asked.

"It was a little nerve-wracking," I admitted. "Fun, though."

"It's a lot easier to get around in the traffic on a bike," Aiden said as he led me to the front door.

The house was relatively small, not a lot bigger than my condo, but it was open and full of sunshine coming through the large windows in the back. The view of the patio and beach beyond was breathtaking.

There wasn't a lot of furniture. In fact, there were more boxes lying around than anything else, including boxes lined up on the couch in the living room. It made me wonder just how long he'd lived here.

"As you can see, I haven't really moved in yet," Aiden said with a shrug. "If I had known I was going to have company so soon, I might have cleaned up a bit. Sorry about that."

"You don't need to apologize," I said. "It's fine—really."

"Maybe you'll be the incentive I need to get the rest of my things unpacked." Aiden stood in the doorway and looked at me a moment. I didn't understand his expression, and I looked at the floor, unsure of what I was supposed to say.

His phone bleeped, and he glanced down as he brought it out of his pocket. He took a moment to type out a text and then tossed the phone onto a table near the door.

"Sorry about that," he said. "Work. I'm technically off until next Monday, but it kind of follows me."

I nodded but didn't ask for details. If I was going to make it through all this, I didn't want to know the specifics.

"Where should I put my things?" I asked.

"Back here." Aiden picked up his luggage and headed down a small hallway, past a bathroom, and into a bedroom. It was more put together than the rest of the house though there were still a couple of boxes stacked in the corner. The furniture was all dark wood in a contemporary style, and the huge bed was neatly made with pure white sheets and matching bedspread.

"There's only the one real bedroom," he said. "The other one is full of my gym equipment. I can take the couch if you want."

"I can't kick you out of your bed." My heart beat faster. "I can take the couch."

"Putting the guest on the couch wouldn't be very hospitable of me," Aiden said. "Besides, it's a mess out there."

"So, we um…we…" My voice trailed off. I couldn't seem to bring myself to say the words.

"Sleep together?" Aiden walked a step closer to me and took my bag from my hand. He placed it on the floor before standing in front of me and taking my hands. "No pressure, Chloe."

"Pressure?" I echoed.

"I'm not expecting anything," he said. "I'm also not against anything that might happen, but I want you to know I'm not expecting it, okay? Nothing has to happen. I didn't bring you here for that."

He brought his hand up and touched the side of my face, and my heart went wild again. I couldn't look him in the eye and found myself staring at top of his chest, trying to understand the markings that went from his neck down into his shirt. I held my breath and ran my tongue quickly over my lips.

"No pressure," he repeated. "We'll just be sleeping in the same bed. It's a king—plenty of room."

"I guess…I guess that's okay." I stole a glance up at him. It wasn't easy because I practically had to bend my neck all the way back to meet his eyes.

"Are you going to end up cuddling me again?" he asked with a smirk.

I blushed and quickly looked down again.

"I'm sorry…I…I…"

"It's okay," he said. "I really don't mind, not at all. I just want you to be comfortable."

I swallowed and nodded.

"Care to check out the beach?"

"Yes, please!"

He dropped his hand from my face but kept his grip on my hand as we walked through the house and to the sliding doors in the back. He released a lock at the top, opened the door to the patio, and led me to the beach just behind the house.

The sun was low behind us as we looked out over the brilliant blue water. The tide was low, and brown sea grass covered the sand near the waves. As we walked to the water, I could see purple and blue jellyfish washed up along the shore. There were very few people on the beach, and the only sound that could be heard was the waves crashing against the sand.

I stood just at the crest of the tide line and looked out over the water. Aiden stood behind me and wrapped his arms around my shoulders to hold me against him. I leaned back, and the sense of security washed over me again.

Alarm!

I shouldn't be here. I shouldn't be doing this. Twelve hours ago, I was checking work email and planning my week. How the hell did I end up here in this man's arms? What was wrong with me?

"You won't believe the sunrise," Aiden said. "Sometimes I get up extra early just to watch it."

"It really is beautiful here," I said quietly. Aiden's arms tightened around me as he pulled me tighter against his chest.

"Not bad for an extended date, right?"

I tilted my head back to look up at him. His eyes were calm and peaceful but still held that sparkle deep inside of them. My skin tingled as he rubbed his hands down my arms and then back up to my shoulders. I glanced down at his hands and the swirling tribal marks over them. On his left hand, the words LOVE LIFE were scrawled, one letter of each word per finger. Instead of the "O" in LOVE, there was a heart.

"Your eyes match the ocean," Aiden said. "The blue's the same shade, and there are all these little flecks of white in them that look like whitecaps."

I looked away, not sure how to respond to his flattery. A simple thank you didn't seem quite right, but I also didn't want to respond with some kind of "I bet you say that to all the girls" line, either. The pause was too long, and the moment passed before I could think of a reply.

"Are you hungry?" Aiden asked. "You haven't eaten much today."

"A little."

"Well, there are a thousand restaurants I can take you to," he said, "but I might prefer to cook you something."

"That would be wonderful."

"Why don't you get comfortable on the patio," Aiden suggested, "and I'll get cooking."

He took my hand, and we walked back through the sand. He sat me down on a lounge chair on the tiled patio and smiled.

"I'm really glad you decided to come with me," he said. He raised my hand to his lips and kissed my knuckles before disappearing inside the house.

I sat in the chair, stared at the ocean waves, and warred with myself internally.

The rational part of me wanted to call a cab and head straight back to the airport. If I caught the last flight back, I'd be home in time to show up for work tomorrow. I could forget all about this as a fleeting moment of insanity and go back to my normal life.

My normal life.

What was that exactly? Boring, that's what it was. Aiden said I wasn't a boring person, but I wasn't so sure I agreed. By his standards, I must be. Why in the world had he even invited me here? There was no way I was his usual type any more than he was mine.

That made me wonder what his usual type might be, and I imagined a vision of long dark hair, a super-slim body wrapped in black leather and thigh-high boots, and tattoos all over. Then I glanced down at my simple tan, scoop-necked shirt and modest, not-too-tight jeans, and skin completely devoid of artwork.

What did he see in me? Someone who was just conveniently drunk at the right time? Despite his words, did he assume because of how I had behaved that first night that I was a target for easy sex?

Was I going to have sex with him, either tonight or any other night I was here?

The fact that I couldn't answer that question scared the crap out of me. I couldn't deny my body's reaction to him, whether it was his build, his bright eyes, or maybe the fact that he was totally not my usual idea of a companion. I couldn't seem to stop myself from remembering the feeling of his lips on mine, his tongue in my mouth, and my body pressed against his. I licked my lips as my mind wandered to visions of myself underneath him on his king-sized bed, my legs wrapped around his waist as he pounded into me.

"Something to get you by." Aiden's voice caused me to jump, and I placed my hand over my heart. "Sorry, didn't mean to scare you."

"I'm fine," I lied. I swallowed and tried to clear my mind even as my thighs clenched together.

Aiden placed the tray he was carrying down in front of me. There were carrot and celery sticks, little triangles of pita bread, and a bowl of hummus.

"I made the hummus myself." He beamed at me. "It's really good."

"Wow, thank you!" I straightened myself in the chair and dipped one of the carrots into the mixture. I was famished and probably would have loved anything he put in front of me, but I had to admit the hummus was the best I had ever tasted. "It *is* really good!"

Aiden's smile broadened.

"You're going to love the rest," he said as he ran back inside.

I tried some of the pita with the hummus and then a couple more carrot sticks. I wasn't a huge fan of raw celery, but I ate one anyway just to be polite. My overactive imagination warned me that if he was a drug dealer, he could have drugged the food, but I reminded myself that if he wanted to hurt me, he'd already had plenty of opportunity to do so. He didn't need to drug me—there was no way I could hope to overpower him if he had less than honorable intentions.

The thought was terrifying and—again—exciting.

My mother would throw a fit if she knew I was here and thinking the things I was thinking. She would tell me to get the hell out—I didn't belong here with this man. I needed a nice, quiet man with a college degree and a steady job. I wasn't supposed to be looking for tattooed bodybuilders who might work for the mafia.

Mafia?

Crap! I hadn't even thought about that. A whole new wave of panic spread over me, and I was about to start hyperventilating when I heard the sliding door open again.

Aiden brought out two glasses of wine and then returned with two plates full of food. There was grilled chicken, sweet potatoes, and seasoned zucchini and yellow squash, and it smelled simply divine. All thoughts of drug dealing left my head as I dove in.

"This is fantastic!"

"Thank you. I usually only cook for myself; it's nice to have someone else enjoy it, too."

We ate as the sun went down, listened to the waves as they crashed against the shoreline, and drank multiple glasses of the sweet, white wine. We talked casually about the beach, foods we both liked, music, and movies.

He was a sci-fi buff, too.

"So, new *Doctor Who* or old?" he asked.

"New," I said without hesitation. "Definitely new. I can't get past the goofiness of the old ones."

Aiden laughed and agreed.

"How about *Torchwood*?" he asked.

"The spin-off series with Jack Harkness, right?"

"That's it."

"I haven't seen it."

"Oh, well you have to," Aiden stated with a nod. "It starts slow, but it fills in a lot of the gaps and Captain Jack is fabulous."

"I like him in the main series," I agreed. "I love how bisexual they made him. It's done so casually and without a lot of fuss."

Aiden grinned but didn't comment. I wondered if I had crossed some line, because the conversation quickly changed back to music. We both hated country and couldn't understand how popular it was.

We talked and talked. We joked and laughed. Throughout the evening, Aiden never made a move on me at all. He didn't even try to hold my hand again.

As the sun went down, I yawned.

"Time for bed?" Aiden asked quietly. The look in his eyes made my skin tingle.

"I guess so."

I helped carry the dishes into the kitchen, and we silently rinsed them off and placed them in the dishwasher before heading into the bedroom. I pulled out my toiletry bag and a pair of pajamas before excusing myself to the bathroom to change.

I stared at myself in the mirror and look a long, slow breath. I could see my own nervousness in my eyes.

"He said no pressure," I whispered to myself.

In the quietness of the bathroom, I doubted. I doubted what he meant, and I doubted what I wanted. I looked down at myself and the short, not quite sheer but still rather revealing pajamas I had managed to pack and wondered what my subconscious had been thinking when I threw them in the bag. In a very short time, I was going to be in bed with him, wearing this.

I could feel my pulse all the way down to my feet as I looked into my own eyes.

He's a drug dealer.

I glared at my reflection. I didn't know that, not for sure. He just said he was in pharmaceutical sales. He could have meant aspirin.

Bullshit. Guys who sell aspirin don't live in a house like this.

There was definitely more to Aiden Hunter than he let on. I was sure of that. I glanced around the bathroom, noticing that the green toothbrush I had used back in Ohio was now in a similar cup next to the blue one on the vanity.

He had packed my toothbrush. He knew I was going to give in and join him.

Or was he just extremely thoughtful?

I'm such an ass.

"You're not being fair," I said softly. "He's been nothing but nice. He cooked and even brought your spare toothbrush all the way from Ohio."

I shook my head, trying to toss the mistrust I felt off of me like a dog shakes water from its fur after a bath. He hadn't given me any reason to think he was going to suddenly change with the moonlight.

He wasn't going to turn into a werewolf or a vampire as soon as we were in bed together.

Did Buffy pack those stakes?

"You are a mess," I told myself. I glared again. "A ridiculous mess. Now stop it."

With a couple of deep, cleansing breaths, I opened the bathroom door and went back to the bedroom. Aiden wasn't in there, so I took the opportunity to quickly slip under the blankets, fretting for a minute about what side of the bed I should sleep on. I remembered that I had been on the left and he on the right when I'd woken up in the apartment in Ohio and decided that was as good as anything.

I checked my phone for messages and saw that it was at half-power. With a sigh, I got back out of bed and poked around in my bag for the charger. Clothes, toiletries, lip balm…dammit.

I hadn't brought it.

This is what happened when you didn't plan. Hopefully, Aiden would have a spare.

Climbing back into bed, I sat up against the pillows with the blankets pulled up to my chest, laid my hands on top of the comforter, and waited. A few minutes later, Aiden came back in the room, dressed in shorts and a white t-shirt. He looked down at me, and I thought he looked a little nervous, too.

"You sure you don't want me to take the couch?" he asked. "It's really not a problem."

"It's okay." I swallowed hard.

"Okay," he repeated. He slipped into the bed beside me and lay on his side, looking into my eyes but not touching me.

I was drawn to the contrast of his tattooed arms against the white sheets of the bed. Even in the dim light, Aiden's dark features seemed to glow.

"Are you glad you came with me?" he asked. "You are really hard to read."

"I am," I told him. "It's so beautiful here."

He stared at me for a long moment, and I glanced down our bodies to visually measure the meager space between us. We weren't touching anywhere, but I could still feel the heat from his body.

"I have to admit I'm a little nervous," he said. "I've never brought a woman here before."

"You haven't?"

"Never. I haven't lived here all that long and haven't dated anyone since I moved here."

"How long have you had this place?" I asked.

"Eight months," he told me.

"Where were you before?"

"I had a place in town," he said, "not on the beach."

"Why did you move here?"

"Came into some money," he said casually. "I wanted to get out of the area I was in, and this place was up for sale. It's hard to get into places right on the beach, but this one was in foreclosure, and I had the cash to make a decent offer. It's worked out well though I'm not here that often."

"Because of work?"

"Yeah, I travel around a lot."

I wondered just what he did to come into so much money but didn't ask. I had the feeling I wouldn't like the answer, assuming he would even be inclined to tell me. It was probably best I didn't know the details.

"Get some sleep." Aiden rolled to his back, leaving his broad shoulders closer to touching me than they had been when he was on his side. "Maybe I'll get you up early to watch the sunrise."

And with that, he smiled and closed his eyes.

SIX

I did not sleep.

As tired as I was, I couldn't. Sleeping in the same bed as Aiden Hunter was nothing like sleeping with my previous boyfriend. Zach was an attractive enough guy, but he had a slim and wiry frame—nothing like Aiden Hunter's body. He took up a good half of the large bed just with his mass. It was impossible to ignore his presence. I was far too acutely, insanely aware of the glorious warm body beside me.

Strangely enough, I found I was a little disappointed that he hadn't made a move on me. I wasn't sure I was ready to have sex with him, but I was surprised he hadn't at least tried for a little more making out. Did he change his mind? Maybe he already regretted asking me to come to Florida with him.

I lay there, listened to him breathe, and stole glances at his muscled chest and arms in the dim moonlight. I resisted the urge to run my hand over the artwork on his skin because I was afraid he'd wake up, and I'd be caught. Instead, I kept myself still and quiet as I watched him sleep. It was a long time before I finally drifted off.

In the moonlight, Aiden's eyes open and he catches me watching him. He takes my hand and places it against his chest before slowly drawing my fingers over his inked skin all the way down to his navel. Without a word, he rolls over and pins me to the bed. He uses his leg to

*spread my thighs, and he's heavy on top of me as he presses me against the
mattress. He's rough. He's grunting as he moves on top of me, and I wrap
my legs around him and hold on as tight as I can...*

I was breathless as I woke from my dream. It was the middle of
the night, and I found myself snuggled up against Aiden's side with
one arm tossed around his stomach. I'd driven Zach crazy and often
out of the bed when we had been dating. He said cuddling made him
hot and sweaty when I did that.

I was definitely sweaty and slightly out of breath. I remembered
my dream and had to take a few slow breaths to calm my pounding
heart before I allowed myself to move. As quietly as I could, I lifted
my arm from Aiden's waist and started to ease away from him. As I
did, I heard Aiden move and felt his fingers tighten around my
forearm.

"Don't go," he whispered in the darkness.

I froze momentarily and then looked up to his eyes. They were
still closed.

"Why not?" I whispered back. I didn't know if I would get an
answer or not. I wasn't sure if he was even awake.

"I like you here," he replied simply as his eyes fluttered open. He
tucked his arm under my shoulders and pulled me against his chest.
"It's nice having someone close again."

"Again?" He didn't answer. His eyes were closed now, and his
breath was slow and steady. I rested my head against his shoulder and
listened to him sigh as he settled back against the pillow.

Curled up against him, I inhaled his warm, musky scent and fell
back to sleep. When I woke, there was sunlight coming through the
window. I was still in the same basic position, and Aiden's arm
remained underneath me, holding me against him.

He was still sleeping, so I decided to ignore my bladder and just
lie there for a while. I breathed deeply and closed my eyes again.
Lying against Aiden was incredibly comfortable. It wasn't just the
physical closeness or the way our bodies seemed to mesh together so
perfectly but more that sense of comfort and security I had felt with
him since he put his arm around me at the airport.

I was warm, safe, and content.

He stirred slightly, and I tilted my head to watch him open his eyes. He blinked a few times, stretched the arm that wasn't around me over his head, and his stomach muscles rippled.

"Hi there," he said as he focused his eyes on mine.

"Hi," I responded, suddenly feeling a little shy. It was ridiculous, but the feeling was there anyway.

"This is much better than the first morning I woke up like this," Aiden remarked.

"Why is that?" I asked, smiling.

"Because today I get to make you breakfast." He beamed as he wiggled his arm out from under me.

"You really like to cook, don't you?"

"I do," he said. "It's a lot better to cook for someone else than just for yourself."

I remembered what he had said in the small hours of the morning and wondered who else he used to have in his life.

"So, who did you used to cook for?" I asked.

"How do you like your eggs?" Aiden asked. "I could do omelets, too. Do you like omelets?"

"I love omelets." I didn't miss his avoidance but also didn't ask again.

"How do you feel about Swiss cheese, green peppers, and mushrooms?"

"That sounds fantastic!"

He grabbed my hand and kissed the back of my knuckles just like he had the night before.

"It will be my pleasure."

Breakfast was fabulous. The omelets were perfectly cooked and accompanied by fried potatoes and orange slices.

"I could get used to this," I remarked. I sucked down another orange.

"I could, too." Aiden smiled slightly before standing up and clearing away the dishes. "Want more?"

"Sure!"

He refilled our plates, and I kept eating despite the full feeling in my stomach. It was just that good. While we ate, we chatted about our favorite foods. I got up to refill our glasses of iced coffee, and Aiden leaned far back in his chair and rubbed his stomach through his T-shirt.

"Damn, I'm stuffed." He looked down at his not-quite-finished half-omelet and moaned. "Can't let it go to waste, though."

"I'm stuffed, too," I said, giggling.

He grinned his intoxicating grin at me. I looked away, and I saw my phone lying on the table.

"Oh yeah," I said, "I was going to ask if you might have a phone charger I could borrow. I forgot mine."

"What kind do you need?" he asked.

"I have an iPhone."

"Hmm," he mumbled. "I only have one for a Galaxy. We could go pick one up for you."

"No, that's okay," I said, not wanting to be a bother. "I'll just switch it off when I don't need it."

"Up to you."

Despite being full, we ate everything Aiden had cooked and then took our coffee to the patio. On the beach, several people with tall fishing poles lined up near the water. Joggers dodged the fishing lines as they went by, and one hopeful teenager walked along the sand sweeping a metal detector in a wide arc.

"That same kid is out there every morning," Aiden commented. "I see him pick things up out of the sand every once in a while, but I have to wonder if it's really worth all the time he spends doing it. He's got to find more roach clips than anything else."

"Roach clips?"

Aiden looked at me skeptically.

"You don't know what a roach clip is?"

"No," I said, shaking my head. "What is it?"

Aiden smirked and leaned back in his chair, watching me closely.

"You really are quite the sheltered one, aren't you?"

I glared at him.

"What does that mean?"

"You're sweet," he said. His smile softened. "That's all it means."

He went back to sipping his coffee.

"Are you going to tell me," I asked, "or do I have to Google it?"

He reached up to scratch the back of his head as he looked toward the water.

"It's slang for the little alligator clip people use to hold the end of a joint."

"Oh." I didn't have another response. I looked down at the ice floating in my glass and bit down on my lip.

"Not your thing, is it?"

"What isn't?"

"Weed." Aiden tilted his head as he looked at me.

"I'm all Clinton there," I said with a wave of my hand.

"You're what?"

"Like President Clinton," I explained. "I tried it once in college, but as soon as I inhaled, I just started coughing. I didn't bother to try again."

Aiden chuckled briefly and then went quiet as he stared out at the teen on the beach. I finished my coffee and set the glass on the patio table with a slight thump. Aiden turned his head to the sound and then looked at me.

"So what would you like to do today?" he asked.

"I'm not sure," I said. "I've never been to Miami. What is there to do around here?"

"Everything," Aiden replied. He stood up, affixed his red cap on his head, and reached for my hand. "A morning beach walk is a good place to start."

We left our shoes on the patio and walked barefoot through the sand until we reached the edge of the water. The overnight tide had left chunks of coral and shells all over the sand, and I bent down to pick up a small, pink shell.

"Are you one of those seashell collectors?" Aiden asked.

"Yes," I said with a blush. "When I was I kid, we would go to Myrtle Beach every couple of years. I always came back with a huge bag of them."

"The pickings are a little slim around here," he said. "There's a sandbar about a hundred feet out, so most of the shells end up out there. There are some nice corals that make it this far."

He was right about the lack of variety though there were plenty of tiny clamshells. I found a few pieces of what might have been oysters, but they were too broken to tell for sure. I kept a few of the more colorful ones in one hand as we strolled along the edge of the water.

"I think I see a good one." I released Aiden's hand and walked a few feet into the cold water to retrieve it. It was a little bigger than the ones I had seen on the shore and had green and blue all over the inside. The waves washed over my feet, disturbing the sand and revealing other shells. I bent over and pulled them out, too.

There was something about shell collecting that had always calmed me. The waves brushing over my feet had a nearly hypnotic effect, and I walked a little farther out to see what else I could find. The warmth of the wind countered the coolness of the water, making a perfect combination.

A gull swooped by and squawked, pulling me out of my shell-searching trance. I looked up, but Aiden wasn't at the edge of the water any longer. I looked up and down the beach and finally saw him crouched near a mound of sand. I rubbed the sand off the shell and walked over to find him holding a small, green plastic shovel. He was staring at it intently, and his eyes seemed far away.

"What have you got there?" I asked.

Aiden jumped slightly before tossing the shovel back into the sand and standing.

"Nothing," he replied. He looked at me and smiled. "Some kid left his shovel on the beach. You still collecting shells?"

"I found some really pretty ones," I said.

He checked out my treasure.

"What are you going to do with them?"

"I have no idea." I laughed. "I think I was always more about the collecting than making any use out of them. I've probably brought thousands home but never even glued them to a picture frame. I think Mom ended up throwing them out when she moved."

"Why would she do that?"

"She threw out a lot of stuff, mostly my dad's things. It was too much for her to try to move it all across the country."

I squinted into the sunlight, remembering Mom's face as she boxed up Dad's clothes to take them to the Salvation Army. She'd remained stoic throughout the day, but it only took one glass of wine at dinner for her to melt down that evening.

"She got rid of all his things?" Aiden asked.

"Yes," I said. "Well, except for a few keepsakes. I held on to some of the things that reminded me of him—mostly books and the little silver tray he always had on his dresser. He kept his watch and change on it."

Aiden nodded, but his expression was strained.

"I don't know how she did it," Aiden said quietly. "Going through someone's things like that and then getting rid of them all, everything they owned—it's like it's a part of them."

"You have to," I said. "Moving forward is part of the grieving process. If you don't move forward, how do you ever get through the loss?"

Aiden looked at me for a long moment before he spoke.

"Maybe you don't. Maybe you shouldn't."

"Life goes on," I said. "You can't live in the past as if the people you have lost are going to show up again someday. You keep them in your memories, but you can't dwell on it."

"Maybe sometimes you have to." Aiden's eyes darkened.

"What do you mean?"

"What if dwelling on it is the only thing that keeps you going? What if it's the only way you can live with it?"

"Is that how it was with your dad?"

"My dad? Oh…" Aiden straightened and looked away for a moment. "Well, yeah. My mom left his den exactly like it was. It's probably still like that."

"Even now? Wasn't that back when you were in school?"

"Yeah, it was my freshman year. I don't know what she did with it all, but it's probably still there. I left home right after I graduated, so I don't know for sure."

"You never went back?"

"Nope."

"But she kept everything just like it was?"

"As far as I know. Like I said, she kinda went off the deep end at that point."

"That's not healthy," I said.

"She's not a healthy person," Aiden agreed. "I don't think I could have thrown out his stuff either. That just seems like…well, like I was trying to get rid of them, trying to forget."

"You don't forget." I reached out and put my hand on his arm. "At the same time, you have to let go."

I felt his arm tense under my fingers. For a minute, he seemed like he was going to say something but took a deep breath instead.

"Ready to find something fun to do?" he asked.

"Sure," I replied.

No doubt, Aiden was good at deflecting.

Aiden shoved his cap into one of the motorcycle bags and dug around in his garage until he found his extra helmet. A few minutes later, I found myself wrapped around him on the back of the motorcycle again. I didn't want to admit it, but it still scared the hell out of me. With me on the back, I was pretty sure he wasn't going as fast as he usually did, and I was grateful for it. As it was, we went plenty fast.

We rode to Oleta River State Park, and Aiden talked me into renting a kayak. He wanted us to each get our own, but I flat-out refused. I'd never paddled any kind of boat before, and I wasn't about to start in an area known for alligators. We got one of those that fit two people, and Aiden did most of the actual work to move us around the canal.

Shortly after we left the dock, I was captivated by the scene around me, forgetting all about the potential appearance of large reptiles. The mangroves were beautiful, and Aiden told me everything I ever wanted to know about them.

"They actually live in the salt water," he said. "Since their roots are all over the edge of the canal, they slow down the waves coming in from the ocean and help with erosion. They also make it a lot easier to navigate the water, and there's a ton of sea life. See?"

Aiden slowed us down near a batch of mangrove roots and leaned over near the water. Just under the surface, three jellyfish bobbed about.

"Watch this," Aiden said with big smile. He reached down and tapped the top of one of the jellyfish.

"Won't it sting?" I asked.

"There aren't any tentacles on the top," he said. "Those are what can sting you. Watch what it does."

I peered over the side, bracing myself as the tiny watercraft leaned with our weight.

"You're not going to fall out," Aiden assured me. "Watch again."

He tapped the top of the jellyfish with his index finger, and the little creature swirled around until it was upside down, reaching out toward the top of the water with its undulating tentacles.

"Is it trying to sting you?"

"Yep." The jellyfish rolled back until it was right side up, and Aiden tapped at it again. Once more, it tried to reach for his finger by spinning upside down.

"They aren't very bright," Aiden remarked, "but a lot of fun to play with. You try it."

"Me? Touch a jellyfish?"

"As long as you only touch the top, it doesn't hurt. It feels kinda cool."

"No way!"

"What's the worst thing that could happen?"

"If anyone would end up getting stung, it would be me."

"So you recognize that being stung is the worst possible outcome?"

"I guess so." I wasn't sure where he was going with this.

"Have you ever been stung by a bee?"

"When I was a kid, yes."

"And you lived?"

"Obviously."

"Compared to these jellies, bee stings are worse," Aiden said. "So, give it a shot. You know you're going to live."

I glared at him, but he just smiled back as he poked another one of the creatures. I took a deep breath, fairly certain he wasn't going to let me get out of it, and reached out to touch the top part of the jellyfish's body,

It was slimy.

"Eww!" I cried as I quickly pulled my hand out of the water. The jellyfish rolled onto its back to try to catch me. "It's gross!"

Aiden laughed, causing the kayak to shake.

"I'll show you gross," he said. He picked up the paddle and maneuvered us closer to the mangrove roots. The water was shallow here, and I could see right to the bottom. Aiden looked over the side, moved us forward a little more, and then grabbed hold of one of the tree roots.

"There's one," he muttered. "Lean to your right a bit."

I did so, and Aiden leaned to the left, shoving his whole hand and arm down into the water. I bit into my lip to keep from squealing as the kayak swayed left. I wasn't enough counterbalance and had to lean over further.

"I got it!" Aiden said as he sat back up, and the kayak rocked right, startling me.

"Warn me!" I cried out as I righted myself.

"You aren't going to fall out," Aiden said again. He leaned forward and held out his hand. Lying in his palm was a brownish mass that resembled a giant, lumpy dill pickle that had been in the back of the refrigerator for far too long.

"What is it?" I asked.

"A sea cucumber," Aiden said. "It's about the most disgusting thing in the world."

"It is gross," I agreed.

"Hopefully it won't do this now," Aiden said, "but when they feel threatened, sea cucumbers have a wonderful defense mechanism."

"What's that?"

"They puke up their intestines."

"They *what*?"

"Basically, it looks like they turn themselves inside out. They go from kinda gross-looking to completely vile, making predators think they are already dead, and therefore, unappetizing."

"You have to be joking."

"Not at all." Aiden looked up, and his eyes glimmered with boyish mischief. "Want me to see if I can piss it off?"

"No!"

"Touch it, then." He held it a little closer, and I cringed.

"Not a chance."

"If you don't," he warned, "I'm going to start fucking with it until it pukes!"

"No!"

"Then touch it!"

"Ugh!" I scrunched up my face, terrified the thing was going to jump out at me, and reached out tentatively with one finger. I stroked the top of it, surprised it wasn't as slimy as it looked. It was still gross though, and I said so.

Aiden smiled as he tucked his hand back under the surface of the water and let the thing go.

"That's twice you've lived today," he said. "Shall we go for number three?"

"I think my quota of touching gross sea life has been reached." I folded my arms over the paddle's handle.

"I had something else in mind," Aiden said. He dipped his paddle in the water and moved us away from the trees.

We paddled a little farther down the canal and closer to the bay. There were plenty of others out and about, mostly in kayaks or standing on paddleboards. There were even a couple of groups led by a nature guide.

The weather was perfect, and the water was perfect, and the whole thing was just beautiful. I relaxed as I became more comfortable moving the kayak around, but I was still glad Aiden was behind me and doing most of the actual steering. When I looked back at him, he was peering over the edge again.

"Hang on," he said as he paddled backward for a moment. The kayak stilled, and Aiden took his cap off and placed it backward on my head.

"What are you doing?" I asked as I grabbed the cap and turned it around the right way.

"Just hold onto the edge of the kayak and brace yourself," he commanded. Then he stood up.

"Aiden!" I cried as he dived into the water, causing the kayak to rock back and forth. A few moments later, he surfaced and swam up to the front of the kayak, grasping the side with one hand.

In the other hand, he held up a giant conch.

"Oh my God!" I screamed. "Is it…is it alive?"

"It is," he said. He turned the huge shell to the side and let me look. Right around the edge where the shell coiled back into itself, I could see the pink flesh of the moving conch, hiding itself from the air.

"I wasn't expecting to find one this big," Aiden said. "A lot of them get taken home by tourists. Sometimes they don't even know it's a living thing—they think it's just the shell."

I reached out without prompting this time, and ran my finger along the edge of the shell. It was smooth and cool to the touch.

"I figured since you liked collecting shells, you'd like seeing a live one."

I looked at him for a long moment.

"I do like it," I said softly. "Thank you."

"You're welcome."

He slowly lowered the giant shell back into the water.

"Now hold on tight again," he instructed. "If you were going to fall out, now would be the time."

"I don't want to fall out!"

"Then hang on!"

Aiden managed to pull himself back into the kayak without upsetting us and sending me into the brackish water, but his dripping body still managed to soak me.

"I might as well have dived in myself."

"I could toss you in," Aiden teased.

"You better not!"

He laughed and began to paddle us around again. Eventually, we had both endured enough sun, and he guided us back to the dock.

"You getting hungry?" Aiden asked as we turned in our paddles and lifejackets.

"Yeah, I am." I realized I was still wearing his baseball cap, so I removed it and handed it back to him.

"Let's go find a good place to eat," Aiden said as he placed the cap on his head. "How about a trip to South Beach, where all the beautiful people hang out?"

"I think I'd be very out of place."

Aiden narrowed his eyes at me and then smiled.

"You're right," he said. "If I take you down there, they're all going to be extremely jealous of you. You could start a riot."

For a moment, my heart lodged in my throat. I knew I didn't fit in with the glamorous and famous people known to frequent that area and wasn't sure what I thought of Aiden's flattery. I hadn't even brought any clothing suitable for a fancy restaurant.

"Most of those places have dress codes," Aiden said as if he were reading my mind. "I don't want to ride all the way back home. If you aren't starving just yet, let's go shopping."

"Buy new clothes just to go out to eat? You can't be serious."

"Why not?" he asked.

"That seems a little…I don't know…wasteful."

"Are you going to throw it all out when you get home?" he asked.

"Of course not."

"Then where's the waste?"

All right, he had me there. Still, when I went shopping, it was always for a specific purpose. I bought clothes for work and leisure when the ones I had were worn out or didn't fit right anymore. I didn't just go buy an outfit to avoid running back home.

"How do we have to dress?" I asked.

"For me, some dress pants, button down, and a jacket of some sort," Aiden said. He looked me up and down. "For you, I'm thinking a nice, short cocktail dress. Maybe red."

He winked.

"This is going to be that kind of place?"

"It's South Beach," Aiden explained. "They're all that kind of place—even the burger joints."

I tried to argue a little more—I didn't mind the trip back to his house—but he was insistent. I gave in to him, which I noticed was becoming a trend.

The kayak rental center had locker rooms and showers. As soon as we were out of our bathing suits and cleaned up a bit, we headed to the Lincoln Road Mall and found a nice department store. I looked at dresses, and a woman came up to me almost immediately to help me with my selection. She gave me a friendly smile and started to talk about the latest styles, but as soon as Aiden walked up, she excused herself and walked away.

"That was rude," I muttered under my breath.

"Happens to me all the time," Aiden said dismissively. He indicated the red cocktail dress I had in my hand. "I like this one."

I checked the price tag and rolled my eyes, but it became very clear very quickly that Aiden wasn't going to compromise on anything, including who was paying for the expensive—and very short—dress he picked out. He claimed it would be the only way I could ride on the back of the bike since a long one would get in the way. In protest against his overindulgence, I quickly bought matching shoes and a purse while he was waiting in line to buy my dress along with the clothes he had selected for himself. He glared at me when he saw what I had done then smiled half a grin.

"Sneaky thing," he muttered.

The attendant at the changing room didn't seem inclined to help us, but Aiden slipped her some cash, and she let us use the store to change into our fancy clothes. He was already done changing when I walked out. The lack of backward cap, the dress pants and blazer made him look like a completely different person from the one in the casual clothes he had worn so far. I almost didn't recognize him without all the tattoos showing.

Of course, when I moved closer, I could still see some of the marking around his neck. I realized I didn't even know what it said though there were obviously words written across his throat. I would have had to get up close to read them, and that just seemed so rude.

We ended up at a steak house right on the beach and sat out on the patio. The evening was perfect, just like the day had been. I had a glass of the best wine I had ever tasted, but Aiden didn't try it. He said he never drank when he had the bike out.

"Are you glad you came?" Aiden asked as we finished our dinners.

"Yes," I said. My face warmed, and I wondered if he could see my blush.

"Good." He sat back and looked around the patio. "See anyone you recognize?"

"No," I said, "should I?"

He leaned close to me.

"Judge Judy is over there, just at the edge of the patio near the gate."

"Really?" I glanced quickly, trying not to be too obvious.

Aiden snickered quietly.

"She lives around here somewhere," he said. "I've seen her a few times. David Beckham and Posh Spice are inside, just by the door."

I tried to look through the window and thought I could see the couple he meant, but it was hard to tell.

"He plays soccer, right?"

"Yeah," Aiden said, "or at least, he did. Now he's starting up a major league soccer team here in Miami. You never know who you might see around here."

Aiden's phone beeped, and he glanced at it. I tried to look around at the other patrons, wondering how many other famous people were around me, but I kept peering back at his face. His jaw tightened as he glared down at the illuminated screen.

Whatever message was on the phone, he wasn't happy about it.

"Ready to go?" he said suddenly.

"Um...sure."

Aiden called for the check and led me back out to his motorcycle. He didn't say a word as he strapped the helmet to my head, climbed on, and started up the engine. I wrapped my arms around him. I could feel the tenseness in his chest as I held on, and we sped north up Ocean Boulevard.

"I have some work to do," Aiden announced as soon as we arrived back at his house. "I'm sorry about that. I had planned on ignoring it while you were here, but sometimes it can't be helped. You want a glass of wine or something? I could get a fire going in the fire pit if you wanted to hang out there."

"That works," I said. I smiled to let him know I didn't mind. "I'm sure you have better things to do than entertain me the whole week."

Aiden turned away from the wine bottle and looked at me.

"Better? No. Definitely not better. Just unavoidable."

"I run into that sometimes," I said. "No matter how many team members are on a project, sometimes nothing gets done unless I spell it out for people."

"Maybe I need you to manage my project," Aiden mumbled.

"Do you work on projects?" I asked. I looked down at the floor for a moment, hoping I wasn't going too far when it came to asking about his work. "With your sales work, I mean."

"Not with the sales stuff, no," he replied quietly. "The sales business is pretty straightforward. I have something, you want it, and we negotiate on price or quantity. Hopefully I come out ahead, and I usually do."

"Do you have a sideline business?" I was pressing. I knew I was, but I couldn't seem to help myself.

Aiden was quiet as he poured me a glass of wine.

"I guess you could call it that," he finally replied. "Did you get enough to eat? I've got more of that hummus. Or maybe some cheese and crackers?"

And he derails the conversation. Again.

"No, I'm still pretty full."

"All right, then," he said as he handed me the wine. "Let's get you settled. Unfortunately, I'm probably going to be a while."

I sat in the cool evening breeze and enjoyed the sound of the waves while I slowly sipped at the wine. The beach was completely empty, which surprised me. It was so beautiful, I guess I expected lots of people out near the water at night. As it was, my only company was the lights from a few ships at sea.

I thought about our kayak trip and dinner. It really had been very nice. I had never considered trying out a kayak before. I wasn't one for physical activities, and doing anything for the first time felt intimidating. It had been nerve-wracking, but Aiden had talked me through it, and I was glad we had gone. I could have done without the slimy jellyfish or puking cucumbers, but the conch had been amazing. I had always wanted to find a conch shell when I was a kid but had only ever found pieces of them. I hadn't even thought about the animal that lived inside.

The air chilled as I finished my drink and brought the glass back into the kitchen. Aiden was in the living room, where he had shoved some of the boxes out of the way and was typing furiously on a laptop. I walked into the room, and he jumped slightly before slamming down the cover.

"All wined out?" Aiden asked with a smile. There was no light in his eyes, though, and the smile seemed feigned.

"I suppose so," I said. "Wine always makes me sleepy."

"Well, don't wait up on my account," Aiden said. "I think I'm going to be a while longer."

"That's okay," I said. "I'll just...um...see you in the morning."

"Goodnight, Chloe."
"Goodnight, Aiden."
And with that, I headed off to bed.

SEVEN

I'd always heard that guys who were tall often had proportional dicks. If what I vaguely remembered feeling against my leg during our first drunken kiss was an accurate memory, Aiden fit the bill. I was certain that man's sausage could feed a developing country of horny women.

"You want sausage?"

"What?" I cried, wondering how in the hell he could read my mind.

"With your eggs," Aiden said. "Do you want sausage with your eggs?"

Oh yeah. Breakfast.

I twisted a little on my seat and tried to hide my blush with a cup of coffee. The thoughts running through my head this morning were troublesome, to say the least. Though the last time we had kissed was next to my car outside of Thirsty's, sleeping next to Aiden Hunter apparently got my hormones going.

Watching him cook breakfast was the sexiest thing I had ever witnessed. I had to grab my phone and pretend to be busy turning it on just to make sure I didn't get caught ogling him.

Every time he switched from one pan to the other on the stove, his ass moved in a way I couldn't stop watching. The cargo shorts he wore weren't tight at all, but that didn't make any difference—the muscles in his ass were quite prevalent anyway. When he shifted his weight, I could see the line of his gluteus maximus muscles through the fabric.

It was quite distracting.

His shoulders were just as captivating. They were broad and as chiseled as the rest of him. The angle of his traps going up to his neck just made me want to draw a line there. Actually, the more I stared as his tattooed skin, the more I wanted to trace every line, every skull, every star, every flower…with my tongue.

I couldn't believe I was thinking this way.

Muscled guys had never been my thing before. I'd always been attracted to the thin, wiry types in white, button-down shirts and Dockers. Tie optional. They never had tattoos or motorcycles or secret business dealings in the middle of the night.

Alarm!

I told the subconscious noise in my head to shut up.

"How about we do something spontaneous today?" Aiden suggested.

"Like what?"

"If I tell you, it won't be spontaneous."

"Not telling me makes it a secret," I said. "That has nothing to do with spontaneity."

"Good point." Aiden shoveled another mouthful of eggs and cheese into his mouth, chewed, and swallowed. "I'm still not telling you."

"Why not?"

"Because I don't want you to back out."

"I can't back out if I've never agreed," I argued, "and I can't agree without knowing what it is."

"Taking a little road trip with me is agreeance."

"It is not. I don't even think that's a real word."

"Sure it is." Aiden's eyes brightened. "Besides, you understood what I meant, right? Isn't that the essence of communication?"

I crossed my arms and looked at him sideways, earning myself another grin.

"So, another ride on the motorcycle?"

"We'll take my jeep," he said. "It'll be more comfortable for a long ride anyway."

We cleaned up breakfast, took our turns in the bathroom, and packed bottles of water for the road before Aiden took me out to the garage and helped me into a bright yellow Jeep Rubicon. The soft top, windows, and doors had been removed, leaving the whole thing open.

"Won't I fall out?" I asked.

"Not unless you do it on purpose," Aiden said as he adjusted the cap on his head. I was starting to wonder if he ever went anywhere without it. "Put your seatbelt on."

I did, and he backed out of the drive and into the road, headed south.

"Where are we going?" I asked. I had to gather my hair at the back of my head with one hand to keep the wind from blowing it in my face.

"Homestead," Aiden replied. "It's just a little ways south of Miami."

"And what's in Homestead?"

"Mostly farms. I get a lot of fresh vegetables down there. It's a great ride on the bike. Sometimes I'll head straight down to the Keys. It's beautiful."

"Is that where we're going?" I asked. "The Keys?"

"Well, not exactly." Aiden glanced at me as his lip curled up. "I think you will be able to see the Keys from where we'll be though."

Aiden continued to evade my questions about our destination as we drove down the coast of Miami, through Miami Beach, west across Biscayne Bay, and then down South Dixie Highway. We went past many vegetable farms loaded with workers wearing their wide-brimmed hats out in the fields, and we passed through a collection of small towns. It took a little while, but eventually Aiden announced that we were almost there.

Aiden turned the jeep into a long gravel driveway and headed toward a large building that looked like a big metal barn. Next to the barn were a small prop plane and a van painted with vivid colors and the words "Skydive Miami." I looked at Aiden sharply as realization hit me.

"You are *not* serious."

"Who me?" He feigned innocence. "I'm totally serious."

"Skydiving?" I cried. "Jumping out of a plane? *On purpose?* I've never skydived in my life!"

"Neither have I," Aiden said. "All the more reason to do it."

"No way!"

Aiden parked next to a couple of other cars and turned to me.

"It's time to live a little, Chloe. Come on, let's just go inside and see what there is to see."

"You are out of your mind," I said firmly. "I am not doing this."

"Why not?"

"It's dangerous!"

"So is driving on the highway," Aiden replied. "You didn't mind doing that."

"I'm used to that," I said with less conviction.

"So we'll go skydiving a few times until you are used to it." I glared at Aiden's smirk.

He came around to the passenger side of the jeep and reached up to take my hand.

"Give it a chance," he said as I pulled back, determined to remain in the vehicle.

The sunlight captured the green in his eyes, and in turn, his eyes captivated me. I gave in and followed him into the building.

Inside, a receptionist handed each of us a large stack of papers to sign and had us sit down to watch a video. To sum it up, both the video and the paperwork said we were going to die.

"I can't do this," I said as I shook my head. "Did you read any of this?"

"Yeah," Aiden said. "It's a lot of lawyer talk."

"Right—because we're going to die."

"Nah," he said. "They just want to make sure if we do, they don't get sued."

I looked down at the papers again, seven pages of all the various ways we could be maimed or dead by the time the trip was over, and the demand that we sign away any right to sue the skydiving company for damages because we recognized that what we were about to do was completely stupid.

"Aiden…"

He lifted his hand to my face and stroked my cheek as he looked into my eyes.

"I don't know what will happen," he said. "That's the excitement of it. That's what makes life worth living. You don't know what will happen next. We'll probably be fine, but there's no guarantee."

He placed his other hand on the other side of my face and stared at me intently.

"There's never a guarantee, Chloe. You never know what life is going to throw at you. We could say forget it, go back to my place, and sit on the beach. It would be nice and peaceful and fun. You could have a heart attack or a brain aneurysm while we sat there. Driving back, we could be killed by a truck full of zucchini. Life isn't about how it ends; it's about what you do while you're alive."

"How much can you do if the guy you are with has a death wish?" I asked.

"I don't want to die," Aiden corrected. "I want to live. That's the point."

"Couldn't we hunt for seashells or something?"

Aiden shook his head slowly.

"I'm doing it," he said definitively. "You join me if you want."

Aiden signed the last piece of paper and walked back up to the counter. I looked down, reread some of the scarier parts, took a deep breath, and signed my name. At the counter, Aiden threw down a credit card and insisted on paying for my jump as well. I wasn't going to argue. I wasn't about to pay for this insanity.

Once the receptionist had all our information and promises not to sue if we died, we were led to a back room where we were both strapped into harnesses and given little helmets. The headgear looked ridiculous, and I didn't see what the point of them was. It wasn't as if they would stop our heads from looking like smashed pumpkins the day after Halloween if we fell out of a damn plane and hit the ground.

We were given very brief instructions about how to fold our arms in front of our chests and lean back when we were ready. The instructors would have the parachutes, and we would be strapped to the instructors. Just as the lesson ended, our instructors came in and introduced themselves as Greg and Mike.

"For your first jump, you always go tandem," Mike said. "I lost the coin toss, so I'll be strapped to the big guy, and Greg here gets the lovely lady."

Greg winked at me and then walked over to check the straps around my shoulders.

"I'm going to get a little personal here," Greg warned. "I just have to make sure everything is on right."

A little personal was right. He ran his hands over the straps around my breasts and around my ass, checking them thoroughly. I caught Aiden watching out of the corner of his eye, but Mike was doing the exact same thing to him.

"You're all set!" Greg said. "Let's go!"

We followed the two men outside and headed toward the plane.

"How many times have you done this?" I asked Greg as we walked.

"Over twenty thousand jumps," he said.

"Really?"

"Really," he repeated. He winked at me again. "Never died once."

My phone rang.

"Crap!" I bit down on my lip as I looked at my mother's picture on the screen.

If I die in the next hour, this would be my last chance to talk to her.

"Do I have time to take this call?" I asked Greg.

"Sure," he said. "It'll be a few minutes before we're ready to go."

I took a few steps away from the plane to dull the noise.

"Hi, Mom!" I said into the phone.

"Hey there! I was just thinking about you. I hope I'm not interrupting a meeting or anything."

"No, not at all." I glanced toward the plane and saw Mike adjusting Aiden's harness. "What exactly were you thinking about?"

"I was going through some old photos," Mom said. "There were some in here of your kindergarten graduation, which got me thinking about high school and college, so I pulled those out, too."

"A little trip down memory lane?"

"I suppose so." I could hear her sigh. "I know I needed to move out here, but I still miss you being around all the time."

"I miss you, too, Mom."

"I thought I might come your way for Thanksgiving," Mom said. "I don't expect you to cook or anything—we could just go out if you like."

"Go out for Thanksgiving? No way!" I laughed. "We can cook together. I'd love to see you."

"I'll make the arrangements!" Mom said.

Aiden beckoned me, and I took a deep breath.

"Hey, Mom? I have to run, but I'll call you back this weekend, okay?"

"Of course. Just don't do anything crazy!"

My heart began to beat faster.

"Um...crazy?" I asked. Was there really some deep mother's intuition at work here? Did she know I was about to do something life-threatening?

Good lord, what was I thinking?

"Well, I know you don't get along with your new boss," Mom explained. "Just don't do anything to get yourself fired or get so fed up you quit without having a backup plan."

"Oh!" I wiped a bit of sweat off my brow. "I won't do that. I swear."

"Good girl. I'll talk to you soon."

"Sounds good, Mom. I love you!"

"I love you, too, dear."

I ended the call and took another deep breath. I turned the phone off and placed it in my purse before walking back to the plane. One of the workers took all our valuables, including Aiden's baseball cap, and promised to lock them up until we got down.

If we got down in one piece, of course.

"All ready?" Greg asked.

"No!" I screamed in my head. Outwardly I smiled and nodded.

Greg climbed up into the plane first and then motioned to me to join him.

"Come on and sit right here," he said as he patted his thighs.

"On your lap?" I asked.

"Between my legs," he corrected. "We're going to be pretty cozy on the way up."

I sat between his legs, and then Mike climbed in and sat between mine. Aiden sat in front of Mike, and we all sandwiched ourselves into the small aircraft. There were three other jumpers going with us —one of them in tandem like Aiden and I were. The other two were experienced jumpers and going on their own.

"Getting personal again," Greg warned as he began to buckle his harness to the back of mine. His hands came around my front as he checked the latches around my chest. I tried not to lean too far back against him, but it was nearly impossible in the close quarters. By the time we reached fourteen thousand feet, my back hurt from trying to sit up straight, so I gave up and rested against his chest.

"We're good!" the pilot called from the cockpit. "Fourteen thousand five hundred feet."

The door on the side of the plane opened, and I peered around Mike's shoulder into nothing but blue sky and a few wispy clouds.

Holy crap! What was I thinking?

The two experienced skydivers made their way to the edge of the door and barely blinked before tossing themselves out into the air, tumbling into the sky with a whoop of exuberance.

I couldn't share their enthusiasm. I was terrified.

Aiden and his instructor moved up to the door, and Aiden looked back at me.

"Here goes nothing!" he shouted. He leaned back against Mike, and a moment later, they both dropped out of the door and were gone.

"Your turn!" Greg said. He helped maneuver us both to the doorway, and I looked out into the open sky and ground below. We were so high up, I couldn't even make sense of the scene in front of me.

"Cross your arms over your chest and lean back against me," Greg instructed.

I did as he said. My heart was beating so fast, I wondered if I would go into cardiac arrest before the chute even opened.

"Ready?" he asked.

I swallowed hard and nodded. I wasn't ready. I wasn't ready at all. This was insane.

"Yes!" I called back.

"Here we go!" Greg leaned forward, then back, and then forward again.

We tumbled into space.

The cold wind bit at my flesh as we fell. I tried to keep my mouth closed, but I was pretty sure a string of curse words were automatically flowing from it. The ground was impossibly far away but getting closer and closer by the second. Below us, I could see the forms of the other jumpers, including Aiden and Mike.

What if we crashed into them?

I felt Greg's tap on my shoulder—the signal for me to spread out my arms. I did so, but it didn't seem to slow us down at all. Greg pushed against me, angling us forward. I could see the fleeting image of Aiden and his instructor as we whizzed past them and through a cloud.

We were still falling. Tears were pulled from my eyes as the wind tore past my face. I tried to look at the meter on my wrist to see how far we had fallen, but I couldn't see it clearly enough to read it. The air was freezing cold on my bare skin, and my stomach did flip-flops inside of me.

With a sudden jerk, my body pulled upward and into Greg. The straps around me tightened somewhat painfully, and our descent slowed as the chute opened.

We floated.

"What do you think?" Greg asked.

"Holy shit!" It was all I could manage to say.

Greg laughed.

"That's the Everglades to your left," he told me. "Key Largo is on the right. See it?"

"It's beautiful!" I exclaimed.

"Let me loosen you up a little." I felt Greg's hands at my back. The harness released, causing me to gasp as I slipped forward slightly. The straps were more comfortable, but my heart remained lodged in my throat.

We floated into a cloud, and for a moment there was nothing but white and a slightly damp feeling on my skin. We dropped below it quickly, and I heard Greg's voice again.

"How about a little spin?"

He pulled on the left side straps, and we spun in a counterclockwise direction. Then he pulled on the right, and we went clockwise. My stomach churned a bit.

"You try," he said as his hand covered mine. I pulled the strap and we spun around again. "Go ahead and turn whichever direction you like."

I did. I moved a little to the left and then a little to the right but kept the motion slow and steady so I wouldn't lose breakfast. Far below, the green of the Everglades dominated the landscape. I could see the fields we had passed in the jeep and the tiny forms of field workers gathering vegetables. The blue water around the islands of the Keys sparkled in the sunlight.

I looked around some more, marveling in the beauty of the panoramic scene below me. I pulled at the strap again and looked out over the ocean, my mind spinning.

Was I really doing this?

I looked up to see two other parachutes above us, but I couldn't make out which one of the figures was Aiden. I glanced over my shoulder to see Greg smiling.

"What do you think?" he asked.

"It's incredible!" I cried. "Really, truly incredible!"

"There's nothing else like it!" he agreed.

We floated through another cloud, and Greg took control of our direction as we began to approach the ground. I could see a wide field below us with two circles of brown grass in the center and several people standing around. The colorful van was parked at the edge of the grassy area.

The first two jumpers landed below us, and their chutes billowed out briefly before the thrill-seekers gathered them up and pulled them away from the circle. Greg turned us again, angling us down and toward the ground.

"Remember, hold your legs up. Leave the landing to me."

We were drawing near the group quickly. I pulled my knees to my chest as we approached one of the small circles in the middle of the field. With a jolt, Greg's feet touched down, and he began to run.

"Feet down!" Greg called out as we slowed. I dropped my feet and rejoined the earth. Greg held my upper arms, keeping me from falling backward as we slowed and then stopped.

Greg hauled the parachute away from the circle and started balling it up. I looked up into the sky and saw the tiny speck of blue and yellow still high up there. I could barely make out Aiden's form, strapped to Mike, as they made their way back to the ground. I watched as Aiden pulled his feet up, and he and Mike landed just outside the circle on the grass. As soon as they slowed to a stop, they both fell backward onto their butts.

I laughed.

"That was fucking incredible!" Aiden screamed as Mike released the harness so he could stand up again. "Holy shit, that was awesome!"

He ran over and lifted me into the air, spinning me in a circle. I grasped his shoulders and held my breath—my stomach was still a little queasy.

"Wasn't that fucking awesome?"

"It was," I agreed with a laugh.

"And you lived!" he exclaimed.

"I did!" More giggling as he dropped me back to my feet.

"You lived," he repeated, "in more ways than one."

"Yeah," I agreed, "I did. Thank you."

I reached up and pressed my lips briefly to his. When I looked at him, Aiden was smiling down at me, his eyes wide and bright with excitement. His hands were trembling at my sides, and I realized mine were as well, but I wasn't scared. I was exuberant.

And with that, I realized what had been missing from my life.

EIGHT

The drive home was spent comparing our experiences as we flew through the sky. I was still pumped up on the adrenaline running through my system and couldn't seem to stop smiling. Aiden was the same way and occasionally stuck his head out the side of the jeep to whoop in joy as we drove down the road.

When we finally arrived back at Aiden's house, a silver Lincoln Town Car was parked in the driveway.

"What the hell," Aiden mumbled under his breath as he pulled around the car and stopped the jeep beside it.

"What is it?" I asked. "Who's here?"

"Just some friends," he said as he exited the jeep.

I climbed out the other side and followed him through the house and to the back patio.

Sitting in the patio chairs were two men. Both were tall with dark skin and massive bodies that would barely fit through a doorway, even one at a time. The darker one was bald and had a bushy black beard. The other, slightly lighter-skinned man had a goatee and short, sculpted hair.

"What's up, Hunter?" the man with the goatee practically screamed as they both stood up.

"Where the hell have you been, motherfucker?" the bald man asked, his voice equally as loud. "You missed a big-ass bash at Redeye's last weekend."

"Ohio," Aiden responded. "Had some business."

"Oh, yeah. How did that shit go?" Goatee asked.

"Later." Aiden glanced quickly at me and then back to Goatee.

"Gotcha."

"And who is this fine lady?" the other man said as he jabbed Aiden in the ribs.

"Chloe," Aiden said as he took my hand and pointed to the darker complected of the two visitors, "this is Lorenzo, or just Lo, we call him."

"Please ta meet cha!" Lo said as he shook my hand.

"Good to meet you, too," I said as I took his.

"And this is Mo," Aiden said. "As far as I know, it isn't short for anything."

"It's short for mo-ron! Ha! Ha! Ha!" Lo said as he belly laughed at his own joke.

The sharpness and volume of the laugh actually caused me to jump.

"Look who's talkin'!" Mo replied as he shoved Lo on the shoulder. He turned back to Aiden. "So where did you find this one?"

"Back up north," Aiden said. "She needed a little vacation in the sun."

"She's too cute for you," Mo said. "Let me take her off your hands."

Aiden took a step forward, standing between me and Mo.

"You keep your hands and everything else to yourself," Aiden said. Though he smiled when he spoke, there was an undercurrent of warning. "She's my guest here."

Mo laughed as loudly as Lo had, startling me again.

"So what's Hunter been doin' with ya?" Lo asked me. "You must be hard up if you're hanging with this loser."

"We went skydiving," I replied.

"Holy shit! Are you serious?" Mo asked. His eyes bulged as he looked at Aiden. "Like, *real* skydiving?"

"Yeah, we went down to Homestead," Aiden said. "I'd always wanted to go, and Chloe needed to let loose a little."

"You crackers are crazy," Lo said as he pointed a finger at Aiden. "There's no way I'd jump out of a perfectly good airplane."

"There's no way you'd fit into an airplane, perfect or otherwise!" Mo said, and they both laughed loudly.

"These guys are characters," Aiden said as he leaned close to me. "Watch out for them."

"There's no point," Lo said as he ran his hands suggestively down his body. Mo began to dance around in a circle with his hands up behind his head. "No one can handle all of this!"

Mo and Lo both started laughing again. Now that I was expecting it, the sound wasn't so jarring. I even smiled a little as Lo sashayed his hips back and forth. I looked at both of them carefully, trying to figure out just what their relationship was. If it wasn't for the variations in skin tone, I would have thought them to be brothers just based on their similar mannerisms.

"You're going to scare the neighbors," Aiden said. "You guys want a drink?"

"Fuck yeah!" they both responded at once.

Aiden went inside and grabbed beer from the fridge. We all sat around the patio table, and Aiden popped open the bottles. Lo and Mo went over some details from the party Aiden had missed, focusing on the obviously insane amount of alcohol they had consumed.

"Vodka roulette, Redeye called it," Mo said. "He's out of his mind."

"He had a dozen flavors of vodka," Lo said, "some good, some not so good. Then there's one shot that's just water."

"That's the worst one to get," Mo piped in.

"No it isn't," Lo corrected. "Nothing is worse than Bakon vodka."

"Bacon?" I repeated.

"Bakon with a 'k' in it," Lo said. "That shit is nasty."

"Crack an egg in it," Mo said, "and it's the perfect hangover breakfast!"

"Dude, you are fucked up," Lo responded seriously. "Nasty, nasty shit."

"So everyone gets a different flavor," Mo continued, "and you don't know what it is until you drink it."

"I got blueberry pancake," Lo informed us. "It's not bad, really."

"That sounds awful," I remarked.

"You can't say no to a shot from Redeye," Aiden said as he leaned toward me. "He'll badger you until you take it. It's easier to just give in."

Mo suddenly stood up and pretended to hold a shot glass out to me.

"You need a shot!" he yelled. "Take this shot! Take this shot right now! Are you disrespecting my hospitality here?"

The three of them laughed.

"That's about right," Aiden said with a nod.

"His name is Redeye?" I asked.

"Not really," Aiden said, "but it's what everyone calls him."

"Why?"

"I have no clue." Aiden grinned and tipped back his beer. "He's a lot of fun, though."

"Is he a bartender or something?"

"Nah, he's in sales, like me."

I didn't press the subject.

Lo and Mo went over more antics from the party, mostly concerning who ended up puking by the end of the night and who hooked up with whom afterwards. None of the names meant anything to me, so I just listened and watched the waves crashing along the beach.

"You want to take a little walk in the sand?" Aiden asked.

"That would be nice," I replied with a smile. The idea of being alone with him for a little while sounded good. He had introduced me as his guest, which was as accurate as anything but still hadn't so much as touched me all evening.

"Good," Aiden said with a smile. "Lo can take you. I need to talk business with Mo for a minute."

"Oh…okay." That was *not* what I was expecting—not at all. I went with it anyway.

I glanced over my shoulder at Mo and Aiden as Lo led me across the patio and onto the sand. They were leaning forward with their heads close together and talking seriously. My curiosity was on high, but Aiden obviously didn't want to share the conversation with me.

"Don't worry about it," Lo said. "They just have some shit to go over."

Well, obviously Lo was in the know.

"I'm not worried," I said. It wasn't especially truthful, but I didn't want him to know that. I was becoming increasingly confused by Aiden's behavior, or lack of expected behavior, but I wasn't about to share that with Lo.

"So how did you meet Hunter?" he asked as we reached the shoreline. I slipped off my sandals and held them in my hand as the water washed over my feet.

"Um…at a bar," I admitted. "He drove me when I'd had a bit too much to drink."

I didn't tell him just where Aiden had driven me or how I had woken up in his bed.

"How long have you known each other?"

"Well…actually, we just met Friday night."

"Ha! Ha! Ha!" Lo laughed. "And he convinced you to come all the way down here with him? Damn, he's good!"

My face heated up, and it had nothing to do with the Florida sun. I bit down on my lip and stared at the sand. Lo obviously assumed that Aiden had brought me here for a particular reason, but I wasn't so sure any more.

Hadn't he said as much yesterday? No pressure, he said, and he definitely hadn't put any on. If anything, he'd done the exact opposite. Was he waiting for me to make a move? That didn't seem right either.

Maybe he'd just changed his mind.

"Hey, I didn't mean anything by it," Lo said in a much softer voice. "I'm really just a bit surprised. Hunter's been alone a long time, and it's not like him to jump into things so quick. It's good to see him with someone. You seem like a nice girl. He needs that."

"Well...thank you," I said. I stared at the sand as it squished between my toes and contemplated for a moment longer before I looked up again. "How long have you known him?"

"We've known each other for years," Lo said. "Um...six or seven, maybe? Met through Redeye at one of his parties. We went through all that shit with him."

"All what shit?" I asked.

"Ah...well..." Lo stammered a bit. "You know—just life and shit. We were there when his last girlfriend dumped him and all. Just life."

I was positive there was more to it than that, but Lo was apparently not going to elaborate. His backpedaling was obvious, but I was also sure he wasn't going to tell me whatever it was.

"Who was she?" I asked just to keep the conversation going. Maybe he'd let something slip that would give me a clue.

"Her name was Megan," Lo said. "Great chick. He was really into her."

"What happened to them?"

"Just one of those things. They weren't in the same place and couldn't get along when shit got real. He wasn't making enough money to give her what she wanted, so she found someone else."

"He seems to do pretty well," I said as I glanced back toward the luxurious house.

"Well now, yeah." Lo laughed again. "He does great *now*."

"How long ago was this?" I asked.

"Three years since they broke up, I guess." He thought for a minute before nodding. "Yeah, about three years ago."

"And he hasn't seen anyone since?"

"Nothing serious," Lo said. "Hunter's always been picky about women he dates. He's been too busy with everything else to bother."

"Busy with what?"

"I bet they're done talking," Lo said without answering me. "We should head back before he thinks I'm trying to steal ya."

He laughed again.

"I wouldn't want the Hunter hunting me! That motherfucker can be scary! Ha! Ha! Ha!"

We turned from the water and headed back up the sand dune to the house. Mo was still sitting outside, but Aiden wasn't there.

"Just in time for scotch!" Mo announced. "Hunter's digging up the private stock!"

"Sweet! Maybe the taste of Bakon vodka will finally be drowned out!"

Aiden appeared with a tall bottle and four glasses.

"You like scotch?" he asked me.

"I've only tried it once," I said. "I didn't care for it."

"You probably never had the good stuff," Aiden said with a wink. He poured out three glasses and handed one to me. "Try mine and see what you think."

It burned my throat but went down a lot smoother than I remembered from years ago when Gabe had convinced me to try some, and it had made me want to gag. Not wanting to be rude, I nodded and smiled.

"It's good."

"See? You just needed to try a good one." Aiden passed the two glasses to his friends and then poured one more for me. He traded glasses with me then stared into my eyes as he turned the first glass around and slowly drank from the same spot I had. He licked his bottom lip. "Extra good."

My heart pounded as I dropped my eyes and sipped slowly, trying to get used to the taste and the feeling the drink left in my throat. It made me cringe a little every time I tasted it, but I just drank slowly and tried to keep a smile on my face.

"Got any new ink?" Mo asked Aiden.

"Of course," Aiden replied. "I always hit up my tat man in Cincinnati."

"What are you going to do when you run out of skin?" Lo asked with a laugh.

"I'll figure something out."

"What did you get?" Mo asked.

Aiden pulled off his shirt to show off a silhouetted bird in a cloud under his right arm.

"Didn't that hurt?" I asked

"Like a bitch," Aiden said with a laugh. "Not as bad as behind the knee, though."

I subtly tried to examine the myriad of pictures all over his torso. There were too many to even try to count. I could make out diamonds, stars, cartoon characters, skulls, numbers, and God knows what else. There were multiple phrases, but I couldn't read them without being far too obvious, so I gave up.

The casual gathering continued as Aiden tossed a few pieces of firewood into a metal pit and lit it up. Mo and Lo pulled out cigars to smoke, and we chatted about nothing in particular until the hour was late, and the two men decided it was time to go.

"It was great meeting you, Chloe," Mo said. "If this guy gives you any trouble, you just smack him over the head with that empty scotch bottle and give me a call."

He and Lo both laughed again.

"I'll do that," I said with a smile.

Lo stepped forward and I squealed a bit as he lifted me into a big bear hug.

"Loved talkin' with ya," he said. He turned his face toward my ear and gave me a peck on the cheek before whispering to me. "Be careful with him. He's more fragile than he looks."

Lo dropped me back to my feet, and as I hit the floor, I felt his hand on my ass. For a moment, I was shocked, but then I realized he had just put something in my back pocket. I glanced at Aiden, and I saw him look between us quickly. He didn't look angry at his friend's familiarity, but there was a hint of worry in his eyes.

Aiden walked the visitors to the door. As soon as they were gone, I excused myself to the bathroom and checked my pocket. There was a business card in it that read "Flux Security Services." It had both Lo and Mo's names on it along with Lo's phone number. I took a deep breath and wondered just what Lo meant about Aiden being more fragile than he seemed. Fragile in what way? Mentally? Physically? Were Lo's words a warning for me to get away from Aiden? That didn't seem right—they were obviously good friends. Fragile was such an odd word to use. It seemed like he was telling me not to hurt Aiden, not that he was dangerous in some way.

Lo had also said Aiden could be scary.

What had Aiden talked to Mo about? What was their business? Aiden hadn't said anything about security, just sales. Then again, if you are a drug dealer, you would need your own security around.

No. I wasn't going to think that way. I didn't want to know. If I knew—if I knew for sure—I'd have to get out. I couldn't stay around if I knew that's what he really did. As long as I didn't know, I could pretend his business was perfectly legitimate.

What legitimate business in sales required a private conversation between him and a security guy?

"You think too much," I told myself in the mirror as I washed my hands. "You're having a good time. Why can't you just leave it alone?"

I already knew the answer to that question; I just didn't want to admit it.

It didn't matter that I had only known him for a few days—I wanted him. I knew I did. I wanted to feel his mouth on mine again. I wanted to be wrapped up in his arms as we sat on the beach. I wanted him to roll me over and take me in the sand. As long as I continued to force myself to believe he wasn't a criminal, then I could let whatever happened, happen.

Aiden had brought me to this beautiful setting. He'd cooked for me. He'd encouraged me to do something I never would have tried on my own, and I had loved every second of it. He'd been a perfect gentleman.

There was no reason for me to be suspicious.

Satisfied with my reasoning, I brushed my teeth and left the bathroom. I quickly changed into my pajamas and then went to find Aiden, who was sitting at the kitchen table, looking at his phone.

"I was going to go ahead and go to bed," I said, giving him a little smile. I hoped he would get the idea from my tone of voice, but I wasn't really sure what tone I should use.

"It is late," he said without looking up from his phone.

So much for subtle hints.

I stood there for a second, wondering if I should just go sit myself down in his lap and make the first move, but he spoke before I had the chance.

"Hey, listen," Aiden said as he finally looked up, "I have a little work to catch up on. I'll probably be up for a while."

"Oh, okay," I said. I tried to smile, but I didn't think it came off well. His eyes were unfocused, and he seemed lost in thought. "I hope I'm not keeping you from things you need to do."

"You aren't." Aiden shook his head slowly before he actually looked at me. I watched his eyes dart down my body briefly before he smiled again. "Don't worry, I'll still be up in time to make you breakfast."

Breakfast was the furthest thing from my mind. Still, I didn't want to bother him when he had other things to do, so all thoughts of trying to seduce him left my head as I said goodnight and went back to the bedroom alone.

I climbed into bed and lay there for the longest time, trying to decide if I had lost my mind or not. Trying to fall asleep without Aiden in the bed proved to be more difficult that it had been when he was there. It was probably just because of the bed I was in, but it felt strange not to have him beside me though we had only spent the one night together.

Well, one that I remembered.

I sighed. Sleep was not coming, and I felt the need to pee again. I shoved myself out of the bed and padded down the hallway.

"I don't give a shit!"

I stopped in my tracks. Aiden was on the phone in the next room.

"It's nothing but bullshit. They knew what they were getting into, and now they're being pussies about it…no, I'm not going to hold back—not anymore!"

I wondered if the beat of my heart was audible as I leaned against the wall and tried not to breathe as I listened to the one-sided conversation.

"I can't right now…no…I've kind of got myself into a complicated thing this week." The chair squeaked as Aiden leaned back.

I stayed still and silent as I continued to listen, wondering if I was the complication Aiden mentioned.

"Oh, Lo told you that, did he? Well, don't read too much into it…I don't know…not yet…"

What had Lo said? Was he talking about me? I folded my arms around myself and bit down on my lip.

"It doesn't matter if it is a chick. I'll fucking kill her if she gets in the way. If it turns out she had something to do with it—*anything*—I'll bury them both in the same fucking hole!"

My legs began to shake. I supposed there was a reason people were warned against eavesdropping, but I couldn't seem to help myself.

"Nothing matters more to me. You know that…I am…no, they haven't found a fucking thing. As far as I can tell, they're useless."

I shifted my weight from one foot to the other, and my toe bumped against the wall.

"Hold on a sec," Aiden said, and I heard him move in my

direction.

Shit!

As quickly and silently as I could, I scurried back down the hallway and threw myself into the bed. My heart raced as I pulled the blanket up over me and tried to lie still.

Aiden's footsteps were at the door. He paused, and I could hear him breathing, but I didn't think he came into the room. I kept my eyes closed even though I was facing away from the door. A minute later, I heard him head back down the hall.

"No," his soft voice echoed. "Just checking on something.

Alarm!

I wrapped my arms around myself as my breathing returned to normal. What was all of that? Was he actually threatening to kill someone? Two someones? Why? What was complicated, and did it actually have anything to do with me?

What had I gotten myself into?

I had to be hearing things wrong. There was no way to tell when you only got one side of a conversation. There was no way for me to know exactly what he meant, and trying to figure it out without knowing even the general topic at hand was impossible. The alarms in my head were premature at the very best. I had no idea what he was talking about, and it wasn't any of my business.

I didn't want to know. I didn't want to imagine there was anything sinister about the man who had bought me a dress just to go out for dinner and treated me so nicely. I didn't want to believe he was anything other than how he seemed when he was around me. Despite everything that I had heard, I couldn't deny how much I still wanted Aiden Hunter.

I still had to pee, but there was no way I was going to get up and go to the bathroom now. I squeezed my eyes shut and tried to forget everything I had heard.

And with that, denial took me into sleep.

NINE

Day four with Aiden, and again, my sleep was restless. Every time I woke up, Aiden wasn't there. I considered going out to find him but didn't want to hear any more of his late-night conversations. Ignorance was said to be bliss, and I was hanging on to that notion.

When I woke in the morning, Aiden was wrapped around me for once instead of the other way around. My back was to his chest with his arms coiled around me. I couldn't recall ever waking up in such a position, and for a moment, I just lay there and *felt*.

He was warm but not too hot. His cheek was against the top of my head, and his arm was bent to allow my head to rest on his bicep. Our knees were slightly bent, with his legs curled up against the back of mine. His arm was around my waist, and his hand was resting on the mattress next to my stomach.

I supposed this was what people referred to as a classic "spooning" position.

I looked down the arm wrapped around my middle, trying to get a better look at the tattoos there. There were stars and a dollar sign as well as the image of a basketball player. The phrase 80's Baby was in red, right in the center of his arm near his elbow, and a long-stemmed rose swept over his forearm.

I remembered what I had overheard on the phone. Frankly, it had scared me a little. If I really thought about it rationally, I'd probably pack up and get the heck out of here. That was the thing, though—I wasn't thinking rationally.

Despite his words on the phone, I still felt safe in his arms.

Why was that? Was it simply a reflection of his strength? Were human women really biologically programmed to seek out someone who was able to protect them physically? If he weren't so muscled, would I still be attracted to him?

That was the crux of the whole thing—I was attracted to him and not just a little. I'd hardly been able to keep my eyes off of him the whole time I had been here and had even dreamed about him.

Aiden shifted in his sleep, pressing his body closer to mine. His elbow bent as his hand moved up to my shoulder, and his grip tightened. There was no doubt in my mind what I could now feel pressed against my ass.

It was long and hard.

I went from warm to hot in a matter of seconds. My thighs and ass clenched involuntarily as I took in a breath and held it. He wasn't grinding into me or anything, but it was still very, very noticeable.

Morning wood.

Like spooning, it was something I'd heard a lot about but never really experienced. When Zach had slept over, he'd always been up before I was. He also wasn't one for cuddling in bed, so it had simply never been an issue.

Is that what it was? An issue?

As I closed my eyes, my mind went a little wild. I couldn't help but have thoughts of him waking, shoving my pajama bottoms down my legs, and pushing inside of me. I could almost feel him kissing my neck as he rocked into me slowly.

The thought made me wonder if he would even be that way—slow and gentle, the same way all my past lovers had been. It didn't seem to fit, and my fantasy quickly switched to him rolling me to my stomach and pounding into me from behind.

I could feel sweat beginning to collect behind my neck and under my breasts. I really had to get out of this position before he woke up. Well, before the rest of him woke up.

He didn't make it easy.

The man had a death grip on me. Trying to move his arm off of me was darn near impossible. He just wouldn't budge. I ended up slithering out from under him, nearly getting my head trapped in the crook of his elbow in the process. Eventually, I fell on my knees at the edge of the bed.

Aiden's face scrunched for a moment as he reached out his hand at the empty mattress. He rolled to his stomach and rubbed his head against the pillow before letting out a long sigh. I remained motionless for a moment until I was sure he was completely asleep, and then I tiptoed over to my suitcase, grabbed some clean clothes, and made my way to the bathroom. I spent a little extra time on my hair. The humidity wasn't doing anything for my curls, and I had been fighting frizz since I had arrived. It was a good distraction.

He was still sleeping when I was done, so I headed off to the kitchen to make coffee. Rain was coming down in sheets, darkening the sand and blocking out the sound of the waves. After the first cup was empty, I decided he wasn't going to wake up any time soon and that I should just find my own breakfast.

Going through someone else's refrigerator was a little nerve-wracking. I wasn't sure if it was as much of a guest faux pas as it was to check out someone's medicine cabinet, but it had to be up there on the questionable etiquette list. It seemed better than going through the cupboards though, so I just made quick work of finding the carton of eggs and some milk.

Scrambled eggs and toast were actually a more elaborate breakfast than I usually made for myself at home but seemed sparse after a couple of days of Aiden's cooking. It didn't taste as good as his, either.

I ate and watched the rain come down, had another cup of coffee, rinsed off my dishes before placing them in the dishwasher, and then sat down at the kitchen table to stare at the rainy beach some more.

Aiden continued to sleep most of the morning. I peeked in on him a couple of times and could only assume he'd been up really late. With the rain pouring down even harder, I couldn't walk along the beach, so I sat at the kitchen table and looked out at the grey sky. Even with the bad weather, it was still beautiful.

I ended up turning my phone back on and playing games. I was down to about a quarter of my battery's power but still considered checking my email. If I were being honest with myself, I would have admitted that I was afraid to check it. I really didn't think giving such short vacation notice would get me fired, but I was also pretty sure Chia Head would have something to say about it. However, Mom's comments about not doing anything rash were echoing in my head.

I played more games. I looked in on Aiden and then made another pot of coffee.

The phone beeped to tell me I was down to twenty percent, so I switched it back off and listened to the wind howl. I picked up Aiden's red baseball cap and fingered the worn inside edge, wondering how long he had had it and if he had ever worn it the right way before placing it back on the kitchen table. Eventually I had to acknowledge that I was running out of options to keep myself occupied.

Boredom got the better of me. Though I felt a little sneaky about it, I started wandering from room to room, just to see what was there. I hadn't had any kind of house tour, but I didn't think it would take long to just peek inside the rooms I hadn't been in yet.

On the other side of the living room was a short hallway with three doors. The first two doors were open, and I found a bathroom behind one and Aiden's weight room behind the other. I recognized the treadmill and a weight bench with a lot of dumbbells lined up in a rack, but there were a couple of machines I couldn't identify. One had a bar running through the middle of it and heavy weights lying beside it, and the other was tall with a barbell at the bottom and handgrips up at the top. There was also a mat on the floor and a free-standing punching bag.

If I hadn't noticed from his physique, this room definitely put him in the serious bodybuilder class.

The door to the last room was closed, and I was pretty hesitant to open it. I was prying—there wasn't another name for what I was doing—and that was ultimately rude. Still, I didn't know what else to do with myself while I waited for Aiden to wake up.

Maybe he already had.

I silently slipped back to the master bedroom and looked in. Aiden was on his back and snoring slightly. He didn't look like he'd be waking up anytime soon.

I went back to the closed door and placed my hand on the knob.

I shouldn't be doing this. All the other doors were open, so why would he keep this one closed unless it was to hide something behind it? What could he have in there? Did he hide his drugs in this room? Weapons? A dead body?

Alarm!

There was only one way to find out. With a deep breath, I turned the knob and pushed the door open.

Boxes.

Labeled boxes.

Piles and piles of them.

I almost laughed at myself. I wasn't sure what I was really expecting, but I probably should have realized that this was what I would find. He had said numerous times that he had never had a chance to unpack. It was no wonder he had a room like this. The only room that seemed fully in place was the kitchen.

Just as I was closing the door, one of the box labels caught my eye.

"Cayden's clothes"

I paused and pushed the door open a little more. There were several boxes labeled the same way. Right behind those were cartons that simply read "Cayden." Some of the other containers had more distinct labels.

"Cayden's bike"

"Cayden's books"

"Cayden's toys"

Toys?

A slight noise from the direction of the kitchen caused me to jump. I shut the door quickly and stumbled out of the hallway and into the living room, sure I was caught. I wasn't, though. The living room and kitchen were empty. I looked around to find the source of the noise when I heard it again—coming from outside. The wind had knocked over one of the patio chairs, and it was now blowing over the stone tiles.

I sighed and sat my ass back down at the kitchen table. My coffee had gone cold, but I drank it anyway.

Who is Cayden?

I wasn't completely sure if Cayden was a boy's name or a girl's name. It sounded like something you would call a boy, but it could also have been unisex. I didn't know any Caydens and had no frame of reference.

I didn't think it was a girl he used to date. Lo said his last girlfriend was Megan, and I didn't even want to think about what kinds of things might have been in a box of women's toys. There was really only one logical answer.

Aiden had a child.

Maybe a boy or maybe a girl but definitely a child. Who else would have a bike and toys in boxes?

Aiden hadn't mentioned a child. In fact, he had said he had no family except his mother, and he didn't speak to her at all. What kind of person neglects to mention they have a kid?

And I was back at square one. What kind of person, indeed? I'd certainly gotten to know a lot about Aiden Hunter over the past few days, but I couldn't say I actually *knew* him. This was insane. *I* was insane. I had no business being here at all.

"Hey there." Aiden's voice nearly startled me out of my seat. "Sorry I slept so late. The rain does that to me sometimes."

"That's okay," I replied automatically.

"I hope you haven't been too bored. Did you at least find yourself something to eat?"

"Yes, I'm fine." I sat up in the chair a bit and held up my coffee cup. "There's still some coffee in the pot if you want some."

"Fantastic," Aiden said with a yawn. He poured himself a cup and sat down across from me. "Has it been raining all day?"

"Yes," I said. "Windy, too. The patio chairs have been blowing around."

Aiden glanced out the window and surveyed the damage with a nod.

"What have you been up to?" he asked.

"Not much," I said, hoping I wasn't giving away my privacy-invasion activities with my blush. "I've been watching the rain and playing on my phone."

"What did we do without smartphones?" Aiden mused.

Snooped around in other people's houses?

I didn't reply. I was feeling really guilty about what I had done. It was so out of character for me to do something like that, and I didn't know what had come over me. Curiosity, I supposed, but that was no excuse.

"You okay?"

I looked up into Aiden's eyes.

"I'm fine," I replied. I wondered if he could tell I'd been doing something I shouldn't have been doing.

"I hope you aren't too pissed off about me sleeping in," Aiden said. "I mean, you could have woken me up if you wanted to. I should have set an alarm or something."

"Not at all," I said. "I figured you had…well, I thought you must have worked late."

"Yeah, I did." Aiden took another drink of his coffee and stared out the window. "Shitty day to do anything outside."

"It is," I agreed. "Then again, I think I've had more outdoor excitement this week than I have had my whole life."

Aiden smiled, and his eyes twinkled at me.

"Was it worth it?" he asked.

"I'm not sure yet," I said. "I'm still trying to convince myself I jumped out of a plane."

"Fucking fantastic, wasn't it?" Aiden's eyes widened with his smile.

"It really was amazing. I just can't believe I did it."

"Are you glad you did?"

"Yes," I said after a moment's thought, "I am."

"Would you do it again?"

I shook my head.

"I think once was enough. I don't want to press my luck."

Aiden chuckled as he stood to refill his coffee. After asking if I wanted anything, he made himself a couple of waffles in the toaster oven and smeared them with peanut butter and jelly.

"That's a little less elaborate than what you have been making," I remarked.

"Well, I'm pretty hungry and don't want to wait," he replied. "Besides, cooking isn't as much fun when it's just for me. I'll have to

114

think of something more interesting for dinner. I could make a stew in the crockpot. Do you like stew?"

"Stew sounds good," I said.

"I was planning to grill out, but I don't think the weather is going to cooperate."

Another patio chair blew over then, right on cue.

"I'd better pull those in," Aiden said. He tossed the half-eaten waffle down on the table and ran out to the patio. He pulled the chairs up close to the side of the house, getting himself drenched in the process.

I ran to the bathroom and grabbed one of the large towels hanging over the shower. Aiden was dripping in the doorway when I got back to the kitchen. His muscle shirt clung to his body and showed his tattoos through the thin fabric.

Wet T-shirt contest, we have a winner!

"Thanks," he said as he took the towel from my hands. "I'm not sure it's going to be enough though."

"Do you want another one?"

"Nah, I need to jump in the shower anyway."

Aiden dripped his way over to the bathroom, leaving his waffle on the table. After I heard the shower start, I wiped the water off of the floor. I was still feeling guilty about poking around in his house and figured the least I could do was clean up a bit.

I also didn't know what to think of the labels on the boxes. I was sure it meant that Aiden had a child, but why wouldn't he mention something that important? Did he think I might not like kids? Was he a deadbeat dad who didn't properly provide for his child?

That didn't seem right. I might not have known Aiden very well, but he did seem like someone who liked to take care of people. He liked to cook for others, and he'd taken me to do all these wonderful things. It didn't seem to fit that he wouldn't take care of a child that was his.

So why would he hide it?

Maybe I was completely wrong, and Cayden wasn't his child. Maybe it was his dog that remained with a pet boarder while I was visiting.

Dogs don't read books or ride bikes.

Oh, yeah.

Aiden reappeared with dry clothes and slightly damp hair. There were water droplets glistening around his neck, encouraging me to think about licking them off. Similar thoughts ran through my head as he pulled out a crockpot and began slicing up vegetables for a stew.

"All right," Aiden said when he had all the ingredients in the crockpot, "what are we going to do today? A motorcycle ride is definitely out."

"I think you are right there," I agreed, glad to have something to think about other than the way water danced around on Aiden's skin. "What else do you have in mind?"

Aiden contemplated for a moment and then suddenly snapped his fingers.

"I've got just the thing to do!" He jumped up and headed down the hallway I'd been poking around in earlier. He came back a minute later with a large black box in his hands. "Xbox! I haven't played this since I moved here."

"Video games?"

"There's nothing like blowing up a bunch of shit on a rainy day!" he announced. "*Team Fortress 2,* here we come!"

For the next couple of hours, we sat on the floor in front of the couch, and Aiden showed me how to work the controls to play the game. We ran virtual characters around on the screen, blowing up members of the other team and burning things down. It was insanely violent and a ton of fun.

"You sure you've never played this before?" Aiden asked as I blew up another one of our opponents.

"Never," I said. "I've always stuck with city-building games."

"Well, you missed your calling." He laughed. "You are putting a lot of fourteen-year-old boys to shame with your mad skills."

I giggled and blew up another opponent.

It was evening by the time we quit for dinner. Along with sandwiches, we ate the stew Aiden had made in the crockpot. He placed a bunch of fruit out for dessert.

"You really are a great cook," I told him.

"Thanks," he said.

"Who taught you?"

He looked away and licked his lips before responding.

"Um, this girl I used to see," he said quietly.

"She cooked a lot?"

"Yeah, at first," he said. "I think she taught me so she wouldn't have to do it anymore."

He laughed humorlessly, and awkward silence ensued.

When he didn't say anything else, I wanted to ask him more about her, but ex-girlfriends were always a bit of a taboo subject. I certainly didn't want to dive into a conversation about Zach. I wondered if the woman he was talking about might have been the same girl Lo had mentioned, but I'd pried into Aiden's life enough for one day.

Maybe she was Cayden's mother?

I hadn't really put two and two together on that. If Aiden had a child, there also had to be a mother in the picture somewhere. Where was she? I could only assume the child was with her, but I couldn't ask him about that. If I did, he'd know what I'd been doing.

"I'm going to clean up," Aiden announced suddenly. He picked up our dishes and took them to the sink.

"Do you want some help?" I asked.

"No, that's okay—it's not much. Do you want to watch a movie or something?"

"That would be good."

"There are a bunch of them in one of the boxes on the couch," he said. "Pick one."

I opened up the first box and found a collection of Blu-ray disks. Action and horror movies seemed to be Aiden's preference, and I was good with that. He had *Fifth Element,* one of my favorites. I hadn't watched it for a long time, so I pulled it from the box and sat it on top of the Blu-ray player. I thought about going ahead and loading it so it would be ready, but something about messing with a man's electronics felt taboo to me.

Aiden started the movie, gathered a couple of pillows from the bedroom, and we sat in front of the couch with the pillows propped behind us. Aiden tossed his arm on the seat cushions of the couch, right behind my shoulders. We had both seen *Fifth Element* enough times to be able to recite our favorite parts, and halfway through it, we were laughing hysterically.

"Bada boom!" Aiden called out as he tossed one of the pillows at me.

I giggled and threw it back.

"Boom!" I yelled out. "Big boom!"

"Multipass!" he cried as he threw it back, hitting me right in the face.

I toppled over, laughing and grabbing for the pillow. The next thing I knew, Aiden was scrambling over my legs, trying to reach the pillow first. I grabbed on and held tight, not wanting to relinquish my only weapon.

We struggled, but I was no match for him. All of a sudden, he was on top of me, and I was pinned to the floor by his body. He grabbed the pillow and dropped it on my head a couple of times before pulling it back and looking down at me as we both caught our breath.

For a moment, there was nothing else in the room—no rain pattering on the roof, no movie sounds in the background, not even any air in the room around us. It was just Aiden's body pressed on top of mine and the beating of our hearts.

His Adam's apple bobbed up and down, and he moistened his lips with his tongue. I couldn't breathe—partially because he was lying on my diaphragm but mostly in anticipation. I'd been here for days, and nothing had happened aside from unintentional morning wood.

I looked up, just waiting. Aiden kept his eyes on mine but didn't move. I felt my thighs tense and wondered if he could feel it, too. My heart was beating so fast, he had to be able to hear it, but he stayed still—his gaze dancing from my eyes to my lips.

He smiled that big, boyish grin that lit up his greenish-brown eyes.

"Bada big boom," he said before rolling off of me.

I sat up, flushed and flustered. I wasn't sure what had just happened.

Aiden fixed the pillows at the base of the couch and leaned back against them. I scooted over next to him, and we watched the rest of the movie in near silence. I glanced at him a few times, but he kept his eyes on the television.

He didn't even put his arm back around me.

What went wrong? I was sure he was about to kiss me, but something stopped him. Had I done something to tick him off? Did I have stew-breath? Had he somehow figured out that I'd gone poking my nose where it didn't belong?

The movie ended. Aiden suggested watching another one, and I agreed with whatever he picked out without really hearing the title right before excusing myself to the bathroom. I nearly raced down the hall, shut and locked the door behind me, and stared at my reflection.

And with that, I started to fall apart.

TEN

"This is not going well," I whispered to myself.

I couldn't help wondering if Aiden had just decided he wasn't interested in me and was now just being polite as he waited for the week to end so he could send me home. I was keeping him from work—whatever the hell that was—and probably cramping his style with my goodie-two-shoes ways. I'd enjoyed our activities together but was still far from being the adventurous person Aiden obviously was.

I had never really even smoked weed—only tried to inhale once —let alone done any other illicit drugs. On the other hand, he was probably selling to all the college students in the tri-county area.

This was why I didn't do things without thinking them through first. If I had spent just a little bit of time considering all the possible outcomes of this trip, I could have saved us both a lot of trouble. If I had thought about it, I wouldn't have agreed to join him.

I'd be at home right now, staring at the television by myself and talking to my action figure dolls.

I swallowed past the lump that had formed in my throat. It had been ridiculous for me to think this was a good idea. I should be home. Yes, I'd be by myself, but I'd be *safely* by myself. I wouldn't be worrying about what I had done wrong. I wouldn't be wondering if the guy I was with was a criminal.

What do criminals do when their date doesn't work out? Would he think I'd learned too much? Would he consider me a threat to him?

Oh, shit.

I closed my eyes for a moment, convincing myself I was not trying to hold back tears. I was way out of my comfort zone, not to mention far away from my home and friends and possibly in danger. I hadn't even told Mare where I was going or with whom.

If I disappeared, she'd have no idea where I went.

A sudden wave of panic came over me. My eyes burned as my attempt to hold back tears failed. I quickly pulled out my phone and turned it on. It beeped immediately, letting me know I had missed texts from both Gabe and Mare. Gabe wanted to know if I could wait until next week to go car shopping, which was perfect. Mare was asking about heading out after work to check out florists.

I sent Mare a text.

Hey there! I just wanted you to know I can't do flowers this week. I'm in Florida with a friend. I should be back next weekend.

Her reply was immediate.

Damn, girl! What friend? You didn't say anything about taking a trip!

I sat down on the toilet.

His name is Aiden Hunter.

I hit send.

Clo are you okay? I've never heard of this guy. Where are you exactly?

I wasn't sure if I was okay or not.

I met him after you guys left the bar. I'm in Miami. Golden Beach.

I wiped a stray tear from my cheek and waited for her to reply.

You met him Friday? And you are in Miami with him now? Alone? JFC

I couldn't argue with that sentiment.

I know. I'm not sure what I'm doing here.

Another instant response from Mare.

Do you want to talk?

I shook my head as if she could see me.

Can't now. He'd hear me.

Are you safe?

Now there was a damn good question.

I think so. I mean, he's been really nice.

A few seconds went by.

Did you fuck him?

Leave it to Mare to be so blunt.

No.

Are you going to?

I took a deep breath.

I don't know. I'm not really even sure if he wants to.

What guy doesn't want to???

Well, that was a good question. However, I'd been pretty much alone with Aiden for the past four days, and he hadn't even kissed me again. He'd been inches away and hadn't closed the gap.

What if he'd changed his mind? What if he wasn't just being polite when he said he'd take the couch the first night but just didn't want to be that close to me? He could have decided that I was just too boring to bother with at all.

"Hey, are you okay in there?" Aiden called through the door.

I hadn't realized how long I'd been gone.

"I'm fine!" I replied. "Be out in a sec."

My phone beeped.

Call me!

I shook my head again.

I have to go. I'll try to call you tomorrow.

You better! You have me worried!

I will.

I shoved the phone back into the pocket of my shorts along with the business card Lo had given me the previous night. After splashing water on my face, I checked myself in the mirror to make sure I looked more composed than I felt.

I didn't.

Something about texting with Mare had me even more on edge. What guy didn't want sex, indeed? If stereotypes were to be believed, men weren't all that picky as long as they were getting laid. If Aiden wasn't interested, what did that mean? Why did he bring me here?

Alarm!

My mind whirled. Could he have brought me here for some other reason? If he really was a drug dealer, what would he want with me?

Or was that too simple—too obvious? Maybe he wasn't a drug dealer but some other sort of criminal. Perhaps he really was in some kind of organized crime ring and planned on using me for…for…for what? He'd had days alone with me. He could have done anything he wanted—raped me, killed me, or sold me off to some arms dealer in trade for weapons of mass destruction.

Aiden was right about me—I had led a sheltered life. I had no notion of the activities of criminals. Aside from a tour of Alcatraz when I visited my mother, I had no knowledge of what sort of illicit dealings people in the underworld might be involved in. He could be planning anything. He could be biding his time, placating me into trusting him so he could lure me into some insane life of crime.

Wouldn't that count as a thrill? Was he testing me with the skydiving to see if I might be enticed into that kind of life? Could he be planning to use me as some kind of patsy for a crime he intended to commit?

Too many questions.

No answers.

Words spoken by both my mother and my father started to fill my head.

Don't trust strangers.

Never get yourself into a situation you can't control.

Think before you act.

If something sounds too good to be true, it probably is.

A free trip to Miami with a gorgeous man—what was that if not too good to be true? I had trusted Aiden enough to come to Miami with him, leaving myself in a situation I couldn't control. I hadn't thought about the consequences, and now I was trapped.

"Chloe?"

Shit!

"Coming!"

When I opened the door, Aiden was standing in the hallway, shirtless. I startled and tried to get myself together while simultaneously letting my eyes drop to his waistline and the deep V shape along with the ink that disappeared into his shorts.

My body warmed, and I took a shuddering breath.

"Everything all right?" Aiden asked. "I hope switching to a horror flick was okay with you. If you don't like horror, we can watch something else."

"I'm fine. The movie is fine." I didn't even know what he had selected, but I couldn't look at that gorgeous, inked, distracting body any longer. I'd made a huge mistake, possibly the worst mistake of my life.

"You don't look fine."

I glanced back at him, trying not to stare at his naked torso but unable to tear my eyes away from the swirling designs and rippling muscles. Angel's wings and a halo touched the center of his chest. Ocean waves crashed around his shoulder, and a long, tattooed necklace wrapped around his neck and trailed down to his navel.

"Where's your shirt?" I asked. I wasn't even sure where the words came from, but it was my voice.

"I spilled my drink on it," he said quickly. "Stop deflecting. What's wrong?"

"Nothing."

"You've been crying," he stated. "Did I piss you off?"

"No. I think I'm just a little tired." I needed to get away from him. I needed to figure out how I was going to regain control of the situation and get myself the hell out of there. "Maybe I'll just head to bed."

His bed. Oh yeah, that was the perfect solution.

I ducked around him and walked quickly to the bedroom. If I could get away from him for a while, maybe I could figure out what I should do next.

Aiden followed me into the room and leaned against the doorjamb.

"What's wrong, Chloe?"

"I'm fine!" I snapped. I dropped to my knees and started digging through my suitcase like I was looking for something, but I didn't have anything in mind. I just didn't want to meet his eyes.

"Very convincing." He didn't try to hide the sarcasm.

"So, does everyone usually call you Hunter, not Aiden?" I asked in a futile attempt to change the subject.

"What?"

"Your friends," I clarified, "Lo and Mo—they called you Hunter. Is that what people usually call you?"

"Yeah," he replied quickly. "Are you going to tell me what's wrong? Did Lo say something to you when you were on the beach last night? I know those guys can be a little intense when you aren't used to them."

"They were fine. Lo didn't say anything."

"What is it then?"

I stopped digging and stood back up, still unsure of what the hell I was doing. All of this had been a bad idea from the get-go, and I felt trapped. My mind was racing so frantically, I didn't even know what direction it was trying to go in.

"Chloe—talk to me," Aiden said.

I made the mistake of looking at him. His expressive eyes were full of concern, and the look caught me off guard. He'd done all these wonderful things for me—the cooking, the kayak trip, the walks on the beach—why was I so mistrustful?

Because he was built. He was tattooed. He was shifty about his occupation. He had strange conversations late at night. He might have a child he didn't want me to know about.

That's not it.

I swallowed hard, and my shoulders slumped. All my previous thoughts of criminal activity disappeared at the revelation that I didn't really think he was dangerous. I was mad because he didn't seem interested in me, and I wanted him to be.

He hasn't done anything wrong.

"Please, Chloe. I'm really confused here."

He was a nice guy. He was fun and exciting. We had a lot of interests in common. The week had been wonderful, but he hadn't even tried to kiss me since we got here. I didn't want to confirm my suspicions that he had decided I was a waste of time.

He wasn't planning to kidnap me or use me for some nefarious plan. He just wasn't interested, and I needed to buck up and get it all out in the open.

"I'm just...just trying to figure out what all this is about." I waved one hand back and forth between us.

"What do you mean?"

I bit down on my lip, not wanting to come straight out and say the words, but I was out of options. Fear and sadness boiled into anger, and I started yelling.

"I don't even know why I'm here!" I cried. "I don't do this kind of thing!"

I covered my face and tried to hold back the tears. After a long pause, he spoke again.

"Do you want me to take you to the airport?" Aiden asked slowly. "I can get you on the next flight if that's what you want to do."

Suspicions confirmed. He wanted to get rid of me. At least I knew it now.

"If that's what you want," I said quietly. I looked down at my suitcase and blinked back tears. I hadn't brought much with me, and it wouldn't take long to pack. I wondered if I should leave behind the red cocktail dress he'd selected for dinner.

"No." Aiden shook his head. "It's not what I want."

"It isn't?"

"No! Jesus, Chloe—I asked you to come here! Why would I want you to leave? What did I do to piss you off so much?"

"You didn't piss me off," I whispered.

"Well, what is it then?" His voice rose and he crossed his arms over his chest. His eyes looked hard, and I took a little step back.

"It's just...I...I don't know what..." I stammered.

His look softened.

"Shit, Chloe—just say it," he pleaded. "Seriously, I don't know what's going on here."

"Well, neither do I!" I cried. "I have no idea what this is all about!"

"What *what* is about?"

"You...me...here..." I couldn't seem to make a sentence in my head, let alone one with my tongue. Too many thoughts were trying to occupy my head at once, and every time I looked at him, I just wanted to know how far down those tattoos really went, driving any linear thinking straight out of my mind and leaving me disoriented.

I shook my head and buried my face in my hands.

"Shit!" Aiden sighed. "I don't know what's got you so upset. Tell me what you want me to do, Chloe."

Everything bubbled out at once.

"The fact is, I don't know what I want!" I yelled. I balled my hands into fists at my sides. "I don't know what I want, and I don't know what you want, and I still barely even know you!"

"I thought that's what this was all about," Aiden said. "Us getting to know each other."

"How well is that working out?" I muttered.

Aiden straightened.

"I thought it was going pretty good," he replied. "You said you liked the kayaking and the skydiving. You did great with the video games, and we obviously like some of the same movies. Chloe, I'm totally lost here."

"I don't understand why you asked me to come here," I admitted.

Aiden dropped his arms and looked confused.

"I thought it was obvious," he stated.

"What's obvious?"

"I guess it isn't." Aiden ran his hand over the top of his head and looked away with a sigh.

"What is obvious?" I repeated.

"I don't remember how to do this shit," he said, his voice rising again. "It's been too fucking long. I just wanted...I *didn't* want to come on too strong. I shouldn't have kissed you like that when you were drunk. It seemed to spook you, and I didn't want to scare you off. I *don't* want to scare you off."

"Scare me off?"

He sighed and dropped his hand.

"You were so cute at the bar—all drunk and helpless without even realizing it. You freaked out so bad when you woke up, I just...I just *liked* you. You seemed so...so sweet. Innocent. I liked that. I *do* like that. I wasn't sure if you'd go for a guy like me. I figured you'd want someone more...I don't know...*sophisticated*."

"You aren't sophisticated? With this house and the pricey scotch?"

He gave me a half smile.

"I was hoping to impress you," he admitted. "Your first impression couldn't have been all that great, cooped up in that tiny apartment and driving you around in a Civic. I barely graduated high school, and you have a college degree. I wanted you to know I was...I was better than that."

Nothing he said made any sense. Why would he want to impress me?

"But...but you've barely touched me since we got here," I whispered. "I...I wasn't sure if...I thought maybe..."

I let my voice trail off, still unable to complete a logical sentence. I didn't want to admit to my own insecurities, and I definitely didn't want to hear his rejection.

"You weren't sure?" he asked. "You think because I *haven't* come on strong that I wasn't interested?"

I licked my lips quickly and nodded.

"Just say the word." Aiden stood up taller and crossed his arms over his broad chest.

"Say...say what word?"

"Chloe," Aiden said, his voice hushed, "it's killing me to hold back, but I've been doing it because you seemed so unsure. I didn't kiss you a while ago because I told myself when we first got here that I needed to let you make the first move. You say the word—you tell me you want me—and I'm going to make it very, very clear that I want you."

I felt my throat tighten, and the muscles in my arms and shoulders tensed. He stepped into the room, heading in my direction. I took a slight step back, but the only thing behind me was a wall. There wasn't anywhere to go, and my heart began to beat faster.

"What are you going to do?" I asked.

"Just say you want it," Aiden continued in the same hushed and deep voice that sent shivers up my backbone, "and I'm going to tear every piece of clothing from your body, hold you up against that wall right there, and fuck you until you scream so loud you drown out the rain and the ocean. I'm going to do things to your body you didn't think were possible. By the time the sun rises again, you are going to be covered in my cum and ruined for every man you ever meet again."

I felt dizzy. I'd never in my life had a man say such things to me. I swallowed past the lump in my throat and fought against the images his words conjured in my head. It didn't work. Inside my head, I could feel his hands gripping my arms, holding me down, and doing whatever he wanted to do with my body.

Aiden stared at me with dark eyes. His strong arms hung at his sides, and his shorts hung low on his hips with trails of ink disappearing below the waistband. He didn't blink or move, just looked at me like he really was a hunter, and I was his prey.

I wanted to be his prey.

"Okay." The word was barely audible as it left my mouth.

"What was that?" Aiden asked quietly as he took a step closer.

I stepped back reflexively.

"I want it," I whispered again. I could barely hear myself, so when he raised his eyebrows at me, I cleared my throat. "I want you."

"That's all I needed to hear."

I barely saw him move.

My back was against the wall, and one of Aiden's hands went into my hair as the other one wrapped around my backside and lifted me off the ground. I might have screamed loud enough to block out the ocean's surf, but his mouth was on mine, and his tongue silenced me.

The gentleness I'd experienced from him thus far was gone. In its place, an animalistic need emerged as my back slammed against the wall. He pressed my knees apart with one thigh, holding me up between my legs as his hand moved up to the top of my shirt. His fingers gripped the neckline, and I heard the distinctive ripping sound of fabric giving way before he tossed my ruined shirt to the floor.

Aiden pulled back and glanced down my body, his mouth slightly open and his breath coming in quick pants. He reached up and cupped my breast through my bra for a brief second before he grabbed the lace and tore it away from my flesh.

"Fuck, you're gorgeous."

One of his hands reached down around my ass and lifted me a little higher as the other wrapped around my breast. He used his thumb to trace my nipple and then pulled his fingers together to pinch my flesh. Sensation spread from my nipple to the apex of my thighs, and I tried to stop the moan in my throat.

"Don't you stay quiet on me," he said as he leaned his body into mine. I glanced at his eyes and found myself paralyzed by the look in them. "I want to hear what I'm doing to you. I want to know how wet you're getting."

"Aiden," I moaned as he lifted me again, pushing me harder against the wall to keep me from falling as his hand grabbed at the front of my shorts, ripped open the button and zipper, and then yanked them and my panties down my legs.

"Kick those things off," he commanded as he looked down my now-naked body.

I complied, and the last of my garments dropped to the floor. Aiden pressed up against me again and used his free hand to release the buttons of his own shorts and pull out the biggest cock I had ever seen in my life.

"Holy shit," I gasped.

"You like that?" He hummed against my ear. "You want to feel that inside of you? You think you're ready for this?"

He reached between my legs and slid his fingers over me. There was no doubt my body was ready for him.

"That's what I wanted to feel," he said as his eyes sparkled. "You're so fucking wet. I should have been able to smell you from across the room."

I sucked in my breath as he took himself in his hand and pressed the head of his dick against my opening. With one hard, quick thrust, he was completely buried in me.

I screamed.

"Oh, yeah," he groaned. "I wanted this since I first saw you. Fuck, Chloe, you're fucking perfect."

He began to slam into me, knocking my backside into the wall with each thrust. He grabbed my ass with both hands and began to pull me against him. He was hard, fast, rough—everything I imagined he would be.

I'd never had sex like this. I'd never felt this kind of frantic need, this desire to be consumed by someone. He wasn't just in my body; he was in my mind, my soul. I gripped the back of his shoulders, wanting to press every inch of our bodies together, and it still wasn't enough.

He leaned back and placed one hand on my shoulder, pressing my back to the wall, and looked down where we were connected. He slowed his movements a little and gripped my hip with his hand.

"Look at that," he said through heavy breaths. "Look at my cock in you, Chloe."

I did as he commanded, and I widened my eyes as I looked at the sight of his shaft moving in and out of me. I watched every inch of him stroke in and out, his cock glistening in the pale light from the bedside lamp. I couldn't breathe right and thought I might start hyperventilating.

"You like that?" he hummed against the side of my face. "You like watching me fuck you?"

"Jesus...Aiden..."

"You do, don't you? Say it!"

"I...I do!"

"You do what?"

"I like...I like watching it...oh, God!"

"That's my girl." He crushed his mouth against mine, and I opened to him. Our tongues meshed together as his hot breath coated my skin. He bit down on my lower lip, pulling it into his mouth and sucking.

I moaned and pushed my hips against him as he continued to pound me.

Abruptly, Aiden pulled out, turned us both away from the wall, and tossed me onto the center of the bed. My chest rose and fell with my rapid breaths as he pushed his shorts and boxers the rest of the way down his legs and crawled on top of me.

I placed my hand against his chest, partially covering the word "Warrior" surrounded by flames. With my fingers, I traced the inked strand of beads cascading down his body.

"Are you on the pill?" he asked.

I looked up into his eyes, suddenly terrified. How could I not have thought about that before? I hadn't been on any kind of birth control since Zach and I broke up.

"No," I whispered.

"I don't have any condoms," he stated.

I slumped against the mattress. This was going to end now before it had really even started. The thought was horrifying.

Aiden huffed out a breath.

"When's your period?"

The bluntness of the words took me off guard. I had to think about it for a moment.

"It's due in a few days," I said.

"I don't want to stop," Aiden said as he stared down at me. His eyes wandered from my breasts to my thighs, hungrily. "I want to fuck you. I don't want to have to worry about pulling out. I want to fuck you hard, and I want to come in you. I don't give a shit what happens."

Christ, if his words didn't make my entire body hum with excitement. I felt like I was back up in the plane, looking down at the earth thousands of feet below, and preparing to jump. Excitement and terror merged, and I could no longer tell one from the other.

What was this if not the ultimate risk? Even when I had been on the pill, I had always insisted on taking the extra cautious route and made guys I had been with use a condom as well. I'd never had a man come inside me in my life.

"Let me come in you." Aiden's hot breath coated my skin. "I want you to feel me fill you with cum. I want to mark you as mine—only mine."

I didn't want him to stop. I didn't want this to end. If I said no, he would stop.

Inhibitions evaporated. I wanted him to mark me. I wanted to be his, whatever that might entail.

"Okay," I finally answered as my heart thrummed beneath my skin. I reached up and gripped his biceps. "Come in me."

He didn't hesitate.

Aiden grabbed my thigh and brought it up over his shoulder. With a single thrust, he buried himself back inside of me. His head tilted back, and I could see the muscles in his neck straining as he pulled back and rammed into me again.

He leaned forward, and my leg dropped from his shoulder. Grabbing my hips with his large hands, he pulled me over his cock as his mouth latched onto one of my nipples.

This was what I'd imagined, fantasized, dreamed about—Aiden's body on top of mine, thrusting into me with so much force it almost hurt. The sweat from his chest and neck combined with mine, and I tightened my thighs around his hips in time with his movements. I could barely keep pace; I could only hold on as tight as I could to his shoulders as every muscle in my body tightened.

"Aiden! Aiden! Oh, God!"

I couldn't hold on. My legs cramped up and dropped to his sides, my knees bent. I pushed up against the mattress as hard as I could, no longer even trying to keep up with him. I coiled my arms underneath his and around his shoulders, holding myself up against his chest in the process. I felt like I was burning from the inside out with every thrust of his hips.

"Scream for me," he grunted against my neck. "Scream for my cock! Scream!"

I couldn't have held back if I wanted to.

"Ahhh!!!"

"That's it! Yeah! Oh, yeah, I can feel you…fuck, you feel so… fucking…good! I'm gonna come in you, baby. Oh, fuck, Chloe…"

Another wave hit me deep in the pit of my stomach. I clenched around his cock as he thrust forward again and held himself motionless. A second later, I felt warm semen filling me.

Oh, shit…

Aiden collapsed on me, his deep thrusts slowing as he moved his arms underneath my body and wrapped me up against his chest. His hot breath coated the skin of my neck and face as he pressed his lips to my throat and then my mouth. Even though I could feel him softening inside of me, he didn't stop. He just moved slowly in and out as he kissed me.

"It's been so fucking long," he mumbled against my lips. "So long since I wanted someone like this. God, Chloe, what are you doing to me?"

I couldn't respond. I could only hold onto him and try to stop my mind from racing. I'd let him come inside of me. I'd had unprotected sex with a man I barely knew. I could still feel it deep inside of me, coating me as he slowly moved back and forth.

He moved his head to the side and kissed a line down my neck, then back up to my ear. He didn't cease the shallow movements inside of me, just slowed down and grinded against me.

"Do you know how good you feel on my cock?" His words made me smile, and he gripped my chin with his hand, kissing me hard. "I could stay like this forever."

His fingers brushed sweat-covered hair from my face.

"Talk to me, Chloe. Tell me what you feel."

Heat coated my cheeks. Sex had always been a quiet affair with me. I wasn't versed in dirty talk and didn't have the slightest idea where to begin.

"I…I don't know what to say," I admitted.

"You could start by telling me if you liked it," Aiden suggested. His boyish smile appeared.

"I did," I said shyly.

"Not too rough?"

I shook my head.

"Good," he said, and he kissed me again. "I couldn't hold back. Shit, Chloe, this is all I I've thought about all week. It's been driving me crazy."

My skin warmed with his words.

"Were you thinking about this?" he asked. He ran his hand down my neck and over my arm.

I nodded, and Aiden licked his lips as he raised his eyebrows.

"Oh, really? What did you think about?"

"You," I whispered with a smile.

"Me doing what?" he pressed.

"What you just did." I suppressed a giggle. I felt like a schoolgirl with her first crush.

Aiden brush the back of his fingers over my cheek.

"You really are a shy thing, aren't you?" He rolled, taking me with him until I had one leg on each side of him, his cock still buried inside of me. "You realize all shyness is negated when my cock is in you, right?"

I snickered, and Aiden pulled me down on his cock to keep from slipping out.

"I'm not done with you yet," he informed me. "I wasn't joking about that sunrise. As soon as I'm hard again, I'm taking you from behind."

He held my hips and slowly moved us together as I balanced with my hands on his chest. I couldn't move my eyes from his, and he just watched me as we moved together. It didn't take long before I felt him growing inside of me.

Aiden was nothing if not a man of his word. As soon as I was able to move faster on top of him, his cock back to its full length, he grabbed me and pushed me face down on the bed. He gripped my sides, pulled me to my knees, and slammed back inside of me.

"I could watch this all day," he said with a grunt. "Watch my cock sliding in and out of you...You're perfect like this."

I groaned, and he leaned over my back, reached around me, and cupped both my breasts. I felt his lips against my shoulder, kissing and nipping at me.

"Tell me you want this," Aiden said. "Tell me how much you are loving this."

"I...I...I want it. God, Aiden—I want you!"

"Oh, you're getting me, baby." He leaned back again with one hand placed on the back of my neck and the other grasping my thigh. His pace increased—fast and relentless. I gripped the sheets with my fingers and cried out with every thrust.

He slowed, stroked my back, and then ran his hands up my sides. I tried to catch my breath, braced for another onset.

Aiden pulled out slowly, and I rolled to my back. He positioned himself again, and leisurely reentered me with a groan. He held himself there, propped up with his hands on either side of me, and he closed his eyes. He pulled back just as slowly and then pushed forward again.

He kept up the slow, deep rhythm as I lay against the mattress with my neck arched and my head pressed against the pillow. I reached up and wrapped my arms around his neck, pulling his mouth to mine. He kissed me gently as I gripped his shoulders and pushed up against him with my hips.

He penetrated me deeply, held himself there, and started grinding himself against my pubic bone. The pressure was incredible, and I felt the buildup between my legs as I pushed back, moaning.

"You like it slow?" he whispered in my ear. "You like feeling every inch of me inside of you?"

"Yes! Yes!" I cried.

He slid his hand from my face down to my breast, brushing lightly over my nipples before reaching down, past my stomach. He used his fingers against me, rotating in time with his brief, shallow thrusts.

There was no holding back.

"Ahhh!" My body tensed, shook, and powerful waves cascaded over my skin, focused, and released.

"Oh, yeah," Aiden moaned. "That's it, baby."

He increased his tempo, returning to that relentless pace he'd used before. I wrapped my arms and legs around him and held on as he grunted, thrust again, and cried out.

"Fuck...yes...Oh, Chloe! So fucking good..."

I felt him fill me again just before he dropped his head to my shoulder, panting.

Emotions I wasn't able to name crushed me. My body shuddered, and I felt as if I had been turned inside out. I held him tighter as my heart continued to pound. It was too much. It was all too much.

Oh, God, what am I doing? What had I done? What is this feeling inside of me?

Tears filled my eyes, and I couldn't help the sob that escaped my lips. Aiden quickly raised his head and looked down at me, his eyes filled with concern as he brought his hand to my cheek, pushing tears away.

"Shh, shh, shh," Aiden cooed. He cupped my face with his hand and began to kiss me, over and over again like he was slowly and gently devouring me. "Don't cry. Fuck, don't cry."

"I'm sorry," I whispered. I tightened my grip on the back of his head and kissed him harder.

He went with it for a moment and then pulled back.

"I didn't...I didn't hurt you, did I?"

"No." I shook my head.

"What is it then, Chloe? What's wrong?"

"I'm just...I'm scared!"

"Scared of what?"

Everything I had been thinking and feeling consumed me, overwhelmed my mind and my senses. My vision blurred with an abrupt onset of tears.

"I'm scared of you!"

And with that, I began to sob.

ELEVEN

Aiden rolled to his side and held me against his chest while I cried. I didn't understand what was going on inside of me; I just knew I was overwhelmed, exhausted, and my emotions were completely out of control.

I'd loved every second of what he had done to me.

That was what scared me.

Deep inside of me, the alarms were still going off. I felt as if I was still falling from the plane before the parachute opened, when everything was still uncertain. I could practically see the ground getting closer and closer as I fell, and this time there wasn't a parachute.

I'd let him come in me.

Twice.

Unprotected sex.

My mother had given me various versions of "the talk" during my childhood and teenaged years. She covered the basics, warned me off of sex altogether until I was older, and then ultimately counseled me on becoming sexually active. There were plenty of rules about making sure it was with the right person, the right situation, and not allowing someone to take advantage of me. Above all others, there was one major rule—use birth control.

I'd failed on multiple counts.

As my sobs dwindled, Aiden kissed the top of my head, hugged me close, and then placed his finger on my chin to lift my face to him.

"You're scared of me?"

"Yes." I sniffled.

"Why?" His voice was a whisper, his expression pained.

"I hardly know anything about you."

"I hardly know anything about you, either," he replied. "What are you scared of?"

How could I even put it into words? It wasn't just that he could have gotten me pregnant, which was enough by itself, but something far greater. It was everything he had made me feel, everything he made me want.

I'm only going to be here for three more days.

"Chloe, what do you think I'd do?" Aiden asked when I hadn't answered him.

"I don't know," I whispered.

"Do you think I'd hurt you? I wouldn't. I swear. I'd never do something like that."

"No." I shook my head, trying to make sense of the thoughts in my mind. "At least, not exactly."

"What is it, then?" he prodded.

"I…I don't know." I took a deep breath. "All of this scares me to death."

"All of *what*?" His arms tensed, and I could hear the frustration in his voice.

"Being here," I said. "Everything about this week, it's just been…well, it's been…"

I trailed off, trying to find the right words.

"It's been wonderful," I finally said, and then I started crying again.

He cradled my head in his hands, staring at me intently.

"And that scares you?"

"Yes." I sniffed and wiped my eyes.

"I don't understand," Aiden admitted. "I mean, if you're having a good time, well…what's the problem?"

Another tear slipped down my cheek, and he wiped it away with his thumb. He stared into my eyes looking as confused as I felt.

"Tell me," he pleaded.

"I don't know what happens now," I said. "Where do we go from here?"

Aiden narrowed his eyes, obviously still unsure what I meant.

"I'm not a one-night-stand kind of guy," Aiden said. "I've got my hand and plenty of porn when it comes down to that. I'm not going to toss you out in the rain now that we've had sex."

"Well, that's good to know." My words were biting, though I didn't really mean them to sound like that. I just couldn't find the right words.

"Chloe," Aiden started and then paused to take a deep breath. "When we first met, you were hesitant about everything. You didn't want me to help you when you were too trashed to drive. You freaked out about waking up with me, and you wouldn't even consider altering your normal schedule. I'm surprised you decided to come down with me at all. Even after we got to Miami, you were more scared than excited. I saw you looking at the cabs at the airport—you didn't even want to ride on the back of my bike. Since coming down here with me, you've really opened yourself up to try shit you haven't done before. You even went skydiving, for fuck's sake, and I had been pretty sure you weren't going to agree to it at all. It was a stretch on my part to even suggest it."

He paused, his looked softened, and he smiled.

"When I looked into your eyes after we were back on the ground, do you know how you looked?"

I shook my head.

"*Alive*," he said. "Really, truly alive. Your eyes were bright and without fear. You looked like you could conquer the world right then."

He ran his thumb over my cheekbone.

"I watched you change. I watched you turn into a completely new and better person right then. It was one of the most beautiful things I had ever seen in my life."

I looked away, trying to process what he had said. Changing into another person was a bit of a stretch, but I *had* felt different after my feet touched the ground. I felt stronger, more powerful. It had been beyond just the thrill of falling through space and surviving. It was like something inside of me, long dormant, had opened up and demanded to be satiated.

I didn't want to lose that feeling.

"What about when this week is over?" I asked. "When I go back home, what happens?"

"I haven't thought that far ahead," Aiden admitted. "I hope we still want to see each other. I'm up your way often enough, and I'd bring you down here again whenever you wanted."

"What if it doesn't work?" I asked.

"Maybe it won't," Aiden said. "That's just life, babe."

I got bolder.

"You're hiding something," I said.

"Yeah," Aiden replied, "I am."

I stiffened at his bluntness.

"Well, that scares me."

"I've got my share of secrets, Chloe." He sat up a little and propped himself up on his elbow. "Everyone does. Someday I might share some of them with you. You've got yours as well, and I hope someday you'll trust me enough to tell me what they are. In the meantime, we learn."

"Learn what?"

"About each other. About what we like and don't like."

"What if we don't like each other?" I asked. "What if I can't handle your secrets? What then?"

"I suppose then we'd go our separate ways," he said. "That's possible with any relationship—you have to know that."

I did, of course. I nodded as I traced the edge of his bicep with my fingertip.

"I don't want that to happen," I said quietly.

"I don't either," he agreed. "I really like you, and I hope you feel at least some of that for me."

"I do," I whispered quietly without meeting his eyes. I focused on the words scrawled across his clavicle and up around his shoulder: "Blood. Sweat. Tears."

"I don't like this shit," Aiden said as he brushed more tears off my cheeks. "I don't like you being so upset, especially not after what I consider to be some of the best sex of my life."

"It was?" I looked up at him.

"For me it was," he said. "You don't agree?"

"It was for me, too," I said. "It's never…well, never been like that."

"How so?" His grin was back, and it made me smile, too.

"Um…fast…a little rough…all that dirty talk." I blushed.

He laughed.

"I can't help myself," he said. "I especially can't help myself with a girl who's so fucking hot, all flushed and breathing heavy before we even got started. I'm surprised I didn't come on the third stroke."

Giggles erupted from my throat.

"I wasn't sure you were ever going to stop!"

He rested his hand on my waist, ran it down to my thigh, and then back again.

"Was it too much?" he asked.

I shook my head.

"Definitely not."

"Good," he replied, "because now that I've had a taste of you, I'm going to want a lot more. I need you to tell me what you like and what you don't like."

"I think I'm good with that," I said with a smile.

He kissed me slowly. I ran my hand up his arm and gripped the back of his neck as he wound his fingers through my hair. He leaned over me, pushing the back of my head to the pillow and kissing me again. When he stopped, he just looked down at me and smiled.

I blinked sleepily as I looked back at him.

"Tired?" Aiden asked quietly.

"Exhausted," I said with a nod. "You wore me out."

"I like wearing you out," he said. "I'm probably going to want to wear you out first thing in the morning, too."

I stared into his eyes as he brushed the hair from my forehead. I remembered the feeling of him pressed against me when he was still asleep and thought about what it would be like to wake up to him sliding into me.

"I think I'd like that," I said.

"Duly noted," Aiden replied. He cupped my face with his hand and kissed me softly. "Get some sleep. You just might need it."

He wrapped me in his arms, and I rested my head on his chest. I was reminded of the first time I woke up like this, hungover and disoriented, and thought about everything that had happened since that Saturday morning, less than one week ago.

I wondered what Wonder Woman, Leia, and Buffy would think now.

The sun was shining through the window when I opened my eyes, and Aiden was curled up against me, breathing steadily. I watched his face for a minute, thinking about how peaceful he looked until my bladder demanded attention.

Disentangling myself from his arms, I crawled out of bed.

Good lord, I was sore. I stumbled a little, barely able to walk down the hall to the bathroom. I could still feel every inch of him inside of me—both in my body and in my head. I felt less emotional than the night before, but I couldn't seem to stop the feeling of dread inside of me as I thought about what we had done.

What if I'm pregnant?

My cycle timing really wasn't right, but I wasn't dumb enough to think that it wasn't possible. That was why you were supposed to always use protection in the first place. I didn't even want to consider the other reasons to incorporate the use of a condom and wondered how I could possibly broach the subject. How do you come out and ask the guy you already slept with if he is clean or not?

That definitely belonged in the "way too late" category.

I plopped down on the toilet, surprised to find my legs were also sore. I guess I had been using them quite a bit during our nighttime undertakings. My back ached, too. Every time I moved, some other part of me protested the vigorous activity that was sex with Aiden Hunter.

I washed my hands and face, trying not to look at myself too much in the mirror. My curly hair was all over the place, and my mascara was smudged. Besides, every time I did look in the mirror, I came up with a bunch of wild notions about what I was doing. Yes, I had been spontaneous in deciding to come here. Yes, I'd taken some risks, and that was all very out of character for me, but I wasn't sorry.

I wasn't sorry at all.

However, I was still feeling a little guilty. I had spent so much time thinking of reasons not to trust Aiden that I hadn't opened my eyes to really see him. I'd been searching for evidence to support my idea that he was a bad person in order to justify my fears. I had judged him based on how he looked and not how he behaved. As it turned out, there wasn't anything about Aiden to fear at all.

I thought about how he had held me and let me cry. I remembered all his sweet words to me and how he admitted that he was afraid, too. This was how it was when you started a relationship with someone. There weren't any guarantees, but that didn't mean you didn't take a chance.

"Like jumping out of a plane," I whispered to myself. "In the end, you are a better person, and it's all worth it."

I smiled as I walked back to the bedroom and climbed back into bed. Aiden's eyes fluttered open, and he reached out to pull me against his chest.

"I dreamed you left," he muttered. He held me tighter.

"Just went to the bathroom," I said softly. "Go back to sleep."

"Hmm…" He tucked his head against my neck. "Don't leave again."

"I'm not going anywhere."

"Promise?" he muttered.

"I promise."

"Okay." His breathing slowed as he drifted off.

Wrapped in his arms, I fell back asleep.

Though we woke up late in the morning, neither of us was interested in getting out of bed. Aiden made a quick trip to the kitchen for croissants, which we ate sitting up against the pillows. As tired as I was, I had to drag myself to the bathroom to shower. I was sticky *everywhere*.

Aiden followed.

With the warm water pouring over my skin, Aiden filled his hands with soap and ran them up and down my sides.

He rinsed his hands, then turned and grabbed my backside. He lifted me up and pressed my body against the tiles as he slowly sank into me. I tensed and wrapped my arms and legs around him, afraid we were going to slip and fall, but Aiden's strength didn't let us down.

"Do you want it slow?" Aiden mumbled against my neck as he pulled back and filled me again. "Or do you like getting fucked fast and hard?"

I groaned as he continued the unhurried pace, gently gripping my ass as he pulled me in to meet his strokes.

"That's not an answer," he chided. "You have to tell me what you want."

I bit my lip and tightened my hold on him, not truly sure what I wanted. The feeling of him inside me was overwhelming and wonderful. I just wanted more of it.

"Faster," I finally said. "Hard and fast."

"Like this?" He picked up the pace as he slid his hands up a little to protect my back from the tiles.

"More," I whispered. I pushed my hips forward and tightened my thighs around his waist. "Harder."

"Yeah, that's what I thought." Aiden tightened his grip and hoisted me up a little higher. "You better hold on."

I tightened my grip as his thrusts deepened. Our tongues met as we kissed, and water poured over our bodies. My heart beat in time to the sound of wet skin on skin as my legs shook, and pleasure swept over my body. My muscles tightened around Aiden's cock rhythmically, and I dug my heels into his backside.

"Oh, you love that, don't you? I can feel how much you love coming all over my cock."

"Yes!" I screamed as another wave quickly followed the first.

Aiden leaned back, holding me around my ass with one arm. He took his free hand and ran it over my stomach and breasts as he dropped his eyes down to where we were connected. He slowed down, pulling almost all the way out as he watched.

"There's nothing better than watching my dick slide in and out of you. Going slow like this…making sure you feel every fucking inch of me. I know how much you crave my cock. You want it in there almost as much as I do."

"God, Aiden…"

"I like the sound of that," he said as his eyes twinkled at me. "Hang on, baby."

I did my best to comply as he picked up the pace, bracing himself against the tiles with his free hand. He grunted with every stroke, and I could feel his fingers tightening on my backside as he pulled me against him each time.

"Fuck, yeah," he groaned as his cock twitched, and he filled me. He leaned forward again, crushing me against the tiles as he breathed heavily. "Damn, that felt good."

He lowered me slowly to my feet and made sure I had my balance before he let go. He kissed me softly and then stepped out of the shower while I rinsed myself off *again*. My legs were wobbly, and I wondered if Aiden's stamina had some sort of endpoint. He seemed to be ready to go at any given moment, and we'd only just started. My experiences had always tended toward the mundane—missionary position in a bed, one round, and then either head home or go to sleep.

I'd never had sex in the shower before. Another first for me.

I turned off the water, slid over the shower door, and stepped out onto the mat. Aiden had a towel wrapped around his waist, and he smiled as he took another towel and stepped up to me.

Without words, Aiden took the towel and started drying me off as I just stood there and watched him. He started with my shoulders, ran the cloth down my arms and then back up again. He dried my skin slowly over my breasts and stomach, then reached around and pressed himself against me as he dried my back. He then knelt in front of me to run the towel around my legs before finishing with my feet.

"There you go," he said softly as he tossed the towel over the shower door. His eyes sparkled as he quickly reached down and wrapped one arm around my waist and the other behind my knees, lifting me into the air. He turned quickly and carried me back to the bedroom like a child, making me squeal. He smacked my ass and told me to hush.

"Ow!" I playfully bit at his neck.

"Oh, we're on to biting, are we? You'll regret that."

"You started it!" I reminded him. "You can't smack my ass without expecting retaliation."

"It was a romantic slap on the ass."

He tossed me in the middle of the unmade bed, and I grabbed at the sheets to keep from bouncing. Aiden crawled in beside me and pulled me up against his chest. He kissed me lightly on the lips and pushed wet hair from my forehead.

"My hair is going to be a disaster," I commented.

"I like it," he said. "It's all over the place. Makes you look freshly fucked."

I rolled my eyes.

"I *am* freshly fucked." I giggled. I wasn't much of a curser, but Aiden's dirty mouth was contagious.

"Yeah," he agreed, "I like that, too."

I found myself tracing the edges of some of the tattoos on his chest. Well, at least where I could find an edge—they all blended together. My fingers ran over one of the more predominant ones over his right pec, where he had DAD inscribed in elaborate, scripted letters with birth and death dates below.

"Tell me more about you," I said.

"Like what?"

"Maybe your family? You don't talk about them much."

Aiden looked away and shrugged.

"There isn't a lot to say. I haven't talked to my Mom in years, and she's all there is."

"Does she ever try to contact you?"

"Yeah," he replied softly. "She calls on my birthday and Christmas like clockwork."

"You don't answer?"

"No."

I had the feeling I was treading on thin ice, but I pushed forward anyway.

"Why not?"

Aiden sighed and rolled to his back, placing his hand behind his head.

"She dwells," he finally said.

"Dwells on what?"

"Dad, having me too young, everything about her life she didn't think was fair—all that shit. The last time I saw her or talked to her, she was sitting in the middle of the living room with all these pictures of my dad from when he played lacrosse. She had another picture of him on the table, and she was talking to it like he was there."

"I talk to my Dad's picture," I admitted quietly.

Aiden narrowed his eyes at me.

"Why?"

I shrugged.

"It's not like I think he's there or that he'll answer me or anything," I clarified. "We were close, and sometimes I just want to talk to him."

"Don't you end up just thinking about him all the time then?" Aiden asked.

"Sometimes. It's taken me a while to get there, but I'm not sad when I think about him anymore. I still miss him, but the good memories outweigh the bad."

Aiden pondered as he stared up at the ceiling. He took a deep breath, and I watched his chest rise and fall.

"Why did you get this tattoo?" I asked as I traced the letters on his chest.

"It was the first one I got," he said. "I wanted...I thought I needed to..."

His voice trailed off as he let out a big sigh.

"He didn't get a grave. We only had enough money to have him cremated, but not buried. Mom still has his ashes. I just thought he needed a marker somewhere, so that's where I put it."

I lay my head down on his shoulder.

"That's actually kind of beautiful," I said.

He shrugged and looked at my face.

"I never talk about this shit," he said.

"Why not?" I asked.

"I don't want to think about him," he said. "I live in the now. I don't want the reminder of what isn't there anymore."

"You can't avoid it forever," I said.

"It's working so far." His voice was flat and a little stern, as if he were trying to put an end to the conversation.

"Is it?" I questioned.

I reached up and placed my hand against his rough cheek, turning him to face me.

"There's room for both, Aiden," I said. "Our past brought us to where we are now. If we ignore part of it, we are ignoring part of ourselves."

He blinked his eyes slowly as he looked at me but refused to comment.

And with that, I knew we both had something to learn.

TWELVE

Unlike the first couple of days full of adventurous, outdoor activities, Aiden and I spent the next two creating indoor adventures of our own as the rain continued to pour down. There wasn't a piece of furniture in the house we hadn't utilized. We'd even had sex on the kitchen counter, some of the sturdier boxes lying around, and the weight bench in Aiden's workout room. He wasn't lying about covering me in cum, either. Eventually, I insisted we run out to the store for a box of wet-wipes.

For better or worse, there wasn't a lot of time left over to talk.

Friday night, the rain finally stopped, and Aiden grilled shark steaks out on the patio. He topped off dinner with sweet potatoes and seasoned green beans that were to die for. He even made sweet iced tea to wash it all down.

We sat outside, watched beachcombers, and listened to the waves as we ate. When we were done, Aiden insisted I relax as he did the dishes. I sat back in the patio chair with a smile on my face and closed my eyes until he joined me back outside.

"Okay," Aiden said as he sat back down. "Now that I've buttered you up with food, I have a question for you, a request, rather."

"What's that?"

"How would you feel about going to a party tonight?"

"A party?"

"Yeah," Aiden confirmed with a nod. "It's at Redeye's place. Just a group of friends, mostly guys, but some of their girlfriends and such will be there. You already know Lo and Mo, so you wouldn't feel totally lost."

I considered it. Though spending time alone with Aiden was also tempting, hanging out with his friends might be an even better way of getting to know him.

"Sure," I said. "That sounds like fun."

"Awesome!" Aiden beamed. "It's not far—just a twenty-minute drive. They're a fun bunch—I know you'll have a blast. Just be prepared for some serious drinking."

Redeye lived in Hollywood, just a few miles inland. It was a nice middle-class neighborhood with a row of houses obviously all designed by the same architect. His house was in the middle of the street, and there were already a lot of cars parked outside. Aiden stopped the jeep a few houses down and we walked up to the front door. It opened before he could knock, and a tall man with a moustache peered out at us.

"Well, look what the fucking cat drug in!" he called out.

"Hunter!" several voices cried at once. I recognized Lo and Mo immediately as they crowded the door.

"Lo said you had a lady with you," the man who had opened the door said. "Quite frankly, I didn't believe him."

Aiden put his arm around my shoulders.

"Chloe, this is Redeye. Redeye, this is Chloe."

"Well, I won't let her taste in men sway my opinion of her." Redeye laughed. He made a big sweeping motion with his arm. "Come on in! Let me get you a shot."

"I did warn you about this guy, right?" Aiden said as we walked in. "If you aren't careful, he'll be shoving shots at you about every five minutes."

"I'll watch myself," I said with a smile.

"It won't help," Aiden warned. He reached up and pushed his cap firmly against his head. "He's pretty insistent."

"Hey there, darling!" Mo said as he pulled me into a hug.

"Don't be hoggin' all that to yourself!" Lo cried.

The next thing I knew, I was trapped in a bear hug between both of them.

"For Christ's sake," Aiden mumbled, "let the girl breathe!"

Their booming laughs echoed through the room as they released me.

We walked through the house and out a sliding glass door to a screened-in sunroom and pool beyond. There were about ten people total, only two of whom were women. Two of the guys came up to us immediately. One had a cute, boyish face and short, spikey hair, and the other wore glasses and had nearly as many tattoos as Aiden.

"What's up, Hunter?" the first one said as he gave Aiden a hug. "Long time, no see."

"Not much, bro," Aiden said. He turned to me. "Chloe, this is Clutch and Dutch."

"Clutch and Dutch?" I repeated. "Doesn't anyone you know have a normal name?"

They all laughed.

"Good to meet you," Dutch said. He tipped his cap and bowed, drawing my attention to his legs, which were covered in green and orange striped socks.

"Good to meet you, too," I replied. "Love the socks."

"Why, thank you, ma'am," he said as he tipped his hat again.

"Tell me this guy is paying you to be here with him," Clutch said as he took my hand and held it. "Tell me there is no way this asshole ended up with a hot chick like you."

"Um…no, I don't think so." I giggled.

"Get your fucking hands off her," Aiden said as he pushed Clutch away. There wasn't any anger in his voice though, and they all laughed afterward as another guy came up to Aiden's side. He was young and wore a hat that looked like it belonged on Crocodile Dundee.

"Hunter," he said as he tipped his hat and shook Aiden's hand. "Good to see you."

"You, too, Lance," Aiden said. "This is Chloe."

"Welcome to the mayhem!" Lance said with a friendly smile. Lance, Dutch, and Clutch then wandered off toward the bar set up by the pool.

Aiden took me around and introduced me to the others, but the introductions went by so fast, I couldn't quite keep up with the names. The next thing I knew, Redeye was standing next to us and shoving a shot glass and a lemon into my hands.

"What is it?" I asked.

"Don't ask questions," Redeye said as he handed a glass and a lemon to Aiden. "Just do the shot, and immediately bite the lemon."

"It tastes like chocolate cake," Aiden informed me. "The lemon is coated in sugar. It's good—really."

Redeye passed out more shots and then held up his own glass.

"Good friends and lots of booze!" he toasted.

I watched Aiden do the shot and then quickly followed his lead. As soon as I bit into the lemon, I was surprised to find out it really did taste like chocolate cake.

I followed Aiden up to the bar, and he made me a vodka and cranberry. I sipped as he poured himself a glass of vodka and Red Bull.

"I guess you don't plan on ever falling asleep again," I commented.

"It's good stuff," he said. "And I'm hoping this will be a long night."

He winked at me.

Music played, and everyone sat around a fire pit chatting about nothing in particular. Aiden was definitely right about Redeye—he brought shots around at least every half an hour, demanding everyone participate. It wasn't long before I was feeling a little tipsy.

When Aiden excused himself to go find the bathroom inside, one of the girls came and sat beside me.

"How do you know Hunter?" the girl asked. I tried to remember her name, but all I could recall was that she was here with Lance.

"We met in Ohio," I explained, leaving out the details. "He invited me down for the week."

"Oh! Are you staying at his beach house?"

"Yes."

"That place is beautiful!" she exclaimed. "I was only there once, but that view—wow!"

"It really is wonderful," I agreed.

"You are so lucky," she said. "Hunter is a sweetheart. I'm glad to see him with someone."

"He doesn't usually bring a date?" I asked, taking the opportunity to get some information.

"Never," the girl said with a shake of her head. "I wasn't around when he was with that crazy bitch, so I never met her."

"Oh," I said. I thought quickly. "You mean Megan?"

"Yeah," the girl confirmed. "I mean, I know I'm not supposed to talk ill of the dead and all, but from what I hear, she really went off the deep end."

Dead? Aiden's ex-girlfriend was *dead*?

"I can't believe all the shit that went down with that, can you?" The girl shook her head slowly.

"Um…no," I said, my mind still spinning, "I can't."

My heart was racing. Of all the ideas I had in my head, I hadn't given much thought to what had happened with Aiden's ex. It never would have occurred to me that she had died.

"Well, when he gets his hands on them," the girl continued, "they don't stand a chance. I have never seen him mad personally, but I hear it's not pretty."

My eyes widened and my head spun. What was he going to do when he gets his hands on whom? What had happened to his ex?

I wanted to ask more, but Lance walked up with Mo and Lo, effectively ending the conversation, and the girl stood to loop her arm around Lance's elbow. I looked at Lo, wondering if I could pull him away from the group long enough to ask him some questions, but he was in some deep debate with Mo over the last *Star Trek* movie.

"Here ya go, Chloe." Redeye appeared on my right with another shot.

"Oh, um…thank you." I watched as he handed out a few others. Mo took his glass before turning to Lance.

"You're watching *The Walking Dead*, right?" he said. "Holy fuck, that last episode!"

"I had to DVR it!" Lance yelled. "No spoilers!"

"Spoilers are the devil's orgasms," Lo announced with a huge laugh. "Don't let the devil come!"

We all drank to the sentiment, but my mind was still on my all-too-brief conversation with Lance's girlfriend. Aiden came back outside, and Redeye penalized him for missing the last shot by making him do two more. He took the first with no problem but cringed after drinking the second.

"What the fuck is that shit?" he yelled.

"That's Bakon!" Redeye announced with a big grin.

Lo and Mo began to cackle.

"I told you!" Lo screamed. "I fucking told you!"

"Holy shit, that's nasty!" Aiden shook his head and took a big gulp of his vodka and Red Bull to get rid of the taste. "Damn, it stays with ya, too!"

"Just a little somethin' to remember me by," Redeye commented as he went out in search of a new victim.

Aiden sat back down beside me, and I couldn't stop myself from staring at his profile as he talked to his friends. What had happened to Megan? He hadn't said anything about her, aside from her teaching him to cook. He hadn't even told me her name—that had been Lo. If she had just succumbed to some disease, wouldn't he have said so?

What happened to her? Did Aiden have something to do with it?

No, I didn't believe that. I couldn't.

I continued to watch Aiden, barely hearing the conversation as the alcohol in my system began to take hold. I wasn't as bad off as I had been the night Aiden and I met, but I also knew I needed to avoid any more shots.

It occurred to me that I could try Googling the name Megan in the Miami area to see if I could find out anything. If she was tied to some crime, maybe I could pull up a police record of some sort. I reached down and took my phone out of my purse.

Apparently, I hadn't turned it back off after texting Mare. It was totally dead. I remembered that I was supposed to have called Mare back days ago but hadn't done it. If she had tried to call me, she wouldn't have been able to get through.

Crap.

"Hey, can you hold these for me for just a second?" Redeye stood at my side, holding two shot glasses in his hand.

"Sure." I said. I was just glad he wasn't telling me to drink another one.

I watched as he poured more shots and then passed a set of two glasses to Aiden, Lo, Mo, and Lance.

"Picklebacks!" he called out as he raised the glasses.

"Um, what about these?" I asked as I held up my hands.

"Those are yours, babe," Redeye said with a wink.

"I thought I was holding them for someone else!" I cried.

"Nope, all yours."

"I think I've had enough," I insisted. I started to look around for someone else to hand the drinks to, but everyone without a drink had gone inside.

"No such thing, sweetheart."

"Really, I'm good."

"Now look here," Redeye said as he leaned down and peered into my face. "This is the best damn shot you are ever gonna taste in your life, and that's a solid fact. I'd be reminiscent in my duties as a host if you didn't take that shot right now."

"Reminiscent?" Mo questioned.

"Translation from Redeye-speak to English," Lance informed us, "he would be *remiss* in his duties."

"He's remiss in his sanity," Aiden said as he grinned at me. "I warned ya. It really is easier to give in."

I cringed and stared down at the glasses. One had brown liquid in it, and I thought it smelled like whiskey. I had no idea what the other glass contained. There wasn't enough light outside to determine its color, but the smell was familiar. I just couldn't quite place it.

Aiden leaned over to me.

"Just give those to me as soon as Redeye takes his shot. I'll take care of them for ya."

I nodded, glad to have an out. Aiden watched Redeye closely and quickly downed first one glass and then the other before switching his empty ones with my full ones. Then he drank those, too.

"What the fuck was that?" Lo screamed. "It's got chunks in it!"

"I ran out of pickle juice!" Redeye yelled back at him. "Had to improvise!"

"Improvise with what?"

"I just put all the pickles in a blender," Redeye explained.

"Fucking awesome, isn't it?"

"That's just wrong," Mo said with a laugh.

"Better than that cheap-ass whiskey he's serving," Clutch said.

Redeye got up in his face.

"Are you disrespecting my hospitality?" he snapped. "Because I'll have you know that's the finest batch of pickles this side of the fucking state!"

"I think you are out of your God-forsaken mind!" Clutch yelled back. "Maybe I need to teach you a little lesson!"

Clutch bumped his chest up against Redeye's, and they stared menacingly into each other's eyes. Dutch walked up between them and put a hand on each of their shoulders.

"What we have here," Dutch said, "is a meeting of the sausages!"

"I better be getting a waffle with that!" Clutch demanded.

"And a chalupa!" Aiden called out.

I looked over to him and raised an eyebrow. Aiden just shook his head.

"The power of suggestion," he said as he pointed to the group. "Any minute now, and someone will run out to Taco Bell and bring back a whole stack of chalupas. Just wait."

"I said sausages!" Dutch roared.

"Hold on!" Lo cried out. "Let me get my camera! I know the perfect porn site for this shit!"

Everyone laughed. My head spun, but I wasn't sure if it was the alcohol or the insane banter between Aiden's friends. I couldn't keep up. All I could think about was what might have happened to Aiden's ex.

The night progressed. Before long, chalupas did seem to magically appear next to the bar, but I wasn't sure who had acquired them. There was more silliness, more banter, and a lot more shots. Aiden managed to save me from most of them though. Apparently, the trick was to take whatever Redeye offered you without hesitation and then wait until he was distracted long enough for you to get rid of it by any means possible.

It worked. By the time everyone began to either crash on couches or head home, I was only mildly tipsy. Aiden was a whole other story. I had to hold on to his arm to help him walk through the house.

"You be careful now," Redeye said as he escorted us to the door. He narrowed his eyes at Aiden.

Aiden leaned over and gave Redeye a quick hug as Redeye mumbled something in his ear. Aiden responded just as quietly, and Redeye grinned.

"It was awesome to meet you, Chloe," he said as he hugged me, too. "Take care of this asshole for us, and don't be a stranger."

Aiden took my hand, and we walked down the sidewalk towards the jeep.

"You had a lot of shots," I said. "Way more than I did."

"Yeah, but you weigh what? A buck twenty?" Aiden chuckled, stumbled a bit, and then got out his keys.

"Aiden," I said as I grabbed his arm, "I really don't think you should drive."

"No fucking kidding," he said with another laugh. He stumbled into the bumper of the jeep and opened the trunk. "However, these seats do go all the way back."

He climbed up into the back of the jeep and fiddled with the seats until they lay down flat. Then he reached out his hand, pulled me in beside him, and closed the back door before falling over, still laughing.

The relief on my face must have been evident. As soon as I positioned myself beside him, Aiden grabbed my face in his hands and kissed me.

"I just found you," he muttered against my lips. "Do you really think I'd risk you now?"

With that, his hands were all over me. He ran one down my front, then under my shirt and back up again. He grabbed my rear end with the other and pulled me into his lap as he leaned against the back of the driver's seat.

"The best way to sober up is with a little rigorous exercise," he informed me as he grabbed his cap off his head and tossed it into the front seat.

He began to kiss down my neck, and I glanced out one of the windows in the back to see Lance and his girlfriend exiting the house and walking in our direction.

"Aiden," I moaned. I turned his face up to mine. "Someone will see us."

"So what?" he asked. He attacked my mouth with his again as he slid one hand into the back of my shorts under my panties and gripped my bare ass. I could feel his other hand fumbling around between us, and I realized he was undoing his pants.

"Aiden!" I called out again. "People are walking by!"

Just then, I heard Lance whoop just outside the jeep.

"Yeah! You go!" he screamed. He and his girlfriend both laughed as Aiden held up one hand and gave them the finger.

They moved on, but I knew there were still others about to leave. Even with the doors on, the jeep had a lot of windows. Anyone could look in on us.

Alarm!

"Aiden!"

"Don't care," he said. He had his dick in one hand and was pushing my shorts down with the other.

Was I really going to do this? Have sex in a vehicle where anyone could walk by and see us? Granted, it was way after midnight, and there would be very few passersby, but anyone still at the party would notice if they came outside.

Aiden started to push me up to my knees so he could get my shorts off, but I grabbed his hands.

"I don't know about this," I confessed.

He paused and looked into my face.

"I'll stop if you want," he said. "I don't want to, but I will."

He took my face in his hands again, kissing me softly once but then pulling back.

"This is *life*, Chloe. Live it."

My skin tingled. I looked back around my shoulder and saw the door to Redeye's house was open, and there were figures silhouetted in it. I glanced back at Aiden.

He was right. This was exciting. This was terrifying.

And I felt *alive*.

"Okay," I said, and my smile matched his.

I pulled off his shirt, and he pushed my shorts and panties down my legs until I could kick them off. They hit the back door of the jeep, and one of the metal buttons clanged, causing me to giggle.

Aiden gripped my hips and pulled me back onto his lap with my knees on either side of him. I reached down and wrapped my hand around him, my heart beating faster at the sound of his moan. He held me up with his hands, and I positioned him between my legs before slowly sliding down on him.

"Oh, shit!" Aiden tossed his head back and arched his hips, pushing deeper inside of me.

My body felt like it was on high alert, and I could feel myself already pulsing around him with the first thrust. I knew anyone could be looking in on us, but I didn't dare look back to find out. I kept my hands on Aiden's shoulders for support, and my eyes locked with his.

"Ride me," Aiden commanded. He moved his hands up to my breasts, thumbing my nipples. "Ride my cock right here where anyone can see you."

His shorts were only opened enough for him to get his dick out of them, and they were chafing the insides of my thighs, but I didn't care. Aiden reached up under my shirt and unclasped my bra. It still dangled from my shoulders but allowed him access to my breasts.

"Fuck," I moaned as he rubbed my nipples between his fingers.

"Oh yeah? There is a little dirty talk in my girl, isn't there? Come on—say it again. Tell me to fuck you!"

"Ugh! Aiden!"

"Say it!" he commanded again. "Beg for it!"

"Fuck me!" I yelled. "Fuck me, Aiden!"

"Hell yeah, I'm going to fuck you!" He dug his fingers into the flesh of my hips and pulled me up and down over him. He kept time with his hips, shoving deep into me every time.

I wrapped my arms around his head, holding him against my shoulder as we moved together at a furious pace. My breasts were bouncing all over the place, and he seemed to be trying to catch them with his mouth as they moved.

He slowed slightly and reached up to palm one breast.

"Tell me how you want it." Aiden slowed his movements further. "Tell me how you want to get fucked, Chloe."

My heart raced. I still wasn't used to all of this talking during sex. It had always just happened without a bunch of discussion.

Aiden wanted to discuss everything.

He stopped moving and held me down in his lap. He took my chin in his hand and stared into my eyes.

"Tell me how you want it, Chloe," he said again. "Tell me how you want to get fucked, or I'm not moving again."

My eyes widened as I stared at him, opened-mouthed and still unsure. How did I want it? Did I even know?

"From behind," I heard myself whisper, and Aiden raised one eyebrow at me.

"Oh really?" he said. "My girl wants to be on her knees, huh? Right here in the back of my car where anyone could walk by at any moment? Is that what you want?"

My thighs clenched around the outsides of his legs. I swallowed hard, unable to make a sound. With a shudder, I nodded.

"Oh, baby," he mused. "You know what I like."

He lifted me, deposited me beside him on my hands and knees, kicked his shorts the rest of the way off, and pushed my knees apart with his legs. He had to lean over my back to keep from hitting his head on the roof of the jeep. He pushed my shirt up to get to my skin, wrapped one arm around my waist, and held his cock in his hand as he pushed it back inside of me.

We moved together, slowly at first. The carpet in the back of the jeep was rough on my knees, but I couldn't bring myself to care about the marks that would be left there. Aiden's hands moved up and down my body, caressing my sides and my breasts. He moved his hands over the skin of my back, caressing me from my shoulder blades down to my ass. I felt his finger slide between my butt cheeks and press against me.

"What are you doing?" I cried, shifting my hips down a bit and tensing my muscles.

"Haven't you ever had a finger in your ass while you're being fucked?" he asked. He wrapped his arm around my middle again, holding me up against his body.

I shook my head and gasped as I felt the tip of his little finger push into me.

"Relax," he whispered. "You won't believe how good this feels."

"Oh, shit," I whispered. The pressure was odd but not

uncomfortable.

"Relax," he said again, and I tried to make the muscles in my back and thighs unclench. "That's it."

He dropped his free hand, stroked over my pubic bone, and then found my clit with his fingers. He stroked me as his cock and finger began to move in and out of me.

"Do you like it?" Aiden's hot breath coated my back. "You like my finger in your ass, don't you?"

"Ugh!" It was all I could manage.

"Yeah, you do," he murmured. "Think about how my cock in there would feel."

He twisted his finger and then coiled it back. At the same time, he pushed his cock deep inside of me and pressed his fingers to my clit. My entire body tensed, shuddered, and electrified just before it released.

My scream was loud enough that everyone still in the house had to have heard it.

I'd never come so hard in my life. My legs continued to shake even as my orgasm passed. I couldn't keep my balance, and ended up slumping down onto my forearms as Aiden kept up his pace, both hands gripping my hips.

"Oh, fuck, yeah!" Aiden groaned. I felt him pull out and looked over my shoulder to see him finish himself off all over my backside.

He closed his eyes, panting for breath. When his eyes opened, he looked at my face and then down to my back and smirked.

"You look so hot covered in my cum. It just makes me want to do it all over again."

"You look very pleased with yourself," I commented.

"I am," he confirmed. He sat up tall…

…and bashed his head on the roof.

"Ow!"

I fell to the floor and began to laugh as Aiden rubbed the back of his head.

"Oh, you think that's funny, huh?" He glared at me as he grabbed for his pants. He fished around in the pocket, pulled out his keys, and tossed them at me. "Just for that, you can drive home!"

I picked the keys up off the floor, still snickering, and pulled my shorts back on. My back was all sticky, but that was just going to have to wait until we got back to the house. Aiden crawled to the front of the vehicle and plopped into the passenger seat. I climbed into the driver's side and placed the key in the ignition.

"You okay to drive?" Aiden questioned. "We can just recline the seats and sleep a bit if you're not."

I sat still and thought about it. I shook my head a little, making sure there wasn't any dizziness.

"I'm good," I told him.

"Well, if you start moving and find out you're not, pull over. I love this jeep."

I looked at his face, and there was something odd in his expression, as if he were going to say something else. He smiled slightly and then leaned over to give me a quick kiss.

"Jeep sex is pretty awesome, isn't it?" he said.

"It is," I agreed with a smile. I turned the key in the ignition and let the vehicle come to life as my mind wandered.

And with that, I began to consider other ways to use the back of a jeep.

THIRTEEN

I felt as if I had just closed my eyes when Aiden's hand began to shake my shoulder.

"Wake up," he said. He pressed his lips to my neck and hugged me against him.

"Hmm?" I hummed groggily.

"It's our last morning," Aiden said. He released his embrace and took my hand to pull me to a sitting position. "You still haven't seen the sunrise over the ocean."

He coaxed me out of bed, took my hand, and led me through the house, across the patio stones, and onto the cool sand. It was still quite dark, with just the slightest glow on the horizon. I was dressed only in my sheer, short pajama set, and my arms broke out in goose bumps. I shivered and rubbed at my flesh to warm it up.

"I love this time of day," Aiden whispered as he stood behind me and wrapped me in his arms. I leaned back against him, fighting the chill in the air. "It's so peaceful. It's like nothing else in the world exists but this time and this place. I'd love to be able to stop time right now."

I turned my head to look at his face, and he brought his hand up to rest against my cheek. For a while, we just looked at each other in the dim light, but then he turned me around and kissed me softly. I wrapped my hands around his head, pressed my chest to his, and stood on my toes to reach him better.

"One more adventure for you." His eyes sparkled as he reached down and picked me up him his arms. I squealed a bit and grabbed his neck though I didn't think he would drop me. He walked a few feet out to the top of the sand dune before dropping to his knees and laying me on my back in the sand.

"What are you scheming about now?" I asked with a giggle.

"Me? Scheming?" he said with feigned innocence. "Never."

"You are a terrible liar," I said.

He straddled me, placed his hands in the sand on either side of my head, and leaned over to press his lips to mine. I opened my mouth to accept his tongue, and he ran his hand down my side before pushing the edge of my pajama top up, exposing my stomach and reaching for my breast.

"Are you serious?" I asked as I broke away and pushed his hand back down.

"I'm always serious when it comes to getting you naked and on your back."

"Out here? I mean...in the back of the jeep was one thing, but..." My words trailed off as I looked out at the beach. I couldn't actually see anyone out there, but I knew there were often people fishing or jogging early in the morning.

"From right here, you can still watch the sunrise and not be seen very well by people on the beach," Aiden said. "Besides, there isn't even anyone out here. They're all still hung over."

He took both my wrists captive as he leaned over to hold my hands above my head.

"Aiden!" I protested.

"You want me to stop?" he asked quietly.

Already, my heart rate had doubled, and my skin was tingling with anticipation. I lay under him, helpless in the sand as he held me down, and knew it didn't matter if someone saw us; I wanted this.

Sex in the sand with Aiden Hunter as our last day together began with the sunrise over the Atlantic.

Yes, please.

I shook my head, feeling the sand lightly scratch my scalp.

"Don't stop," I said.

Aiden smiled as he pushed his free hand further up my stomach and over my breast. He kissed my throat, and the wetness of his tongue caressed my flesh, leaving it cool as he moved to another spot. His fingers pinched lightly at my nipple, and grains of sand rolled around on my skin.

"You're getting sand all over me," I said.

"And I've barely even started," he replied.

He covered my mouth, stifling any further protests, and I gave in to the feeling of his mouth on me, quickly forgetting the discomfort of the sand. He ran his thumb over the waistband of my pajama shorts with his free hand, then hooked it inside and pushed them down my legs and off.

He released my wrists, and I reached for his boxers, sliding my hands inside and moving them down his thighs. He arched his back to lift his hips and help me remove his clothing completely. I stroked his inked skin with my hands, marveling at the beauty of the markings on his flesh, the intricacies and the flow of the lines as one image merged into the next. I wanted to memorize them all, but there wasn't enough time. I marveled at the story the pictures told, laid out on his skin for everyone to see but no one to understand.

The hidden truth was both beautiful and sad at the same time.

Aiden knelt over me, kissing down the center of my body and brushing sand from my skin as he moved toward my stomach. His tongue circled my navel, and then moved down as he took both my legs in his hands and lifted them over his shoulders.

I groaned shamelessly as his tongue met my sensitive flesh. He covered me with his mouth, teased me with his tongue, and nipped at me with his lips. I clenched my ass, reflexively raising my hips off the sand to increase the pressure as Aiden's grip around my thighs intensified, holding me to his mouth.

With a gasp, I tossed my head back and stretched down to grasp his shoulders. I couldn't quite reach him, and had to sit up slightly to feel his skin on my palms as my body started to convulse, sending waves of pleasure from the point where his tongue circled, outward down my legs and up my torso.

I felt a moan begin in the back of my throat, and I held my lips together to keep from screaming out loud as my body shuddered. I dropped back into the sand, unable to hold myself up any longer as my breath exited in short pants into the air.

Aiden lowered my legs and crawled back over me, covering my mouth with his. I could taste myself on his smooth lips and tongue as he parted my legs with one of his knees. He poised himself over me as he kissed down my throat. He stopped at my shoulder and turned his head toward the water.

"Look at that," Aiden whispered in my ear.

I turned my head in the sand and watched as the sun rose over the horizon, igniting the water and sand in brilliant rays of red, orange, and yellow. A group of seagulls took flight with their raucous morning calls, announcing the sun's reappearance to the world. The whitecaps on top of the waves sparkled in the light; the sand glistened, and a new day began.

Aiden's hand brushed over my cheek.

"Do you see that, Chloe? Do you realize what it is? The sun over the ocean, the beach, the gulls flying over the waves...and you and me, like this. That's *life*, Chloe. That's *living*."

He kissed my mouth and then made a trail down my neck to my chest. Each of my nipples received the attention of his lips and tongue in turn. He sucked briefly, licked, and then sucked again. I moved my hands down his sides to grip his toned ass as he entered me slowly, allowing me to feel every inch slide into my depths.

He held himself buried inside of me, not moving. I touched his cheek with my hand, and he opened his eyes to stare down at me, the glow of the sunrise lighting up the side of his face.

"You're so beautiful," he whispered, his eyes wide as he stared down at me, "every part of you bathed in the red morning sun. You're like a painting in brilliant light and color. I want to capture you like this, keep you exactly as you are right here and now."

I swallowed as his words poured over me. I could see what he was imagining, reflected in his eyes, and the image transformed in my head until I saw myself captured in ink on his skin—forever part of him, forever part of his story.

He shifted then, pulling out only slightly before tilting his hips to bury himself again. He wrapped one arm under my shoulders, and I raised my legs to lock them behind his back as me began to move inside of me.

All the roughness was gone. The fast, hard strokes I had come to expect were replaced with unhurried, deep, and methodical penetrations. He kissed me with every movement, his hand caressing me softly from my neck to my breast as I let my hands memorize the feeling of his back against my fingertips.

"Oh, Chloe…Chloe…Oh, God! I don't want this to end…"

My body began to tense. Sensations from my breasts down to the pit of my stomach and then focusing between my legs caused me to shudder as I pushed up against him with my hips and dug my ankles into his back. I bit down on my lip, not wanting my screams to be heard down at the beach, and let go.

My body relaxed into the sand, and I wrapped my arms around his head.

"Aiden," I whispered. "Oh, Aiden…"

"You feel so good," he moaned. "So good, oh, baby…"

Aiden squeezed his eyes shut and held himself against me as he let out a muted gasp. I tightened my legs around his waist as I felt him fill me, holding on to him as tightly as possible.

I didn't want to let go. I never wanted to let go.

"All good things," I mumbled to myself in the bathroom mirror. I took a deep breath and blinked back tears, not wanting Aiden to notice how upset I was about going home.

The past week with Aiden had been both thrilling and terrifying. There were so many things I never would have considered doing in the past and still hardly believed I had done—riding on the back of a motorcycle, skydiving, sex in the back of a car and on the beach. If anyone had told me a week ago that this was what I'd be doing, I would have laughed at them. I didn't do those things.

Now, I wouldn't have traded my experiences for the world.

The idea of returning home to my steady job and lackluster life was downright depressing. I could hardly imagine myself returning to my office and sitting at my desk all day, dealing with Chia Head's ridiculous demands and spending my evenings with my collection of superheroines.

Routine had lost its appeal.

If Aiden had ended our beach encounter by asking me to stay with him, I would have agreed immediately. In that moment, I would have ditched my entire existence back in Ohio and stayed in Florida to experience life, *real life*, with him here on the beach.

But he didn't ask, and I hadn't suggested it.

With my bag packed, I walked to the front door and glanced around for Aiden. At first, I didn't see him, but then noticed movement out on the patio and went to find him. He was standing at the edge of the sand, looking out over the water.

"You had a good time, right?" he asked. He fiddled with the edge of his cap nervously.

"I did," I confirmed. "It was the best."

"I should have booked your flight back for Sunday," Aiden said as he looked at me sadly.

"It's all right," I said. It wasn't. It wasn't all right at all, but I was willing to make excuses. "I kind of need a day to recuperate."

He chuckled and then glanced at his watch. He sighed.

"I guess it's time to head to the airport," he said.

"I guess it is."

We piled in the jeep, and Aiden drove slowly out of the driveway. I kept my purse with my driver's license and boarding pass, wrapped around my right wrist. I was always a little paranoid about losing important documents when traveling and kept checking to make sure they were in there with my credit cards and a little cash.

Aiden didn't say much, just stared at the traffic as he followed signs to the airport. I alternated between looking out the window to glancing at his profile but didn't have any more words than he did.

We'd talked about making plans to see each other in three weeks, when Aiden would be back in Ohio. He didn't have an exact date but promised to let me know as soon as his flight was booked. It seemed like a lifetime away.

I reached over and placed my hand on his thigh. Aiden glanced down, smiled slightly, and covered my hand with his. I watched him move his fingers over my knuckles, trying to burn into my mind the image of the intricate flower on the back of his hand and the tribal marks covering his fingers. Memories of his hands on my breasts, my legs, and holding my face as he kissed me invaded my mind and threatened to cause me to break out in a flood of tears.

I was trying to be strong.

I wasn't ready to go. I wanted more time. There were still so many things about him I didn't know and desperately wanted to learn. I had no idea what would happen after we parted ways, and something deep in the pit of my stomach warned me that long-distance relationships rarely worked.

Sure, we'd keep up over the phone for a while, but that wouldn't last. We both had lives outside of the week we had spent with each other, and those were going to take precedence. Phone calls would change to text messages, and even those would eventually decrease and end.

This could be the last time I see him.

What could I do? My friends were in Ohio, and Aiden's in Florida. Despite my post-coital thoughts, it wasn't like I was in the position to just pack up and move to Miami, and I wouldn't dream of asking him to move closer to me. I had my career to think about, and he had his…well, whatever it was.

Despite everything I felt, I knew he was hiding something big.

I had to come out and ask him. I had to bite the bullet, as it were, and demand he tell me exactly what he did for a living. Without knowing for sure, I couldn't even begin to think about what the future might hold. If my initial suspicions were right, and he was a criminal, it would make any decision easier.

Just as I had gathered up enough courage to open my mouth, Aiden's phone rang. He released my hand and grabbed the phone from the center console.

"Yo, Mo," Aiden said in monotone.

I pulled my hand back from his leg and placed it in my lap. Outside the window, tall, white birds poked their long necks into puddles in the roadside ditches, looking for their breakfast. I swallowed hard, thinking about the grilled tomatoes Aiden had made to go with our omelets that morning.

"Fuck!" Aiden screeched.

I jumped in my seat, looking around quickly to see if we were about to hit another car or if he had possibly just avoided a collision, but there were no other cars near us. I looked back to see his face contorted with fury.

"You found them? Where?" Aiden was practically shouting into the phone. "You stay on them! Do not let them out of your sight! I'm heading that way right now."

Aiden tossed the phone into a little cubby on the dashboard and then quickly changed lanes, darting for the closest exit as the tires squealed.

I was flung into the door of the jeep as he turned swiftly and pressed his foot to the gas. He barreled around another car, nearly hitting it.

"Aiden!" I cried. "What are you doing?"

"Sorry, babe," he said without looking at me. "I really, really hate to do this to you, but this is the best chance I've had for months, and I can't let it slip."

"Can't let what slip?"

He ignored me. He held the wheel with one hand and jammed his finger at the GPS with the other, entering an address.

"Route confirmed. In four hundred feet, turn right."

He barely slowed down to make the turn.

"Shit!" I grabbed onto the handle of the door, holding on tightly.

"I'm sorry, Chloe. I really am."

"Sorry for what?"

He didn't answer. His fingers were turning white as he gripped the steering wheel with one hand and the gearshift with the other. His arms were shaking.

I had no idea what was happening, and his driving was terrifying me. I could barely hold on as he sped down busy roads, dodging traffic and ignoring traffic signals.

"Aiden, please! You're scaring me!"

"I'm sorry," he said again. "Shit, I'm really sorry! I didn't know this was going to happen...not now."

"I don't know what this is!" I cried again.

Aiden swerved, barely missing a bicyclist in the intersection. He slammed the jeep into second gear, slowed just enough to make a U-turn, and then veered into a parking lot. He pulled into a space in front of a strip mall and slammed on the brakes, throwing us both forward and causing my seatbelt to lock.

"You aren't going to make that flight," Aiden said. "I'll get you another one."

"Aiden, what the hell is going on?" I stared at his face, barely recognizable from the boyish grins I was used to seeing.

"You know those secrets we talked about?" He turned, and he stared at me with intense and frightening eyes.

My heart stopped, and my throat started to close up so I couldn't take a breath. My head began to pound as I looked into his face. His eyes were wide and wild. Every muscle in his body was tense, and I could see the tightness of his jaw as he clenched his teeth.

"What secrets?"

Aiden switched off the car, pulled the key from the ignition, and turned to unlock the center storage unit. He reached in and drew out a sleek, black revolver. He reached in again and pulled out a clip, sliding it with a loud click into the handle of the gun.

Alarm! Alarm, alarm, ALARM!

"You said I was hiding something," Aiden said, "and you were right—I am. You are about to find out what that is."

And with that, I went from suspicious to terrified.

FOURTEEN

"Stay here," Aiden commanded. His fingers tensed around the grip of his weapon. "Don't get out of this fucking car for any reason, you hear me?"

I couldn't answer. I still couldn't breathe, much less speak. I'd never so much as *seen* a gun in real life unless it was holstered on a police officer's belt, let alone been so close to one. I couldn't take my eyes off of the gleaming black metal.

Aiden opened the driver's side door and started to get out, the gun clasped tightly in his hand.

"Aiden?" I managed to croak as I tore my eyes away from his hand and back to his face.

He paused, halfway out the door.

"I'm so fucking sorry," he said again.

"What are you doing with a gun?" I whispered. I felt like my body was trying to shut down, and I wondered what going into shock felt like. For a second, the phone call from my mother informing me of Dad's heart attack filled my head. At this moment, the feeling of all my blood leaving my veins was similar to how I had felt when she had told me he was gone.

I focused on Aiden again and couldn't understand what I was seeing.

Everything my subconscious had been warning me about Aiden Hunter began to fill my head. All this time, I'd been telling myself not to judge him. All this time, I'd been convincing myself that everything was fine, that *he* was fine. Since the moment I had met him, I'd been trying to convince myself that the only danger was in my head.

But it wasn't.

The Aiden in front of me wasn't the man I had known the past week. His face was barely recognizable. His eyes were dark and full of hatred. His jaw was locked, his teeth clenched. He had gripped his hands into fists, one of which held a deadly weapon. This man was not the one who cooked breakfast for me. This was a man consumed with raw fury.

Echoed words from Lance's girlfriend flowed through my head: "I have never seen him mad, personally, but I hear it's not pretty."

No, it was not pretty. It was not pretty at all.

"Aiden." It seemed to be the only word I could utter.

"Stay here," Aiden commanded once again, and he slammed the door.

I looked out through the windshield, and I tried to make sense of the scene in front of me. Mo was outside, standing on the sidewalk near the strip mall. Aiden walked up to him, spoke to him quickly, and Mo glanced in my direction before tapping his ear and speaking into a Bluetooth device.

I sat there, frozen, as Aiden marched away from Mo and up to one of the doors of the strip mall, gun still plainly visible, and disappeared inside. Over the door was a sign for a Cuban restaurant, promising the best pulled-pork sandwiches in Dade County.

Mo yelled something, but I couldn't hear his words through the windows of the jeep. He had his hand on his hip, resting on another gun. He took off after Aiden just as I heard a noise to my right, and the passenger side door of the jeep opened.

I screamed and tried to push away the hands that came at me. The seatbelt was still locked from the sudden stop, and I could barely move. I screamed again, but then I recognized Lo's voice as he told me to relax—everything was all right.

"It is not all right!" I screamed back at him. "Aiden has a gun,

Lo! He's got a gun!"

"I know, babe," Lo said calmly as he reached over to unlatch the belt and bodily remove me from the vehicle despite my struggles. "Just come with me. I gotta get you out of the way."

"Get off of me!" I cried. I swung my arm and smacked his meaty shoulder with the purse still attached to my wrist. I wasn't even sure why I was struggling, only that I felt like I should be in the jeep, and I wanted to stay there. It was familiar. It was safe.

It had a gun in it the whole time.

"Don't argue with me, Chloe!" Lo tightened his grip on me. "Not about this!"

I shuddered. My eyes burned, but tears wouldn't come. I couldn't get a good enough grasp on the situation to understand what I was feeling. I only knew I didn't want to leave where I was. Aiden told me to stay in the car. He said not to leave—not for any reason.

Was I really still listening to his instructions?

I heard gunshots followed by screams. Two young men barreled their way out of the restaurant, grasping at each other and yelling in Spanish as they ran across the parking lot and into the street.

"What's happening?" I yelled at Lo.

"I am getting you out of here!" he yelled back. He grabbed me and pinned my arms to my sides before lifting me up and off my feet. I kicked uselessly as he dragged me away from the jeep and into the back of a dark Chrysler.

More gunshots.

"Get down!" Lo screamed as he shoved me inside and slammed the door.

I pushed myself up on my hands and looked out the window of the back door. Lo was crouched beside the car door with his shoulder pressed against it and yet another gun in his hand. With a shaky hand, I pulled at the door handle, but the child locks were engaged, and I couldn't get out. A glass partition separated the front and the back seats, blocking any exit that way.

"Lo!" I screamed.

"Get down, Chloe!" he snapped back.

I didn't listen. I pulled at the door handle again, still shaking. Movement caught my eye, and I watched a man and woman come out of the side door of the restaurant. The man also carried a gun and ran backwards, shooting toward the building as the woman pulled at his arm. They jumped into a red sedan at the end of the parking lot, and the tires squealed as the couple sped from the area.

Aiden and Mo came out of the door as they sped off.

"Goddammit!" Aiden turned and kicked the door closed with a bang loud enough to make me jump. He jerked his head up and looked at the jeep.

"Where is she?" Aiden screamed. He spun in a circle, darting his eyes all around the complex.

"I got her!" Lo yelled back. "She's fine, Hunter! I got her!"

Aiden looked toward me, and our eyes met for an instant. I had no idea what he might have been thinking, only that his shoulders slumped a little as I stared back at him. He shook his head once and then turned to Mo.

"We have to follow them," Aiden said. "We can't lose them!"

"Not now!" Mo replied as he grabbed onto one of Aiden's arms. "Holy shit, Hunter, have you lost your mind? The police are on their way!"

"And they're going to do what, huh?" Aiden snapped. "They can't do a fucking thing, and you know it!"

Lo stood and ran to Aiden's side. In the distance, I heard sirens.

"You gotta relax, man," Lo was saying. "You gotta go calm your girl down before she freaks out completely and says something stupid."

They surrounded Aiden with their huge forms and coaxed him back to Lo's Chrysler. Mo opened the door, and Aiden sat in the back next to me, but he didn't look in my direction. He had his hand clenched into a claw where it rested on his thigh, and the other one still held his gun. His chest rose and fell as he took long, labored breaths which he hissed out through his teeth. His leg began to shake.

Suddenly, Aiden screamed.

He screamed at the top of his voice and repeatedly punched the seat in front of him until his knuckles began to bleed. I crawled to the other side of the car and pushed my shoulder against the door, pulling futilely at the handle. Aiden kept yelling, and I curled my feet up and wrapped my arms around my head.

The tears came, followed by choking sobs.

"Oh, fuck, baby," Aiden moaned. "No, no, please! I'm sorry, Chloe. Fuck! I'm sorry!"

I felt his hand on my arm, and I lurched away.

"Don't touch me!" I screamed as I pressed my body into the door of the car.

"Please don't," Aiden begged. "Please don't do that, baby. I'm sorry—I'm so fucking sorry! I didn't mean for you to get caught up in this, I swear. Please, Chloe…"

He gripped my arm again, pulling me away from the door and into the center of the car. I fought against him, screaming and crying. He could have forced me to him, but he didn't. He let go, and I crawled back to the other side of the car and continued to sob.

"Shh, Chloe, please," he whispered. "I'm sorry, I'm sorry, I'm sorry…"

Over and over again, he whispered those words to me. He reached out and touched my hand, but I pulled away. Mo was calling his name from just outside the car, and when Aiden looked up, Mo shook his head slowly.

"What's happening?" I finally choked out. "Aiden, what is going on?"

"It's a long-ass story," he said. "I didn't want you tied up in any of this shit. I didn't even want you to know."

"Know what?"

"We gotta move," Mo said through the car door.

Lo was suddenly on my right, opening the door and helping me out.

"Fuck!" Aiden slammed his fist on the bench seat before running his hand over his head.

"Company has arrived," Mo said with a sigh.

"Yeah, I see that," Lo responded.

The sound of sirens invaded my ears as several police cars pulled into the lot. Aiden got back out of the car and went around to the front where Mo stood. They leaned close together, speaking quickly and glancing in the direction of the sirens as my heart raced.

There was no capacity for comprehension in my head. It was just too far beyond my experience. Guns? Running into restaurants and chasing people out? And now police? I couldn't cope with it all.

I shook my head slowly from side to side as I stood in the parking space next to Lo's car. I couldn't speak. As tears flowed down my cheeks, I could only watch.

"It won't do any good," I heard Mo say. "People in there know you."

"Fuck my life," Aiden muttered.

"It's still progress," Mo said as he placed his hand on Aiden's shoulder.

I couldn't do this. I couldn't cope with this. Everything inside of me revolted against what was happening. Whatever this was, I couldn't deal with it.

I took a few steps back, just behind Lo and out of his view. He didn't move, just kept watching Mo and Aiden as they spoke to each other. Police were getting out of their patrol cars, and some had their weapons drawn. I stepped back again, but no one seemed to notice.

One of the police officers addressed Aiden and his friends, telling them all to put their weapons down. Aiden raised his hands up over his head, the revolver dangling by his thumb near the trigger. He lowered it slowly to the ground and backed away from it, leaving his hands on top of his head.

Just like a pro.

I realized I was still walking backward when I hit the edge of a car several spots away from the scene. I jumped and stopped a scream from coming out of my throat as I covered my mouth with my hand and smacked myself in the shoulder with my wrist-purse.

I have to get out of here.

I turned and looked around quickly. No one seemed to have noticed me at all—everyone's focus was on Aiden. I had everything in my purse I needed to get myself out of here. I walked swiftly around to the far side of the vehicle and ducked down a bit until I was sure no one had seen me. Sweat dripped between my shoulder blades and down the side of my face, mixing with my tears. My breath was coming in choppy gasps. I looked over to the other side of the street and saw a gas station and a restaurant.

My hands were still shaking, and I could barely keep my knees from giving out on me. All of my instincts had been dead-on, and I hadn't listened to them. Aiden was a criminal. He carried a gun, shot at people in restaurants, and God knows what else.

Was I going to be arrested? Would the police even believe me if I told them I didn't know anything?

I was an idiot and had nearly been trapped by Aiden and his accomplices. I'd heard Aiden say that the police couldn't do anything to them. What did that mean? Was he so big in the crime world that the police couldn't touch him? Was he that corrupt? What would he do with me now that I knew more than I should? I had to get out of there. I had to get out of there as fast as possible.

I ran.

Nearly tripping over the curb, I raced across the street just as the light was changing. My legs were scratched by bushes as I pushed through them and into the parking lot of the gas station. That was when I heard Aiden screaming.

"Chloe! CHLOE!"

I turned my head and looked back over my shoulder. Aiden's wide eyes were clearly visible in the bright Florida sun. The same sun gleamed off the shiny handcuffs around his wrists as two police officers pushed his head down and shoved him into the back of one of the cars.

Terrified, I kept running.

And with that, I'd had enough excitement.

FIFTEEN

More than two weeks had gone by, and I was still having nightmares.

Sometimes they were about being in the parking lot surrounded by gunshots and sirens. Sometimes I was trapped in the back of a car with Aiden screaming, his face contorted. I'd even had one where I went out on the patio to watch the sun rise over the water and found the bodies of the couple who had run from the restaurant, covered in blood, lying near the fire pit.

Sometimes I dreamed he was making love to me on the beach.

That was the worst.

No, it wasn't. The worst was waking up and realizing I was only holding my pillow.

I hadn't told anyone what had happened. The cashier at the gas station had pointed out a nearby hotel that had a shuttle to the airport, and I gave the valet a twenty to get me on it. I had to pay to have my plane ticket changed to a later flight, but I'd gotten myself back to Ohio. Eventually, I found a taxi driver willing to let me pay an outrageous fare for him to take me all the way to the north side of town and home.

Once I had my phone plugged back in and charging, I'd found a dozen text messages and missed calls from Mare. Not wanting her to hear my voice over the phone, I texted her back to let her know I was home, safe and sound. She had sent me several texts over the next week, asking about my time away, but I had dodged them by saying I would tell her in person. Since then, I had avoided being alone with her.

We had been friends for far too long for her not to know something was wrong, and I didn't want to answer her questions. If I did, I was going to break down and tell her everything, and I couldn't risk that. I didn't want to admit how stupid I was, and I was also terrified to say anything about my last few minutes with Aiden. I didn't want to even think about what had happened outside that small, Cuban restaurant my last day in Miami.

I'd made an absolute fool of myself by not listening to my inner alarms, and I was positively ashamed. The last thing I wanted to do was admit my stupidity to someone else.

Aiden had tried to call three times that first week I was back. I didn't answer, and he didn't leave a voice mail. He didn't try to call again after that. For all I knew, he was on his way to prison.

I just wanted to forget it all.

So I was back to my normal, boring routine. Chia Head was pissed that first Monday morning, and he gave me quite a lecture on giving vacation notice, but he didn't fire me. He did make it clear that my actions would be reflected on my next review, though.

Asshole.

I was tired of putting up with Kevin and his idiotic Chia-head demands. As much as I hated the idea, I decided it was time to find a new job. I told Nate I was in the market, and he said he'd get his old recruiter to call me.

In the meantime, I got up with the alarm every morning. I fought traffic on the way to work but still managed to be there on time every day. I went to meetings, answered emails, and kept projects on track. Gabe called to let me know he'd already found a car and didn't need my help. Mare must have told him about my spontaneous trip because he asked me how I liked Florida, but he got another call, and we didn't have time to talk about it, thankfully.

I'd avoided any happy hours at Thirsty's Oasis with excuses ranging from extra workload, to car problems, to headaches. I knew there would be questions, and I didn't want to answer them. It was also the place I had met *him*, and I didn't need the reminder.

I was doing everything I wasn't supposed to do when it came to getting over a loss. I was avoiding talking about it, thinking about it, and ultimately, I wasn't dealing with it at all. My thoughts had me tied up in knots, but I didn't know what to do about it. I had actually considered calling Lo to find out what had happened after I left, but every time I picked up the phone, I couldn't bring myself to make the call.

At night, I went to bed early and tried to force the memories from my head. It rarely worked, and my sleep was fitful at best. I woke up every night feeling cold and alone, refusing to admit that I missed his presence beside me. I considered bringing Buffy to bed but couldn't bring myself to be quite that pathetic.

Maybe I needed a cat.

So I trudged on, denying everything.

"I'm going to need updates on all your projects before you leave today," Kevin said as he appeared at my desk right before five o'clock. "I need the budget numbers and all the key performance indicators."

"The budget numbers won't be accurate until accounting gives their final blessing," I said. "We just talked about that in the last meeting."

"Well, I need something for my presentation tomorrow."

"The KPIs are in your email."

"I need the budgets!"

I looked up at him and felt my stomach tighten.

"I don't *have* all the budget numbers," I repeated. "Like Jeff from accounting said, they can't confirm anything until the board meeting on Thursday. They'll sign off on them after the third quarter numbers are in."

"I don't know why you are trying to undermine me," Kevin snapped. "I ask you for the simplest things, and you just can't seem to deliver."

I sat up straighter in my chair, trying to figure out just where this tirade originated.

"I'm not sure what you expect me to do," I said, feeling my face beginning to warm. "I can't give you something I don't have, and I can't just make up budget numbers."

"I promised them to the execs for tomorrow's meeting!" He raised his eyebrows and stared down at me like he thought the numbers might just start scrolling across my forehead. "You already have one strike against you due to your mismanagement of vacation time. I really don't think you can afford another."

I stared back at him. Was he really threatening me because of something he'd done wrong? I took a deep breath. I felt as if my toes were on the edge of some deep chasm, and the urge to jump was strong.

Kevin leaned closer to me.

"So why don't you get off your pretty little ass," he sneered, "and get me the fucking numbers."

I froze. My face felt tight, and I clenched my teeth against the sensation. In the back of my mind, I heard the door on the side of a plane open, and the wind began to howl outside. I stood up and mentally moved to the edge. I looked at Kevin and in my head saw the vast openness of the ground far, far below.

I jumped.

"If you have promised something to the execs that you can't deliver," I said, my voice getting louder, "then maybe you need to inform the execs that you made a bit of a mistake. Or maybe you can go to accounting and ask them for numbers they don't have. Better yet, walk into the board meeting and ask them for the budget."

He took a half step back, but I just stepped forward and stared up at his Chia-head face. Others in the cubicle-farm were taking notice. There were a few people who had stopped in the hallway as well.

"And the next time you refer to my 'pretty little ass,'" I practically screamed, "I'll just invite you to the next meeting with HR!"

I kept my eyes on him, completely unmoving. His face had gone white, and he checked over his shoulder at a few of the people who were standing around, listening in.

Including his boss.

I smiled. My chute opened, and I began to float.

"I'm heading home now," I stated, "because I already worked through lunch to get you all the things it is within my power and job description to get you. If you have a problem with that, we can discuss it with Mr. Thompson in the morning."

I nodded toward Kevin's boss as I picked up my purse and prepared to leave.

Kevin just stood there, mouth agape. As I turned down the aisle to the stairwell, I heard Mr. Thompson's voice.

"Kevin, I'd like a word with you."

I landed in the circle in the middle of a green, grassy field, and my smile grew wider.

The autumn wind was cold as I marched to the parking lot to find my car. I had to break down and start up the car's heater to ward off the chill. The air smelled dusty and burned my nose the entire drive home from work. I couldn't stop thinking about what I had said and how fabulous it felt to stand up for myself.

Just like jumping out of a plane.

I pulled into the garage, switched off the heater, and tried to remember if I had ever gotten around to having my winter jacket cleaned last spring. I was going to need it soon.

I bet it's warm in Miami.

"Shut up," I said to myself. I didn't want my mood ruined, but apparently that was all it took. Memories began to flood my head, and despite the good ones, they all ended with that last afternoon in a strip mall parking lot.

I switched on the Tuesday night sci-fi movie and found that my favorite channel was playing *The Fifth Element*. I groaned and switched to the home and garden channel instead, then decided to polish up my resume.

I updated my work experience and shot out a couple of emails to people I thought would give me good references. I hated the whole job-hunt thing, but it was a great distraction, and maybe it would help keep me from losing my mind.

"It's probably already happened," I mumbled to myself. I glanced up at Wonder Woman, who seemed to agree.

I got up to make myself some dinner. The only thing that sounded good was breakfast food, which I had totally refused to make for myself ever since I returned home. I pulled out the half-dozen eggs I had in the refrigerator and threw them in the trash before dumping some cottage cheese and pineapple into a bowl and calling it a meal.

"I can't even turn the damn stove on," I muttered.

I shook my head. I had to stop thinking like this. I had to stop letting every little thing that reminded me of Aiden Hunter get to me. It was like when my dad had first died, and I couldn't even bring myself to look at his picture for the longest time. Every time I did, it brought tears to my eyes.

Walking across the room, I grabbed the picture of my father off the bookshelf and held it in my hands. I ran my finger along the edge of the frame and smiled sadly.

"I miss you, Dad," I said. "I have the feeling you'd be really disappointed in me right now, but I still wish I could talk to you about it."

I didn't even take any pictures of Aiden.

A tear slipped down my cheek, and I wiped it away quickly. I placed Dad's picture back on its shelf and headed to the bathroom for a shower. I had run myself clear out of shower gel and ended up using shampoo to wash off. Once I was as clean as I was going to get, I stepped onto the bath mat and tossed the empty shower gel bottle into the trash. It hit the white, cylindrical pregnancy test I had taken the week before.

Negative.

Thank God.

My period had started the very next day, and I'd sat on the toilet and cried for an hour. I should have felt relieved at the additional confirmation, but all I felt was emptiness. I had even considered going to one of those clinics that tested for STDs, but I didn't actually seek one out. I was due for a yearly exam next month and figured if there was some kind of bad news, it could wait until then.

I lay down on the couch and stared at the kitchen remodeling show that was on. I wasn't actually listening to it, but staring at the moving screen was at least enough to lull me a little. I closed my eyes and tried to take slow, calm breaths.

The phone rang, and I looked down at the unfamiliar number. I didn't usually answer when the number was unknown, preferring to let it go to voice mail and calling back whoever it was later if the call was legitimately for me. However, I was hoping for a call from Nate's recruiter, and I didn't want to miss an opportunity to talk to him, so I answered.

"Hello?"

"Hey, is this Chloe?" The voice on the other end was vaguely familiar, but I couldn't quite place it.

"Yes," I answered tentatively.

"Chloe, this is Redeye. I was hoping maybe you could spare a little time to chat with me."

Oh, shit.

It was completely unexpected, and I considered just hanging up. If Lo had called, I might have been less shocked, but I also would have recognized the number. I'd added it to my phone just in case I ever needed it before throwing away the card he had given me.

"You still there?"

"Yes," I whispered.

"Would it be all right if we talked?" he asked again.

"Um…well, I guess so," I said. "What about?"

As if you don't know.

"It's about Hunter," Redeye confirmed. "I know you all didn't exactly part under the best of circumstances, but I'm at my wit's end here. I'm about to give up hope."

As his words and tone sank into me, my fingers and toes went numb. I almost dropped the phone. Had something horrible happened to Aiden?

"What's wrong with him?" I asked.

"It's not good," Redeye said.

A thousand things went through my head. Had he gone to jail as I had suspected he might? Was I going to be subpoenaed as a witness? What would I say to a judge about what I had seen? What if he'd gotten away from the police, gone after those people again, and been shot? What if he was dead?

My hand started to shake, and I switched the phone to the other one.

No, that couldn't be it. He had tried to call me—I just hadn't answered. Besides, Redeye wasn't talking about him in the past tense. I took a deep breath as Redeye continued.

"Well, I'm not sure exactly what's wrong," Redeye said. "He won't talk to me. He won't talk to anyone, which is why I was hoping you could help."

The words were far from what I was expecting. He wouldn't talk to anyone? What did that even mean? Why would Redeye reach out to me anyway? Was he now trying to pull me into whatever the hell was going on?

I was not going to be made a fool of again.

"I really don't think I want to talk to him," I said definitively. I sat up straight on the couch. The distance between Redeye and me and the impersonal vibe a phone call creates made me feel braver than I would have felt in person. "In fact, I'm sure I don't."

"I was afraid of that." Redeye sighed. "I was just thinking you might be the only one who can get through to him right now."

"Why would I do that?" I asked. "The last time I saw him, he was waving a gun around at people, and that's not really the kind of thing I need in my life right now."

"Yes, I can understand how you would see it that way."

"That's how I see it," I confirmed. "So I wish you all the best, but-"

He cut me off.

"Please hear me out," he said. "Just for a minute, Chloe."

I paused and swallowed past the lump in my throat.

"All right," I said, relenting, "but I'm not agreeing to do anything other than listen."

"I can live with that," he agreed. "Just promise you'll listen with an open mind."

"I'll listen," I repeated. "I can't promise anything else."

"Well, I'll take what I can get."

I could hear him taking a few breaths on the other end and realized I was breathing along with him. I wiped my sweaty palm on my thigh and switched phone hands again.

"Hunter's one of my best friends, Chloe," Redeye said. "I can't imagine what you think is going on, but I can assure you that you don't know the whole story."

"What is the whole story?" I asked.

"Well, frankly that isn't mine to tell," he said. "Even if it was, we'd be on the phone all night. As it is, what I can tell you is this—that boy was different when you were there with him, different than he's been for years. I was fucking thrilled to death when you showed up on his arm, and I could tell he was, too. He needs somcone like you in his life."

"I'm sorry," I said quietly. "I don't think I can do that, not after everything else."

"Well, yeah, I understand that." Redeye paused, and I could hear him sigh another deep breath. "The thing is, he really needs someone right now. No one has been able to get through to him. Lance and I even went over there and broke into the damn house, but he wouldn't talk to us. He just sits there."

"Sits where?"

"In that back room filled with his kid's stuff," Redeye said.

With everything else that had happened, I'd forgotten all about my discovery in Aiden's back bedroom. Redeye's words were the first real confirmation that Aiden had a child.

"He hasn't gone out, hasn't gone to work—nothing. He just sits in that room, holding on to some stuffed animal and not talking. I don't think he's even eating anything. He's just shut down, Chloe, and I don't know what else to do. I'd haul him to a damn hospital if I didn't think he'd kill me for the effort."

He let out a short, humorless laugh as an image filled my head—an image of Aiden in that small room, surrounded by boxes and refusing to talk or eat. Why would he do that? Because of me? No, that couldn't be it. We'd only been together a week. There had to be something else.

"I…I don't know how I could be of any help," I admitted.

"I've known Hunter a long time," Redeye said, "and I'm almost positive he'd open up to you. We all talked about it, and we think you're the only one who can get through to him. We even took up a collection to get your plane ticket and shit."

"We?"

"Me, Lo and Mo, Lance—everybody," he said. "We all saw the same thing in him that night you guys were here. We all saw how different he was with you. Lance said you all were even getting it on in the jeep, and that's just unheard of for him. You really mean something to him, girl."

I didn't say anything. I couldn't seem to even open my mouth.

"He'll open up to you," Redeye continued. "I know he will."

"I...I don't know," I said quietly.

"He *needs* you, Chloe. He fucking needs you."

"I can't," I whispered, shaking my head. The image of Aiden, broken and alone, continued to invade my mind. I felt pressure behind my eyes and blinked a few times.

"Please, Chloe—I'm begging you. We're out of options here. We don't have anyone else to turn to."

Redeye might as well have been holding out a shot glass because he was not to be deterred. Unfortunately, I didn't have anyone else to take the drink for me. I had Aiden for that before. He'd stepped in for me, knowing I couldn't handle it all on my own. He'd been there for me.

He had taken the shots for me.

He had been there with me when we fell from the sky.

He held me in the sand and showed me what was really important in life.

He didn't have to do any of that. He'd taken me out of my sheltered world and taught me that there wasn't anything to fear out there and that risks were just a part of living. He'd done all of that for me and I was...I was...

I was grateful.

He'd changed me. Regardless of what kind of mess he was caught up in, he'd changed me for the better.

Was I really going to turn my back on him now?

There's more to the story than I know.

I wanted to know the rest. I owed him that much.

"All right," I whispered. "I'll come down there."

And with that, I called in sick and headed back to Miami.

SIXTEEN

"I can't tell you how glad I am that you agreed to do this, Chloe." Redeye tossed my luggage into the back of his car. "Lance is going to meet us there. Hunter's in bad shape, Chloe. I hope you can get through to him."

"I'll do what I can," I said. I climbed into the car and buckled my seatbelt.

He pulled away from the terminal and headed to the highway. I couldn't help but think of my ride with Aiden on the motorcycle. The route wasn't exactly the same—Redeye took the highways more than the back roads—but similar enough to evoke the memory of holding tightly to Aiden's body as we sped down the streets.

Redeye focused on his driving and didn't talk much, which was fine with me. I could barely believe I was back here already, planning to see the man I had run away from just…how long had it been? Eighteen days. Eighteen says since I ran from Aiden in the parking lot. Eighteen days since I had decided to close the book on that chapter of my life.

Thoughts of returning had been the furthest thing from my mind. I wanted to forget it all. I wanted to pretend it never happened. But I hadn't forgotten. Not only did I remember, but I also knew how much I had changed because of it. Aiden had shown me something inside of myself I didn't realize was there, and I was grateful to him for it.

Drug dealer or not, I couldn't just ignore him if he really needed someone. I didn't know what I was going to find, but the image of Aiden, broken and alone in the back room of his house, continued to haunt my thoughts.

I began to recognize the houses on the side of the road, and I rolled down my window to smell the ocean breeze. Another block down, I saw the bright flowers that lined the property, and I knew we were close. As Redeye pulled into the driveway, I recognized Lance, sitting on the retaining wall near the front door. He stood up as we approached.

"No answer?" Redeye asked as soon as he opened the car door.

"None," Lance said with a shake of his head. "He's in there, I'm sure. The Jeep and his bike are in the garage, but he won't answer."

Lance turned to me and gave me a hug.

"Thanks for coming, Chloe," he said as he patted my back. "It means a lot to us."

"You're welcome," I replied automatically. Lance released me, and I took a quick glance between him and Redeye. I was touched by how close Aiden and his friends seemed to be. There was no doubt Lance and Redeye's concern was genuine, not that I had doubted it. After all, they'd paid for my plane ticket to come back down here. The loyalty and friendship they shared with Aiden was so evident, I wasn't sure what I could do that they could not.

"We going to go through the back again?" Redeye asked.

"Yeah. Mo disabled the alarm system."

"Good. I hate that fucking alarm."

I followed them both to the back of the house, trying to push the memories away as I only let myself glance at the patio furniture and beach view. Though it hadn't been that long, it seemed like ages ago when I was last here, believing the only thing that was wrong was my own inhibitions.

Lance and Redeye went up to the sliding glass door that led into the house. They pressed against the glass, lifted it up to disengage the door from the track at the bottom, and slid it to one side. They made it look easy, and I considered making a comment about their breaking-and-entering skills but decided against it.

"Mo and Lo had to work the football game today," Redeye said, "or they'd be here, too. They'll come by when the game is over. They're real anxious to see you."

"Football game?" I asked.

"Yeah, they have a security business. I thought you knew that."

"I guess I did." However, I hadn't thought of their jobs as something that would involve football games. I pictured them in the back room of a seedy bar, standing behind Aiden and protecting him from any drug deals that might go bad. Checking backpacks for unauthorized beer didn't fit the impression I had at all.

Lance walked in first, heading straight for the little hallway off the living room. He came back a moment later and pointed over his shoulder with his thumb.

"He's still in there."

"Is he okay?" Redeye asked.

"As good as he was the last time."

Redeye let out a long breath.

"I guess this is where you come in," he said to me. "We'll stay out on the patio. Holler if you need us."

He placed his hand on my shoulder and gave it a squeeze.

"Good luck," he added.

I nodded and walked into the house, maneuvering past the boxes in the living room and then into the hall. I glanced into the weight room and bathroom as I went by, but all was quiet in there. The last door was open this time, and I could see a patch of sunlight in the doorway. I peeked my head around slowly, peering inside.

The scene before me wasn't unlike the image I already had in my head.

Aiden was up against the wall in the far corner of the room, surrounded by boxes and a few empty beer bottles. His beard, usually meticulously trimmed to the same length as his hair, was scraggly and reached down his neck. He sat just beneath the window with his knees drawn up to his chest and his head resting against the drywall, staring straight ahead. There was a plush horse in his hand.

He didn't look up. As far as I knew, he had no idea I was even there.

I took a few steps into the room and then stopped.

"Aiden?"

He didn't move.

"Aiden?" I said again.

He moved his head slightly and shifted his gaze from the space in front of him to his hands. I watched him for a moment before speaking again.

"Will you talk to me?" I asked. "Everyone is really worried about you."

He closed his eyes and then opened them again as he looked at me blankly. I watched him wet his lips with his tongue before he looked back to the stuffed horse.

"Trying to figure out if you are actually here," Aiden said in a raspy voice, "or if I've totally lost it."

He continued to look at the horse in his hand.

"I'm here," I told him.

"Why?" he asked.

"Redeye called me. He said…well, he said you weren't doing too well."

"Did he?" His tone was mechanical, monotonous—soulless.

"Yes." I took a few more steps into the room. "Aiden, what's going on?"

"I kept hearing your voice," he said. "I kept hearing you cry, and then I'd see you running away. I knew I'd fucked it all up so bad. I didn't mean to, but I did."

He looked at me again.

"I lost you," he said flatly. "I fucked it up, and I lost you."

I had no idea what to say. If this all came down to Redeye convincing me to come here because Aiden was pining over me… well, I wasn't sure what I was going to do. I wasn't prepared to tell him I'd come back to make up with him. The strange thing was, in the past I probably would have. I would have made up with him and played along just to keep him from being sad, but Aiden had changed me—I wasn't that person anymore. I wasn't going to tell him everything was all right between us, because it wasn't.

I wasn't entirely sure what I was hoping to accomplish.

"Redeye said you were in bad shape," I said. "He thought maybe you'd talk to me."

Aiden was looking at his hands again, twirling the stuffed horse around with his fingers. I wasn't sure if he had heard me.

"This was his favorite," Aiden said quietly. "It wasn't even his. He went to this daycare for a while when Megan was working. He was two years old then. He'd walk around with this horse every day and throw a fit when it was time to go home because he had to leave it behind. They started letting him take it home at night, and eventually I just bought a new horse and traded with the daycare so he could keep this one."

He chuckled dryly.

"Megan was so pissed I had spent money on the replacement. It was only ten bucks, but we were having trouble paying the bills. He loved this thing so much, though. I didn't want to ask the daycare to just give it to him. That didn't seem right."

I took the last few steps across the room and knelt beside Aiden. The muscles in his arm flexed as I reached out to lay my hand on his shoulder. He stopped spinning the toy.

"You didn't tell me you had a son," I said quietly.

"I know." Aiden's shoulders rose and fell as he breathed. "I didn't want to tell you."

"Why not?" I ran my hand down his arm before lacing our fingers together. He stared at our interlocked hands for a long moment before he spoke.

"Because if I tell you, then I also have to tell you why he's not here."

I'd considered a few different possibilities and wasn't surprised to hear Aiden's reasoning. The most logical conclusion I had drawn was that Cayden had been taken away from Aiden after Megan had died. I figured whatever illegal activity Aiden was involved in had caused him to lose custody.

"Don't you think maybe I deserved to know about it?" I asked.

"Yeah, probably," he agreed.

"Probably?"

"It's not that easy." He sat back and bumped his head against the wall a couple of times before he looked in my direction again. He didn't meet my eyes. "I liked you...I really liked you. I was...I was afraid if you knew everything that was going on, you would run."

He shook his head.

"I fucked it up. I should have told you."

I wasn't sure whether it would have mattered. If he had told me he was into illegal activity…if he had told me there was a gun in the jeep, I wasn't so sure I wouldn't have just run anyway. Aiden's having a child from a previous relationship didn't seem as big a deal as it might have been otherwise.

There was more to it, though—Redeye had said as much. I was missing something important.

"Redeye said I didn't know the whole story."

"He didn't tell you?"

"No."

Aiden's eyebrows knitted together as he looked at me quizzically.

"Then why did you come?"

"He said he was worried about you," I said. "I was worried, too."

"You were still worried about me? You still don't know, and you were worried?"

"Well, yes," I said, unsure why this was such an obviously strange concept to him. "Of course I was."

"But…but you ran off."

"I was scared, Aiden," I said. "I had no idea what was happening —I still don't know what happened. You scared me half to death, and I couldn't think straight. I'm still not completely sure myself what I'm doing here. I don't think I can reconcile all of this. Kayaking and skydiving were far from the norm for me, and I'll admit I wasn't comfortable with that at first, but this is entirely different. I'm not even sure I want you to tell me. Guns and police? That isn't me, Aiden."

"No," he agreed, "it's not."

"So what am I missing here?" I asked again. "Aside from having a son, what were you keeping from me?"

"I didn't tell you what happened to my last girlfriend," he said. "I didn't want you to know how she died. I didn't want you to know …"

His voice trailed off, and the words seemed to have lodged in his throat.

"Know what?" I prompted.

"I didn't want you to know what happened to him," Aiden whispered.

"Are you going to tell me now?"

I watched his Adam's apple bob up and down as he swallowed and then nodded his head.

"I'll tell you," he said. He tightened his hold on my hand. "I don't know what you are going to think afterward, but I'll tell you."

My legs were starting to cramp, so I sat down next to Aiden and leaned back against the same wall. I let him keep his grip on my hand —he seemed to need it—as he began to tell his story.

"It's been over six years since it all started," Aiden said. He took in a long breath and blew it out slowly. "Megan and I, we had known each other for a while and had just gotten more serious, but we were young. We were talking about moving in together when she found out she...that she was pregnant. She gave birth to Cayden the next spring."

He traced the edge of my hand with his thumb.

"Everything was going okay, you know? I mean, at least I thought it was. Yeah, we were usually strapped for money, but we were making it all right. Daycare was so expensive, she decided to quit her job and just stay home and take care of him. She was in retail and wasn't making much anyway, so I figured it would work out. I picked up a second job so we could afford what we needed for Cayden, but it was never quite enough."

"I don't know exactly when it all started falling apart," Aiden continued. "I don't know if I should have seen it coming. Since I was working two jobs, I wasn't around as much as I should have been, but I was only doing what I had to do to keep things going. Eventually, she met this other guy."

I felt him tense.

"Jackson Harper." Aiden said the name with a sneer. "If she had just found someone better than me, I could have lived with it. I still loved her, but I wouldn't have tried to stop her if that was the case, but it wasn't. He was bad news. I knew it. All our friends knew it, but she didn't listen to anyone. He promised her the world, and she believed him. When she left me, she moved right in with him."

"He was into all kinds of shit," Aiden said. His eyes had gone dark and cold. "Bad shit. Drug trafficking, knocking over convenience stores, mugging restaurant workers as they left with the night's deposit—all that kind of shit. He had a record, had done a little pen time in the past, and had met some seriously rough people while he was there."

"The thing was, he was also stupid. He had no idea how deep he had gotten into it, and he thought he could play one of the big-time drug lords off another one. He was wrong. He pissed off the wrong guy and ended up with a price on his head."

"Megan, she…she wasn't into that stuff, but she believed every lie he told her. I don't know if it was the money he was bringing into the house or not, but she ate it all up like fucking candy. I barely recognized her when I saw her. She'd changed her clothing style, her hair, her attitude—everything—just to please him. By the time she understood what was really happening and called me, it was too late. I was so pissed off at her for having Cayden around that asshole, I couldn't even think straight. If I had known…if I had really thought about it…fuck!"

"What happened?" I whispered as a cold feeling closed over my heart. "What happened to Megan and Cayden?"

"We switched off weeks with him," Aiden explained. "I wasn't going to settle for that every other weekend shit, so we alternated whole weeks—Sunday to Sunday. I couldn't stand being around Jackson, and to avoid making a scene, we would exchange him at Sugarman—this candy store off of 20th Street. It was right between where we lived, and Cayden loved the place, so it was easy to occupy him there for a little while if one of us was late or something."

"They were late. They were usually late, but they were *really* late. An hour went by, and Megan wasn't answering her phone. I finally got sick of sitting around and drove to Jackson's apartment."

He looked up at me.

"I knew something was wrong," he said. "I could feel it in my gut. When no one answered the door, I kicked it in."

His eyes became glazed, and his voice dropped to nearly a whisper.

"They came for him. They came to kill Jackson, and Megan and Cayden were there too. I found them all in the bedroom. All shot. All dead."

Aiden's grip on my fingers intensified. He leaned forward as he squeezed his eyes shut, and every muscle in his body contracted. Tears formed in my eyes as the words sank in. Cayden had been taken away from him, just not in the way I had assumed.

"He was…he was still holding onto the horse. His fingers were locked around it. Even when I-"

He stopped, unable to continue as his voice grew ragged and strained. He tightened his grip around the stuffed animal and my hand but couldn't seem to take a breath. When he finally did, it came out as a gasp.

"Oh my God, Aiden." I pulled my hand from his and wrapped both arms around his head. I held him against me, feeling his body shake with sobs as he tried to keep going.

"I…I picked him up. I knew he was gone, but I didn't want him to be on the floor there. He was so cold. When I picked him up, he still held on to the horse. It didn't fall out of his hand until after the police and paramedics showed up and took him away from me."

He turned toward me and wrapped his arms around my waist. I held on to him as tightly as I could, rocking slowly back and forth as his tears soaked my shirt.

"They came for Jackson but killed Megan and Cayden, too. They didn't have to fucking do that! He just turned four…he wasn't a threat to anyone…he was just a little kid."

All the thoughts in my head were spinning around like a tornado. All the storylines I had imagined were falling apart—none of them fit with this information. It was as if the puzzle I had nearly completed had just been tossed on the ground, and all the pieces had separated and scattered on the floor.

There was still a lot missing, and I knew it. His story had explained what happened to his family but not why he was in a parking lot with a gun, chasing people out of a restaurant. It didn't explain what he did for a living, and it didn't explain why he was falling apart now.

One thing my father had always impressed upon me when it came to grieving patients was the need to take things slowly. I had the distinct impression that this story was not one Aiden often told, and pushing him to tell me more right now wouldn't get me far. He needed to get past this piece before he could move on.

So I held him. I held him, and he cried, and I cried for him and the loss of his little boy. The sunbeam shining through the window moved slowly over the boxes in the room, highlighting the box of Cayden's toys before retreating up the wall and finally disappearing. At one point, I saw slight movement at the doorway as Redeye checked on us, then quickly retreated. I continued to hold on to Aiden.

Aiden's shaking gradually slowed and then stopped. I kept holding on to him until he pulled back and sat up, looking at the window and away from me. My back and legs were stiff, and I had to imagine his were far worse.

"How long have you been sitting here?" I asked.

Aiden just shrugged.

"Have you eaten?"

Aiden nodded toward a pile of empty beer bottles.

"That doesn't count."

He shrugged again.

"Have you slept?"

"Not really."

"Come with me," I said. "I'm going to get you something to eat, and then you're going to bed."

I held on to his hand, pulling at it slightly as I stood. He didn't move at first, but I stared at him until he surrendered. He stood up slowly, grimacing and rubbing at his back. I wrapped one arm around his waist and led him to the kitchen.

I saw Redeye and Lance look up at us from the patio. Redeye's face broke into a grin as he watched me sit Aiden down at the kitchen table and start making him a sandwich.

"I didn't know they were here," Aiden said.

"Redeye picked me up from the airport," I informed him. "I told you they were worried."

"I'm all right," Aiden said. He blinked a couple of times and made a face at the sandwich when I put a plate in front of him

"Don't argue," I said sternly. "You are going to eat that, and then you are going to get some rest."

I opened up cabinets, looking for the huge container of protein powder I remembered Aiden drinking in the mornings. I found it right next to a large box of individual packets of Swedish Fish. Remembering that Aiden liked them, I grabbed one of the bags.

I mixed up the protein powder in a blender cup, and then placed the cup and the bag of sweets on the table. Aiden stared at the bag as his face lost color.

"Aiden?"

He shoved himself away from the table, slammed into the wall behind him, and looked over to me with his eyes blazing.

"I'm not fucking hungry!" he screamed. "I don't even know why the fuck you are here! You already left once. Isn't that enough?"

I took a step back, surprised by the outburst. I saw Lance stand up from where he was sitting outside, but Redeye grabbed his arm and held him back.

Memories of my mother shortly after Dad's funeral played through my mind. We had gone to dinner with a few friends, and Mom had yelled at the server when he got the orders turned around a bit. I had never known her to lash out like that before, but I understood her anger wasn't directed at anyone in the restaurant. She was angry with life and with the hopelessness and fear that accompanied Dad's death. She was angry at him for being gone, and she had lashed out rather than feel the pain of losing him.

I remembered Aiden buying Swedish Fish when we were in the airport before we flew down to Miami together. I'd picked on him for getting candy, and he'd gone quiet and cold for a while. I was starting to understand why.

Aiden's anger wasn't directed at me now any more than it had been then. This was grief, not anger.

"Aiden," I said as I took a step toward him. He clenched his hands into fists and pressed them against the wall at his back. "What is it? What is it about Swedish Fish?"

He took in a gasping breath as he looked sharply away from me. He clenched his teeth along with his hands.

"Aiden, tell me about the fish."

"No," he said. His jaw was still tight.

"Why is the candy important to you?" I prodded, afraid I was pushing too hard but feeling like it needed to be done now, or the opportunity would be lost. This was important. This was key. I was sure of it.

"It's...it's not," he said, but the venom was gone from his voice.

"Tell me," I said softly as I moved a little closer again. "Tell me about them."

Aiden's shoulders slumped and he looked down at the table. He dropped back into the seat, and a single tear fell down his cheek as he reached out and ran his finger over the bag of Swedish Fish.

"They were Cayden's favorite," Aiden said quietly. "We always shared a bag of them, watching TV. He didn't like the yellow ones."

I walked up beside him and put my hand on his shoulder.

"Why was that so hard?" I asked.

"Because...because it hurts to think about it."

Like a flash of lightning over the ocean, I saw the issue with perfect clarity. Aiden had never grieved for his son any more than he had for his father. Though my father had died much more recently, I'd spent my time mourning his death. Aiden had never let himself feel the loss, never allowed himself to grieve.

"You have to feel it, Aiden," I said quietly. "If you don't let yourself feel the pain, it stays with you forever."

"I can't," he whispered. "I can't think about it."

I ran my hand over his cheek and turned his head to face me.

"You can," I told him. "I'm going to help you."

He stared at me.

"Why?" he asked.

"Because you need help," I said simply. "Besides, I owe you one."

"You owe me one *what*?"

I took a deep breath as I stared straight into his eyes.

"As much as you talk about living for the here and now, you are completely stuck in the past," I said. "You helped me learn how to deal with life, and now I'll help you learn how to deal with death."

Aiden was in no shape to continue our conversation. He needed to eat, and he needed to sleep. While he ate the sandwich and drank the protein shake, I went back outside to talk to Redeye and Lance. They stood as I walked out.

"Looks like you made more progress than anyone else has," Redeye said with a grin. "I knew you would. I fucking knew it!"

"We'll see," I said. I wasn't sure how I felt about him being so pleased with himself. "For now, he needs to sleep. I'll stay with him. You guys can leave if you want."

"Are you sure?" Lance asked. "I can just park on the couch or something. I've been here the past couple of nights, but I don't think he's noticed."

"No," I said. "I'm fine, really. Take a break. I don't know how all this is going to turn out."

Lance nodded.

"If you're sure," he said.

"I am."

They both hugged me.

"You're good people," Redeye said. "I knew it as soon as I met you. You're going to be great for him."

"I don't know about that," I said. "I don't know where all this is going to lead, but I'm trying to be open-minded about everything."

"I left your luggage by the front door," Redeye said with a grin.

I narrowed my eyes at him, annoyed with his smugness. He had been right though. I couldn't deny him that.

Lance smiled and tipped his hat at me before they both walked back around the house to the front. I went back inside as Aiden finished up his food. A couple of minutes later, I heard their cars starting up.

"You need to sleep," I told Aiden as I took his empty plate away and put it in the dishwasher.

"You're going to stay?"

"Yes."

"For how long?"

"I don't know yet," I said. "That kind of depends on you."

"I haven't told you everything yet," Aiden said.

"I realize that." I ran my hand down his arm. "You can tell me in the morning."

We walked out of the kitchen and to the bedroom. I helped Aiden find some clean shorts and ordered him into the shower. While he cleaned up, I tried to sort through all the new information in my head.

Yes, Aiden had a child, but I had been completely wrong about what had happened to him. Aiden hadn't even tried to get over his loss, much like the picture he painted of his mother after his dad had died. He didn't have a role model when it came to grief and didn't know how to cope with it.

The death of a child. Was anything worse?

After holding my ear up to the bathroom door and confirming Aiden was still moving around in there, I meandered to the kitchen and made myself a quick sandwich. I hadn't eaten since I'd left home, and I was suddenly famished.

I knew I was in over my head, and Aiden ultimately needed professional help. Being the daughter of a psychologist didn't make me an expert though it did give me the tools to help get him pointed in the right direction.

I still didn't understand what had upset him on the phone in the airport or his violent words during late-night phone conversations at his house. His explanation didn't account for the gun and everything that followed. It didn't clarify Aiden's occupation or what had happened after he was arrested. There were still plenty of things I didn't know, but I would have to save all of that until morning.

With the sandwich devoured, I collected my luggage from where Redeye had left it and brought it back to the bedroom. I found my phone charger—it had been the first thing I packed—and then my toiletry bag and pajamas. The shower went silent, and I knew Aiden would still be a couple of minutes, so I went ahead and changed clothing where I was.

Aiden emerged from the bathroom, still scruffy-faced, but clean. He stared at me for a moment before he climbed into bed. I took a deep breath and then slid in beside him. He placed his hand on my waist, and I felt myself stiffen reflexively. I had no idea what he was expecting.

"I won't make a move," Aiden said quietly. "Not until you tell me I can."

"I appreciate you telling me this time." I relaxed immediately then reached up and stroked his cheek. I was torn between not wanting to get his hopes up and simultaneously not wanting to crush them. I still didn't know what would happen in the morning.

I knew I couldn't be in a relationship with a criminal.

I looked at his red-rimmed eyes, and my heart went out to him and the long-overdue pain he was experiencing. Could I be friends with him, regardless of everything else? That would put us on a completely different level, but could I do it? Could I remain friends with Aiden once I knew everything, even if I couldn't reconcile his activities with my own conscience?

As always, there were too many questions and not enough answers. For now, I would leave it all alone and let him get the rest he needed.

And with that, I pulled his head to my shoulder and waited for him to sleep.

SEVENTEEN

Aiden dropped off almost immediately. I wondered how long it had been since he'd actually slept. I had the impression he'd been right where I had found him for some time and could have been sleeping, leaning up against the wall for all I knew.

It was only early evening, and despite the plane ride and emotionally exhaustive discussion, I wasn't tired enough to sleep. Instead, I lay against the pillows and watched Aiden. Even in slumber, he still looked pained.

As I always did, I questioned my thoughts and feelings as I held him. I was torn between the empathy I felt after learning about the horrible and violent way Aiden had lost his family and the reservations I had about the questions that remained unanswered.

He turned restlessly, and I moved a little closer to wrap my arm around his waist. He settled with a sigh, and his hand slid around my back and landed on my shoulder blade. I lay my head on his chest and listened to him breathe.

The need to make a decision, to know what I was going to do when all of this was over, was pressing. Aiden had suffered a terrible loss and would need ongoing support, but I didn't know if I would be able to provide it.

As much as I enjoyed my time with Aiden, and as much as I had learned from him, I knew in my heart that I couldn't support someone who lived his life outside the law. Thrill-seeking within certain parameters was one thing, but I didn't have it in me to be in a relationship with a criminal.

You still don't know everything.

I feared when I learned the truth, I would have to leave him.

Yet here I was—back in his bed, back in his arms. I couldn't take my eyes off the way his skin looked next to the white sheets, and I couldn't stop thinking about the feeling of his hard, muscled body against my flesh. With his arm around me, the feeling of security was undeniable, and I realized how much I had missed him.

So I spent my evening holding Aiden, watching him sleep, and tracing the line of his bicep with my finger. I examined the tattoos running up and down his right arm, trying to understand the significance of each. I remembered the feeling of his hands on my body and the words he would say to me—both the dirty and the sweet ones—when we were having sex.

The ceiling fan turned slowly above my head, casting shadows on the walls. The small slits in the blinds over the window let in strips of light, brightening the dark wood of Aiden's bedroom furniture. It was all so familiar, so normal.

Aiden stirred, and his eyes fluttered open for a moment. He blinked at me slowly before moving his hand to touch me face.

"Are you a dream?" he asked quietly.

"No," I said with a smile. "I'm here."

"She took Cayden and left in the middle of the night," he said. "I just woke up, and they were gone."

I could see it in my head: Aiden waking up to an empty bed, checking his son's room and looking round the house only to find himself alone.

"I'm not going anywhere," I promised. "I'll be right here when you wake up."

He nodded as he tightened his arms around me and closed his eyes again.

Eventually, I slept.

When I woke, Aiden was still asleep. Soft rain pattered on the window, and I hoped the sound of it would help him get all the rest he so obviously needed. I untangled myself from his arms and made a quick trip to the bathroom. It was only seven-thirty, so I called my boss and left a voice mail that I was still sick. I returned to the bedroom and climbed in beside Aiden just as he was opening his eyes.

"You're still here," he said, sounding surprised.

"I told you I would stay."

He brought his hand up to my cheek and ran his fingers over my skin. His eyes were still red from yesterday, and his voice sounded scratchy when he spoke.

"I'm sorry you saw me like that."

"You don't have to apologize," I told him. "Sometimes, you have to let go of it all."

"I've never fallen apart like that before."

"What about when...when you found them?"

Aiden shook his head slowly.

"I never cried about it."

I considered the implications of what he was saying. How could a father not cry over his child's death?

"You didn't?"

"No." He looked at my eyes. "Not even when they buried him. I just...I just kept thinking it was all a nightmare, and I'd wake up and he'd be there, asking me to get his tricycle built for him. I was going to do it that week, but I never had the chance."

I knew everyone dealt with grief differently, but crying seemed to be the ultimate outlet of emotions. I'd always been taught that it was important to cry when you felt loss. I didn't understand how all this time could have passed without Aiden allowing himself to cry.

"It's all right to cry, Aiden," I said.

"I know," he responded with a shrug of his shoulder. "I just never did."

"Now you have," I pointed out. "Maybe you needed to."

"I guess so." He yawned. "Right now, I just need coffee."

We made breakfast together. The rain stopped as we ate, but it was too wet to sit outside. Aiden moved the boxes off the couch, and we sat in the living room.

"You want to know the rest?" he asked quietly.

"I think I need to," I replied.

"You do." Aiden rested his hands in his lap as he gathered

himself. "Since that day—the day I found them—I've spent my life trying to put it right. When I wasn't working, I was at the police station, talking to people around town, and doing everything I could to figure out who had done it. I stopped talking to the girl I had recently started dating, stopped going out with friends—I didn't even go to a movie for the next two years."

He turned to me.

"You're the first girl I've been with since that day," he said as he looked back at his hands. "I just felt drawn to you, like maybe you were what I needed to keep me going. I was starting to give up hope, and I thought you could…I don't know…bring me out of it."

"I didn't want to tell you about it," he continued. "I didn't want you to know because when someone finds out, they want me to talk about it. They want me to explain, and that's just…it's just *hard*."

"You didn't tell me because it hurts," I said.

He nodded.

"It was nice," he said, "not to have to talk about it. Even with the guys, it comes up because most of them are trying to do something about it."

He glanced at me, and his eyes were dark.

"I need to make the people responsible for it pay, Chloe. I can't even consider anything else until that happens."

I thought about what that might entail.

"You can't go after a drug lord," I said. "Aiden, that's not a thrill. That is insane."

"I'm not," Aiden said. "I don't blame the guy who put the hit out on Jackson. That shithead had done it all to himself, and he deserved what he got. But those who were there—they're the ones who decided to take it further. They're the ones who decided they had to get rid of the witnesses."

"Who are they?" I asked.

"I'm not telling you the name of the drug guy. You don't need to know it, and it could put you in danger, but the name of the guy who went after Megan's boyfriend is Chris Marc. From everything I've heard, it wasn't his first hit, but he had a girlfriend with him— one who was new. Her name is Corinne Hayden. Apparently, she wanted to get in on the business. They're both out of their minds, kind of like Woody Harrelson and Juliette Lewis in *Natural Born Killers*. A couple of psychos who think everything they're doing is *fun*. She was there with Marc when they went to Jackson's apartment. She might have done it herself—I don't know. I don't know which one of them pulled the trigger."

"That's the couple who were at the restaurant," I said as the realization hit me. "They are the ones who ran out."

Aiden nodded.

"So why did you go there?" I asked. "Were you going there to… to kill the people who killed Cayden?"

"No!" Aiden shook his head vehemently. "As much as I want them dead, that's not what I went there for. Mo got a tip that they were back in town, and we were just going to hold them there until the police arrived. They're the ones who started shooting, not me."

"So, you called the police?" I questioned.

"Mo did, right after he talked to me."

"But they arrested you."

"Yeah, because of the gun," Aiden said. "People at the restaurant were scared, and I can't blame them for that. I only ended up spending the night in jail. They could tell the gun hadn't been fired, and my attorney was there first thing in the morning. After everything that happened with Megan and Cayden, I'd had words with most everyone at that police station, so they knew me there."

"So, are you out on bail? Do you have to have a trial?"

"Oh, no," Aiden said, "nothing like that. I don't have a prior record or anything. I was arrested for disorderly conduct, but given the circumstances, it was reduced to a city ordinance violation. I paid the fine, and it's all done."

"So you…you've never had a record?"

"A few traffic violations," Aiden said. He shrugged and grinned. "I like to ride fast."

I didn't know what to say. All the assumptions I had made, all the things I had assumed were Aiden's transgressions—I was completely wrong. I hadn't seen Aiden for the man he was. Instead, I had judged without ever giving him a chance to explain.

"But…but your job…" I stammered.

"What about it?"

"Pharmaceutical sales?"

"Yeah," Aiden said. He narrowed his eyes a bit. "I go around to doctors' offices and sell drugs for a pharmaceutical company, mostly generics as the brand-names become available. It's not a great moneymaker, but I get to set my own hours. Better than what I used to do."

"What was that?"

"Shoe sales," he said with a laugh.

"Why…why were you so dodgy about it?" I demanded.

"Uh, well…" Aiden said as he scratched the back of his head, "the whole idea was to bring you here for a little excitement. What could be more boring than going around to doctors' offices hoping they'll take a few samples?"

I was completely flabbergasted.

"Wait—what about this house? You can't make enough to afford this place."

"Oh, well, like I said—I came into some money."

"What money?"

Aiden took a long breath.

"When Cayden was born, Megan and I hired an attorney to draw up wills for us. Neither of us had a lot to do with our families, and we wanted to make sure Cayden was taken care of if something happened to us, you know?"

I nodded.

"It was all very simple—if I died, she got everything of mine, and if she died, I got everything of hers. If we both died, Cayden was going to be raised by Megan's aunt in Tampa, and everything would go into a fund for him until he was eighteen."

"We had some life insurance," Aiden continued in a quiet voice. "That was just enough to bury them both. What I didn't know was that Megan's aunt had passed away about two months before…before everything else. She left Megan everything, and Megan hadn't changed the will. I'm not sure Megan even knew her aunt was gone. I ended up with it all—an estate worth about two million."

"Wow." It was the only word I could manage.

"I honestly didn't want it, but Megan didn't have any other family that I knew of, and there wasn't anyone coming out of the woodwork and demanding a cut. After about a year, my lawyer called and told me it was all mine. I used most of the money to buy this place and the jeep. I invested the rest."

Everything fell into place, and it all made sense.

"Aiden, I'm so sorry."

"What are you sorry about?"

"I never gave you a chance to explain," I said. "I just made all kinds of assumptions about you and what was going on."

The corner of his mouth turned up, and his eyes twinkled at me.

"You thought I was a drug dealer, didn't you?"

I blushed, and Aiden shook his head.

"I ought to be pissed off about that," he said. "Before they got to know me, a lot of the cops around here thought I had to be a bad guy because of the tats. They thought I had to be a lunkhead because I did all the bodybuilding shit. They tried to sweep the murders under the rug, figuring I wouldn't pursue it out of fear that they'd find out I was also mixed up in that shit."

He gritted his teeth.

"If they had moved sooner, they might have gotten to Marc and Hayden before they left the state. They didn't listen to me for the longest time, even when I had evidence that they were in Ohio. I hired my own private investigator up there to find them. He finally made progress about a month ago."

"That's who you were talking to in the bar the night I met you." I remembered the man in the blazer who had been sitting across from Aiden.

"It was," he confirmed. "He had turned over all the surveillance information to the police down here, and they said it wasn't enough to go on."

"Why were you angry with him?"

"Because he said he couldn't get the cops to do anything with it." Aiden sighed. "We got together the next day for a conference call with them, and it was basically worked out. What I didn't know was that Marc and Hayden were on to me. They knew I had found them, and they headed back down here."

"Why would they do that?"

"Best guess, they thought the guy who hired them to kill Jackson would protect them. He won't, though."

"How do you know that?"

"Because he's the one who gave me their names," Aiden said. "I may not be involved in crime, but that doesn't mean I'm ignorant as to who is. Mo and Lo have their contacts —a lot of them. You can't be in the security business without knowing who the lowlifes in the area are. They knew exactly what was going on after making a few phone calls."

"I guess that makes sense." It did, too. In fact, everything was falling into place. "Is there anything else I need to know?"

"Only that they ran," Aiden said. "The police are searching for them. The security cameras at the strip mall caught the car and license plate, but it was a stolen vehicle. They might still be in it, though. It hasn't turned up anywhere."

"What happens if the police find them?"

"They've got arrest warrants outstanding," Aiden said. "Aside from car theft, Chris Marc is wanted for robbery up in Orlando as well as suspicion of homicide on another count as well. If they're caught, they're going to go to prison. I hope they get the fucking chair."

Aiden looked exhausted, and I decided he needed a break from all of this. He went to take a shower while I cleaned up in the kitchen and sorted through all the new information in my head. More than anything, I felt guilty for all my critical theories about Aiden's life. I had been afraid to ask questions, and my hypotheses had been completely wrong.

Aiden came out of the bathroom, his beard neatly trimmed, and he was dressed in his usual shorts and muscle shirt. I looked down his body slowly before moving back to his eyes, only to find he had an eyebrow raised at me.

Caught ogling, I blushed. I wasn't ready for the heart-pounding feelings I had when I was in his presence and needed to get myself back on track. We still had important things to discuss. I looked down at my hands for a moment, twisting my fingers around as I got my thoughts in order.

"Aiden," I said, "I owe you an apology."

"You aren't the first person to think that I was the bad guy," he said, his voice sounding sad. He picked up his red cap and ran his finger over the edge of it before he placed it on his head. "My mother started telling me that right after the first tat. She said I looked like a gang member and would never get a decent job."

"I don't care if I was the first or not," I insisted. "I still made the assumption, and I'm sorry for that. I...I should have asked. I should have made you tell me all this before. Maybe then, I wouldn't have run away. I wouldn't have refused your calls."

Aiden swallowed visibly.

"That hurt," he admitted quietly. "I really thought you...that maybe you could be the one who understood. I thought you didn't have those kinds of notions about me. I thought you had seen me for who I was."

I walked over and took his hand before leading him back to the couch so we could sit more comfortably, and I laid my hand on top of his.

"I did see you, Aiden," I said. "I just let my own fears get the better of me, and I'm sorry for that. I really am."

He turned his hand over and locked our fingers together.

"I'm sorry I didn't come clean earlier. I could tell you had your reservations, but I didn't want to have to live through it all again. I didn't want to explain what was happening, and it drove you away."

"I'm here now," I reminded him.

"Yeah," he said with a smile, "you are."

He brought my hand up to his lips and kissed my knuckles.

"Where do we go from here?" he asked.

I squeezed his hand, and he looked at me expectantly.

"I don't know what happens next," I admitted. "I came here because Redeye asked me to and because I was worried about you. I called in sick to work, but I can't keep that up for long. I need to go back home."

Aiden nodded slowly.

"I guess my cooking hasn't convinced you to stay here forever," he mused.

I chuckled.

"I don't know about that just yet," I said. "I'm still trying to wrap my head around all of this."

Aiden flexed his fingers and furrowed his brow. He took a deep breath and licked his lips before speaking.

"Do I have another chance with you?" he asked. "I know I fucked up the beginning of this by not telling you everything sooner, but I have to know if there's still hope here."

I wasn't sure how to respond at first. The last few days we had been together, before the fiasco at the restaurant, I had certainly felt like we were a couple, but we hadn't put a name on it. The way it all happened was so foreign to me, I hadn't even considered it.

So where did that leave us now? Putting a name to it made it all the more real, and I wasn't sure I was ready for that. There was still so much about each other we didn't know, and even with some of the misunderstanding cleared up, we had distance to consider. I was also still hesitant, still afraid. I hadn't talked to Mare or my mom about him. None of my friends had met him.

I had my doubts, but they were focused more on my own insecurities and fear of the unknown than anything else I might learn about Aiden. Before I had heard about Cayden and the people who destroyed Aiden's life, I had been focusing on my concerns about Aiden and his supposed lifestyle. My perceptions were different now. If I had known everything from the beginning, would I have doubted him in the first place?

No, I wouldn't have.

Everything was clearer to me now. The distance was going to be a challenge, but weren't there challenges in any relationship? There might be other things I didn't know about Aiden Hunter, but learning about each other was part of the excitement. He had some baggage, certainly, but didn't we all? It was a risk, but if I had learned nothing else from my time in Miami, I had learned that risks could be worth it.

"Yes," I said, "there's hope."

"Really?"

"Really."

"You aren't just saying that because you think I've gone off the deep end?"

"I'm not just saying it," I confirmed. "However, I might want you to agree to some conditions."

"Conditions?" He took a deep breath. "Honestly, I think I'd agree to almost anything right now, so give it your best shot."

I watched his face carefully, but he seemed sincere.

"I want you to think about seeing someone," I said.

Aiden looked confused.

"I thought…I mean, I thought we were talking about me seeing *you.*"

"Not that." I shook my head. "Aiden, you need to deal with the loss of your son. You need to see someone professionally and work it out. I'll be here for you, but I won't be enough."

He dropped his eyes.

"You're talking about a shrink, right?"

"A psychologist, yes."

He stared into my eyes, and he didn't look pleased at the idea. Anticipating his objections, I decided to strike first.

"If your leg was broken, would you have a doctor fix it?" I asked.

He raised an eyebrow at me.

"You saying my head's broken?"

"No, not exactly."

He laughed.

"Yeah, it is," he said. "At the very least, there are some dark corners I don't care to think about on my own."

"So what do you think?"

He scratched his head.

"Okay…yeah. If that's what it would take to bring you back here, then yeah, I'll do it."

I reached up and ran the backs of my fingers over his jaw.

"Thank you," I said. "If you can do that, I can certainly consider trying this long-distance thing. I'm not sure how well it's going to work, but I'm willing to give it a shot."

"Fair enough," he replied. He turned his body on the couch to face me and took both my hands in his. "Thank you, Chloe."

"For what?"

"For coming here," he said. "For giving me another chance."

"Thank you for not holding all my assumptions against me," I replied.

"I guess they were understandable," he said. "I wish you had just asked me."

"I'm not very good at being straightforward like that," I admitted.

"Then that's my condition," he stated.

"What's that?"

"If you have doubts, you tell me," he said. "No more making stories up in your head. If you are wondering something about me, ask and I'll tell you."

"Deal."

He pulled me closer to him tentatively. When I didn't resist, he ran his hand up my arm, cupped my face, and placed his lips on mine. He was slow at first, but when I wrapped my hand around the back of his head, he opened his mouth and kissed me deeply.

My body became electrified, remembering the sensations he had brought to me in the past.

"Will you let me try to convince you?" he asked.

"Convince me?"

"I want you, Chloe," Aiden said. He stroked my cheek with his thumb and stared into my eyes as he spoke. "I want to know I'll have more days of waking up to you in my bed. I want to make you breakfast again. When I walk down the beach, I want you beside me, looking for seashells. I want you in my life, Chloe. I want to convince you that you want it, too."

He kissed me again and again. I trailed my fingers up his arms, feeling the strength of the muscles there before landing on his broad shoulders. He pushed against me until I was lying beneath him on the couch.

"What do you think?" he asked.

I smiled up at him.

"I think I'd like that," I said.

He smirked, his devilish grin reaching his eyes as they sparkled with life. He leaned in and brushed his lips over mine.

"Do you know what I've been thinking about all morning?" Aiden whispered against my lips.

"What?" I pressed my mouth against his, tasted his tongue with mine, and let my fingers slide through the short hairs on his cheek. He sucked my lower lip into his mouth and then trailed kisses over my chin and down my neck.

"I was thinking about how good it felt sliding my dick into you." His breath was hot against my throat, but all the skin on my body warmed as he spoke. "I was wondering if you still liked watching my cock move in and out of you, like you did that first time we were together. I was thinking how good you look lying on your back underneath me when I come in you."

I closed my eyes as he ran his nose up the side of my neck to my ear. My skin tingled as he took my earlobe between his lips and sucked at it gently.

"I'd love to spread your legs and taste you right now," he whispered. "I want to make your clit sing with my tongue. I want to feel your legs shake as you come all over my face, and then I want to fuck you so hard and so fast you forget your own name."

"Jesus, Aiden..."

He chuckled against my ear.

"You love that, don't you? You love hearing all that dirty talk."

"Stop teasing me," I said with a groan.

"I'm not making a move," he mumbled as he kissed down the side of my neck.

How in the world he didn't consider all of this "a move" was beyond me. I felt like my skin was on fire. I grabbed his head with both of my hands and turned him to face me.

"Aiden Hunter," I said as I stared straight at him, "make a move."

His eyes twinkled.

"That's what I needed to hear." He slid his hand up to cup my breast over my shirt. "We're going to have to do something about all this, though."

He reached down to pull off my shirt, and I did the same to his. Our shorts and underwear quickly followed until everything was in a heap next to the couch. Aiden climbed back on top of me, straddling my waist.

"That's better," he said. "Now spread your legs for me, knees up."

I licked my lips and did as he said, bending my knees at his sides and raising my hips slightly. He looked down at me as a slow smile spread across his face. He looked back at me, pressed his lips against my shoulder, and then moved up my neck.

"Are you ready for this, Chloe?" he cooed in my ear, the softness of his voice contrasting with his words. "Are you ready to get fucked?"

"Yes," I whispered back. "Please."

I wrapped my arms under his and held tightly to his shoulders, preparing myself for the onslaught. Aiden held himself over me, balanced on one hand as he took the shaft of his cock in the other and slowly pushed into me.

"Oh, yeah…Oh, fuck! I missed this…" Aiden buried his face in my neck and moaned.

It seemed like forever since I had felt him inside of me and heard his intoxicating words invade my ears as he pounded into me over and over again. The blur of his marked body swirled in my eyes as he moved, keeping me from being able to focus on anything other than the full, tight feeling of his body meshing with mine.

With soft strokes, I ran my hands over the lines of ink on his chest and arms. I traced the cross covering his shoulder and bicep, using my fingertip to write over his name inscribed down the middle of it—A HUNTER. For a moment, I wondered what it really meant. Was it simply a representation of his name or a declaration of his mission to bring his son's killers to justice?

He gripped my hip with his hand, and my fingers slid up around his shoulder and down his back, landing on his ass. I gripped the muscles there, feeling them tighten and release as he plowed into me. I closed my eyes and just let myself feel his hands on me, caressing my sides, stroking my breasts, and running up and down my legs.

With my thighs gripping his sides, I pushed up, deepening his penetrations and crushing his hand between our bodies. He continued his quick movements over my clit, and I shuddered, giving in to the intense feeling as I cried out for him.

The muscles of his ass tightened beneath my hands as he pushed forward a final time. I felt the warmth of his semen inside of me as he shuddered.

"Chloe, Chloe…oh, baby, you're so fucking perfect. You're perfect for me."

I wrapped my arms around his head and held him against my shoulder as both of us tried to regain control of our breathing. His lips pressed to the side of my neck, and I leaned my cheek against the top of his head.

All the feelings of security and comfort I'd had in the past returned—this time without reservations.

And with that, I knew I wanted to make this work.

EIGHTEEN

"Will you come back for the weekend?" Aiden asked as he carried my bag toward airport security. "I'd just head up there to see you, but the police want me to stick around town in case they locate Marc and Hayden."

"I'll have to see," I said. "I'm going to be behind at work—I'd just gotten caught up from being here before, and I kind of had it out with my boss the day before I left. I have no idea what I'll be walking into tomorrow. I may have to work this weekend to make up for some of it. Maybe the next weekend?"

"At least I'd have something to look forward to," Aiden said with a smile. "That might keep me going through the week."

At the security checkpoint, we had to part ways. Aiden leaned down to kiss me softly, and I squeezed his hands.

"Hang in there," I told him as I ran my fingers up over his inked arms. "I'll call you when I get home."

"You'd better!" He gave me one last hug.

The flight back was uneventful, leaving me to continue my ponderings. Now that I understood everything that had happened, I was able to focus on the whole idea of a long-distance relationship instead of what secrets Aiden might be hiding from me. It should have been easier, but I found I was almost as distressed by the idea of trying to make things work from so far away as I had been when I wondered about Aiden's occupation.

At least now I would be able to talk to Mare about it. She was going to laugh at me for being so distrustful now that I knew the truth, but I could live with that. I was also dreading my return to work in the morning, which was actually a decent distraction.

As promised, I called Aiden when I got home. We talked about the mundane for the most part, but I did make him promise to seek out his friends over the weekend instead of staying home by himself. He said he would, and I threatened to follow up with Redeye to make sure he made good on that promise.

Opening up my laptop for the first time in days, I checked my personal email. I found a message from Nate's recruiter, Brian, who said he had a couple of opportunities that seemed to fit my skillset. I emailed him back with my availability for a lunch meeting sometime next week.

It was good to have something promising. I only hoped it would work out.

At work the next day, I walked into a firestorm.

"Hey, Chloe!"

I looked down the hall to see Matt, the guy in charge of major problems with the IT systems. It was never a good thing to have him searching for me before I even got to my desk. He bustled down the hallway, holding a pad of paper under his arm. He had a pen shoved between his teeth as he tapped on his phone.

"What's going on, Matt?"

"Can you get on the conference bridge?" he asked. "Those servers for the acquiring software have gone haywire."

Fabulous.

I was on the phone for the next three hours. The server techs managed to restart the systems eventually, but they weren't in good shape and were bound to fail again. In the meantime, we'd incurred a lot of fines from our customers who couldn't use the system.

As soon as the call ended, Kevin and his Chia-head face appeared at my desk.

"Those servers have been over capacity for months," he said.

"I'm aware of that," I replied.

"Well, why haven't you done anything about it?"

I looked up at him, stunned. These were the very servers I'd warned him about, but he had disregardd my recommendations and axed the project anyway.

"You cancelled the project," I reminded him. "This was all part of the upgrade we had in the pipeline since June, but you said the funding was going elsewhere."

"Don't you try to put this on me," he said, pointing his finger at my face. "You were in charge of that project. If you couldn't be bothered to make the risks known, that's on your head, not mine!"

I couldn't believe what I was hearing.

"I gave you all the data on those servers," I said. "I told you there was risk."

"You most certainly did not," he said, "and now your lack of foresight has cost this company more than the upgrade would have!"

He leaned back with his arms crossed over his chest, smirking.

I tightened my hand around my pen enough that it nearly broke. I gritted my teeth together as my head began to pound. Slowly and deliberately, I stood up and put my hands on my hips.

I had officially had enough.

"*My* lack of foresight?" My hands were starting to shake as my heart beat wildly in my chest.

"You were the project manager." Kevin continued to stare me down. "You should have made the risks obvious."

"I did," I stated. "You are the one who wouldn't listen. You wouldn't even look at the data."

"You didn't provide me with any data," he sneered.

I lost it. I dropped back down into my chair, stabbed at the keyboard to pull up my sent emails, and opened seven documented requests sent directly to Kevin, explaining the exact risks of not upgrading.

"There you go," I said as I shoved my chair back away from the computer. "And at this point, here I go."

I grabbed my security badge out of my purse and handed it to him.

"What's this for?" he asked.

"I quit," I said. "I'll send you my formal resignation by email before the end of the day."

My heart continued to pound as I gathered my things and walked away from Kevin and his accusations. I could barely believe what I had just done. It went against everything ingrained in me. I had no backup job. I had no other means of supporting myself, and I was in deep shit.

But I didn't stop.

As soon as I got to my car, I locked the doors and called Nate's recruiter to let him know I was available immediately. Then I called Mare, told her what I had done, and started to cry.

"Holy shit, Clo!" Mare bellowed on the other end of the phone. "What are you going to do?"

"I don't know!" I blubbered. "I just…I just couldn't take any more!"

"Well, damn, girl!" Mare let out a whistle. "I knew you weren't telling me something, but I wasn't expecting this. Does it have anything to do with that guy in Florida?"

"No…yes…I don't know!"

"Hang in there," she said. "I'll be over with a bottle of wine before you know it. We're going to get this sorted out."

True to her word, about five minutes after I got home, Mare was at my door with a bottle of merlot gripped in her fist.

"I thought you were never going to tell me what was going on," Mare said as she sat down on the couch and pulled a corkscrew from her enormous purse.

"Do you have glasses in there, too?"

"Of course not," Mare said. "They'd break."

I laughed and grabbed a couple of wine glasses from the cupboard.

"So, tell me everything," Mare said. "You never avoid me on purpose, which you've obviously been doing. I couldn't decide if it was work or what. Start at the beginning, although I'm pretty sure it's the night you met this Aiden guy."

"I think you are right," I confirmed. "It does start with him."

"So, out with it!" Mare poured the wine, and I started to tell her about meeting Aiden at the bar, waking up in his bed, and then agreeing to go to Florida with him.

Like a good friend does, Mare sat and listened to my story, filled my wine glass when it needed it, and didn't interrupt unless she needed some clarification. She only stopped me once.

"Skydiving?"

"Yeah."

"You went *skydiving*?"

"I did." I couldn't stop the smile on my face.

"Holy shit."

"I know, right?" I giggled.

Mare narrowed her eyes at me.

"I know I'm getting ahead of myself here," she said, "and normally I don't like spoilers, but at the end of the day, this Aiden guy is really good for you, isn't he?"

"Yes," I agreed quietly, "he is."

I continued, telling her about my time with Aiden and then the whole fiasco in the parking lot. Her eyes widened at that part, but she didn't interrupt me again. Once I told her about going back to Miami and finding Aiden in the back bedroom of his house and the story about his son, there were tears in her eyes.

"All that time," she said when I finally finished, "you didn't really know what you were getting into. You didn't know if your suspicions were correct, but you stuck it out. Then when push came to shove, you were there for him anyway even though you didn't understand until the end."

"Yeah," I said. "I guess that's true."

"Damn, Clo." Mare tilted her head to look at me from another angle. "You're in love with him."

I opened my mouth to deny it, but the words wouldn't come out. An image of Aiden's laughing, boyish grin and twinkling eyes filled my head, causing my skin to warm. I missed him already, but beyond that? I just didn't know.

Tears cascaded from my eyes and rolled down my cheeks.

"It's okay," Mare said as she reached over and hugged me. "He's in love with you, too."

I grabbed a tissue and wiped at my face.

"You can't know that." I narrowed my eyes at her as I blew my nose.

"Oh, yes I can."

"You haven't even met him."

"I don't need to," she said. "No wait—yes, I do, but not to confirm that. It's obvious."

"Don't be ridiculous." I stood up and walked across the room, dismissing her comments with a wave of my hand. I couldn't be in love with Aiden Hunter—it was just too soon. He certainly wasn't in love with me.

"You don't see it, do you?"

"See what?"

"Even that friend of his—Redeye—he could see it. All his friends could, so why can't you? Why else would they have put up the money for a ticket to fly you down there? They knew you loved him or else you wouldn't have agreed to go back after all the misunderstandings. They knew you could get through to him because they knew he was in love with you, too."

I shook my head, but her words were difficult to deny. I turned away from her and found myself looking at the plastic faces of my superheroine collection. They all seemed to be grinning at me with amusement and possibly even psychic knowledge.

"I'm not ready for that," I finally said. "He lives a thousand miles away, and I'm completely jobless right now. Isn't that why you came over here anyway?"

"Yes, it is," Mare said as she coaxed me back to the couch and refilled my glass. "As long as you are in denial, we might as well talk about that. Now, what happened at work?"

"I told off my boss," I said with a shrug and then quickly gave her the details. "I couldn't put up with his crap anymore, so I quit."

"No backup plan?"

"Not really." I ran my hand through my hair, getting my fingers tangled up in it. "I talked to Nate's recruiter, and he's going to get some interviews lined up for me, but I don't have a real plan, no."

Mare leaned back against the couch and looked at me for a long moment.

"You really are different," she said.

"What do you mean?"

"The Chloe Ellison I know never would have done that," Mare explained. "She never would have given that jerk a piece of her mind, and she never would have walked out of a job without another one lined up."

I slumped. She was right.

"I fucked up," I said.

Mare laughed.

"The Chloe I know never says 'fuck' either."

I pursed my lips and scowled at her.

"I do...sometimes."

She laughed again and evenly distributed the remainder of the wine in our glasses.

"You didn't fuck up," she said. "You stood up for yourself, and I'm proud of you."

"You are?"

"Definitely." Mare tipped the glass to her lips, peering at me over the edge. "I've told you before about saying what's in your head. You're always so concerned with other people's opinions and reactions that you never do it. You keep it locked up inside."

"I don't want to hurt people's feelings," I explained, fully aware of how many times we'd had similar discussions. "You have to think before you act, and that includes opening your mouth."

"Don't you see, Clo?" Mare said as she leaned forward. "That's exactly what you *weren't* doing with Aiden. You took a lot of risks and came out okay on the other side. Not just okay, but better for it —stronger. Don't you see that leaving your job is just another one of those risks?"

"And you think I'll be stronger for it in the end?"

"I do."

"And poorer," I pointed out.

"I bet you have some reserves stashed away somewhere," Mare said, eyeing me.

She was right. I did. I'd read an article years ago about having six months of living expenses tucked away in case something unexpected were to happen. I really did have plenty of time to look for another job before I was in danger of losing my condo or anything like that.

"Fine," I said. "You're right—I'll be okay for a while."

"So what are you going to do now?" Mare asked.

"Work on finding another job, I suppose."

"I meant about Aiden."

"Well, he was asking me to come down for the weekend. I thought I'd have too much work to do, but I guess that's not an issue now."

"So you'll go see him again."

"Yeah," I said. "I guess I will."

Telling my mother about Aiden didn't go as smoothly as my conversation with Mare. She was furious about all the dangerous things I had done, the risks I had taken, and kept repeating the same phrase over and over again.

"You jumped out of a plane, Chloe? A *plane?*"

I sighed *again.*

"I'm fine, Mom," I reminded her.

I told her about Aiden's son but decided it was not in anyone's best interests to tell her about all the tattoos and the assumptions I had made about him while I was down there. She was mad enough as it was, and I didn't need her flipping out on me more than she already had.

"You have to promise me," she practically yelled into the phone, "*promise* me you will never do anything crazy like that again!"

I opened my mouth with my agreement on my tongue but then paused. I didn't have any desire to go skydiving again, but what if Aiden came up with another activity? If he suggested bungee jumping or parasailing, I would undoubtedly agree, and I wasn't going to lie to my mother about it.

"I don't have any current plans to do anything crazy," I told her. "That doesn't mean I'll never do anything exciting again."

"This is beyond exciting, Chloe Ellison! You quit your job, for goodness' sake! What in the world were you thinking?"

I bit my tongue, holding in the words I wanted to use. I didn't want a prolonged argument with Mom, and I didn't want her to worry about me. I needed to just tell her I was wrong. Maybe I could see about getting my job back.

Alarm!

My body jerked in response to the internal alert. Had I learned nothing in the past few weeks? I didn't need that job—I could always find another one. I wasn't wrong to quit. Had I taken a risk? Yes. Was I afraid? Yes. But wasn't that all just a part of life?

This time, I listened to the alarm in my head.

"Here's what I was thinking," I said. I kept my voice calm and controlled. "I was thinking that the stress my boss was putting on me wasn't worth the job and that I'm a highly skilled professional that lots of companies would want to hire. I was thinking I might even take a couple of weeks off to go to Florida and get to know Aiden a little better because I think he's been really good for me. He's sweet and he's kind and he's a fantastic cook. He's taught me how to live life without being afraid of everything, and I really needed that. He's also just now starting to deal with the loss of his son, and I'm going to be there for him while he works through it."

I took a deep breath.

"Now if you don't like that, I'm sorry, but it's what I'm going to do. I hope you are still planning to come for Thanksgiving because I'd like to invite him to join us."

There was silence on the other end of the phone for far, far too long. I checked the phone, but we hadn't been disconnected.

"Mom?"

"I'm here," she replied tersely. "Just give me a minute."

I bit down on my lip and held my breath. Finally, she spoke again.

"Is he really good to you?" Mom asked quietly.

I let my breath out in one big burst.

"Yes, he is," I confirmed. "He really is."

"It sounds like he has a lot to work through," she commented.

"I know he does. I think he'll be okay, though, eventually."

"I hope you are right." I heard her sigh again.

"So, we're good?" I asked tentatively.

"It's your life, Chloe," Mom said quietly. "I don't have to like all of your choices, but I will respect them."

"I hope you'll give my choice in Aiden a chance."

I heard her sigh.

"I will, dear," she said. "You better invite him to Thanksgiving because I have quite a few questions for him."

"I suppose I can't begrudge you that."

"No, you can't," she agreed. "Now I have to get my flight arranged. It sounds like you do, too."

"Thank you, Mom."

"You are welcome, dear. I love you."

"Love you, too."

I hung up the phone. The call had lasted much longer than I had anticipated, and Mare's wine was catching up to me. I ran off to the bathroom. When I was washing my hands, I looked at my face in the mirror.

I was smiling.

"You really are learning a few things, aren't you?" I asked my reflection. I nodded to myself, just to solidify my feelings. "It's about fucking time, too."

I giggled and then went back to the living room to call Aiden to let him know I was coming for the weekend after all.

And with that, my life started to fall back into place.

NINETEEN

I lay on my back in the jeep, panting.

"Is this going to become a habit after all of Redeye's parties?" I asked, wondering if I was going to have to add a package of wet wipes, tucked away in one of the back corners.

"Depends on if there are shots," Aiden replied.

"There are *always* shots."

"I guess you have your answer." He rolled to his side, propped himself up on his elbow, and gazed down at me with a drunken grin. There was still sweat covering his neck, leaving little droplets making trails through the ink on his chest.

Cool air blew into the back of the jeep, and I shivered. I grabbed the blanket Aiden had so thoughtfully tossed in the back of the jeep before we left his house—as if he knew this was going to happen again. I pulled it up to my chest and wrapped my arms around myself.

"You're beautiful," Aiden said as he reached out and ran his fingers over my arm. "I'm so glad you came back."

"I'm glad I'm here, too."

He ran his hand up and down my arm, warming it with friction. I reached behind his head and pulled his face to mine, nipping at his bottom lip with my teeth and wondering how long this was going to last.

I didn't want it to end.

"Still worried about the job?" Aiden asked.

"Not as much. It will work out eventually."

"Is it okay if I hope it doesn't?"

I looked up, expecting to see his characteristic smirk, but it wasn't there. He was completely serious.

"Why would you say that?" I rolled to face him and leaned against my elbow in the same fashion as he.

"Because it means you might stay here longer," he said with a smile that didn't make his eyes twinkle.

I stroked the side of his face.

"With your cooking, how can I resist?"

Aiden laughed and hugged me against his chest.

"I can't drive," he stated. "I'm still fucked up."

"Me, too," I said.

"I guess we'll lie here a while." Aiden grabbed the edge of the blanket and scooted up against me, wrapping it around us both.

"Seriously, are you two at it again?" Lance called from the sidewalk. I could hear his girlfriend, Jennifer, laughing, too. At least I remembered her name now. "Get a room already!"

"This is better than a room!" Aiden yelled back. "Now fuck off!"

Everyone laughed.

"What's the plan for today?" I asked as I cleared away our breakfast plates.

Aiden sipped his coffee as he tapped the back of one knuckle on his laptop.

"Well, nothing in particular," he said. "I could use some help picking out a head-shrinker."

I looked at the screen to see a list of local psychologists specializing in grief counseling.

"You know they don't really prefer that term," I informed him.

"Tough shit," he replied. "I said I'd do it. That doesn't mean I think it's going to help."

"Thank you for trying anyway." I kissed the top of his head.

We went through the list until we found one with a profile Aiden thought sounded right. It was Sunday, but he wanted to go ahead and leave a voice mail.

"Uh, okay," he said into the phone. "My name is Hunter, and my girlfriend says I need to talk to someone about some shit, so, uh…yeah…call me back sometime."

He left his number, hung up, and tossed his phone onto the kitchen table.

"Really?" I rolled my eyes at him.

"I figure it's best if she knows what she's getting into," Aiden explained. "I'm a cranky son-of-a-bitch."

"No, you aren't."

"I can be," he argued but didn't meet my eyes as he spoke. "I don't want to do this, Chloe. I will, but I don't want to."

His hands were shaking a little, just enough for me to notice. I stepped up beside him and placed my hand on his shoulder.

"Do you want to talk to me about it?" I asked softly. We'd spent some time talking about Cayden over the last day, but it was clearly painful for him.

"No." He leaned back in the chair and rubbed the heels of his hands in his eyes. "Not today."

"We need to find something fun to do, then," I suggested. "Maybe we need to ride a whale or go skinny dipping with piranhas."

That made him laugh.

"Maybe slightly less adventurous," Aiden said with a smirk.

"Outside sounds good. Maybe start with a walk on the beach?"

"Don't you have enough shells by now?" Aiden got up from the table and placed his coffee cup in the sink.

All right, he had a point. I'd found one of his empty moving boxes and nearly filled it with shells I had found in the sand.

"Well, it would be nice to do something outdoors," I replied. "What were you thinking of?"

"There are a few indoor games I know." Aiden waggled his eyebrows at me.

"You have a one-track mind!" I accused.

"Hide the cock is a great game." He wrapped his arms around

me and backed me into the wall separating the kitchen from the living room. He found my neck with his lips and started running kisses up to my ear. "I know just the place, too. You'll never find it."

"I have the feeling I'll be able to tell where it is."

"I can be very sneaky," he said.

"But not very subtle!"

His hands trailed up my sides, and he started wriggling his fingers, tickling my sides. I was insanely ticklish and immediately pushed at his hands and tried to escape.

"Stop it!" I screeched, but I couldn't stop laughing. I ducked under his arm and ran for the living room. There were too many boxes around to move very quickly, and he was right behind me.

"Not a chance!" Aiden grabbed me around the waist and tackled me to the ground. I landed safely on the carpet with his arms wrapped around me.

In the kitchen, Aiden's phone went off, but he ignored it.

Aiden rolled me onto my back, and his mouth was on mine a moment later, but he kept tickling me while simultaneously trying to push my shorts down. I kept screeching. He paused for a moment to let me catch my breath, and I heard the distinct sound of tires on the stone driveway as the phone began to ring again.

"Cut it out!" I squealed as he managed to get his hand into the front of my shorts. "Your phone is ringing, and someone's here!"

"Don't care," he said. His fingers were sliding between my legs, rubbing against my clit and causing me to feel lightheaded.

"Aiden!"

The phone rang again. I couldn't hear anyone coming to the door and wondered if I had been mistaken. Maybe someone was just turning around in the driveway.

"Are you going to get that?" I giggled and pushed at his shoulders without success.

"Nope," Aiden said. "I have better things to do."

I felt the button and zipper on my shorts release, giving Aiden better access to me. I was moaning, but not giving up. I twisted my legs around and tried to push him off of me that way, but it was futile. The person trying to call was just as insistent.

"Dammit!" Aiden said with a growl. "I'm going to kill whoever keeps calling!"

"Ugh! Just answer it already!"

Aiden pushed himself off of me and stomped into the kitchen. I started to follow, zipping my shorts back up along the way. There wasn't any reason to make things easier on him, and I was enjoying the game.

"How the fuck did they get the address? Christ, Mo!"

I fluffed up my hair. The carpet had already tangled it all up. Aiden's escapades were murder on my hairstyle.

"Chloe, get in the bedroom," Aiden said.

"What?" I asked as I paused outside the kitchen to adjust my shirt. I heard another noise outside and tilted my head to look out the window at a red sedan in the driveway. It looked familiar, but I couldn't place it right away.

Aiden was suddenly beside me again, grabbing me by the waist and pulling me back into the kitchen. My feet slipped out from under me, and I nearly fell.

"Don't look out there!" he yelled. He grabbed my arm roughly and yanked me to his chest.

"Aiden!" I cried as he pulled me backward. "What the hell?"

"How far away is Lo?" Aiden said into the phone, ignoring my protests.

I turned to look back at his pale face. He was looking from the front door to the back quickly. The phone was wedged between his jaw and his shoulder, and his eyes were wide.

"He better hurry. They're already here," Aiden said bluntly before he let the phone drop to the ground.

I screamed as I heard a crashing sound from behind me. Glass was suddenly everywhere—all over the kitchen and part of the living room. The top half of the sliding door to the patio had been smashed.

Aiden dragged me toward the counter and grabbed one of the larger kitchen knives just as I saw a huge rock slam into the bottom half of the patio door, adding to the shattered glass on the floor. The two people who were just outside now stepped through the broken door.

I knew who they were immediately, even before I realized the car in the driveway had been the same one that sped off from the strip mall. I recognized them as the man and woman who had been firing guns at the restaurant's back door as they fled. These were the people responsible for the death of Aiden's son.

Chris Marc and Corinne Hayden were in the house, and I was staring right down the barrel of the gun in Corinne's hand. Chris had one pointed at Aiden, and the cold smile on his face stopped my heart.

It wasn't a dream. We weren't "Red Shirts" in a movie or television series. There were people in Aiden's house, people with one thing on their minds. They weren't vampires, and I didn't have any stakes. They weren't supervillains, and I wasn't wearing any bulletproof bracelets. They weren't going to offer us some long discussion about how their plans weren't to be foiled.

In fact, only three syllables were uttered.

"Say bye-bye," Corinne said.

"No!" Aiden screamed.

Everything happened so quickly, but I remembered every second of it like it was etched into my brain. There was a flash from Corinne's gun. At the same time, the front door burst open, and I heard Lo's voice.

"HUNTER!"

Aiden was in front of me so fast, I never saw him move. He was just there, blocking my view of Chris and Corinne as a blast made my ears ring so badly I went deaf for a moment. Then Aiden was on the floor at my feet, and Lo and Mo appeared around the corner from the kitchen with guns in their hands, screaming at Chris and Corinne to get down.

Seconds really can last a lifetime.

There was blood on the tiles, seeping through a hole in Aiden's shirt. I was sure it hadn't been there a moment ago. I blinked a few times and shook my head. I still couldn't hear properly. The kitchen knife had fallen from Aiden's hand and bounced underneath the table.

"Aiden?"

Mo had Chris down on the carpet near the back door, surrounded by glass, his knee in the center of Chris's back. Chris was screaming about being cut. Lo had Corinne up against the wall, yelling at her to stop moving as he clamped handcuffs around her wrists.

I blinked again. Aiden's head rolled slightly to the side, nudging against my foot. I knelt slowly, unable to fathom what was happening around me, and placed my hand on his chest. My hand got sticky, and red fluid oozed between my fingers. I didn't understand where it was coming from.

"Aiden?" I slipped my hand under his head, pulling it onto my thigh. His eyes closed briefly and then opened again, staring up, but not seeing anything. I place my other hand on the side of his face, smearing his cheek with red. There was shouting all around me, but nothing made sense. I felt cold, and my mind was blank.

Flashing lights.

Sirens.

There was noise all around me. Unfamiliar voices spoke quickly and violently as the room filled with people. My knees hurt as I knelt on the tile floor with Aiden's head in my lap. He was staring up at me with blank eyes, and his chest rose and fell with quick, staccato breaths. He was shaking. No…wait…*I* was shaking as I held him.

A woman in a blue uniform was speaking to me, but I couldn't comprehend her words. A man in white and green crouched in front of me and held Aiden's wrist between his fingers.

"Please, ma'am, we need you to back away."

I looked toward the sound of the man's voice but didn't move. Arms were linked around my shoulders, pulling me from the floor as the man took Aiden's head and laid it on top of a rolled up towel.

"Aiden? Aiden!"

"I got you." Lo's voice was in my ear as his arms went around my shoulders, pulling me back. "Take a breath, Chloe. I got you."

More people dressed in white and green gathered around with bags in their hands, blocking my view. I knew in the back of my mind that something was seriously wrong, but I couldn't grasp what it was. What was the red on the floor? Why wasn't Aiden moving?

My head jerked back as it all hit me.

The barrel of the gun, pointed right at me. Aiden's quick movement. The blast. Aiden on the floor, covered in blood.

"Aiden's been shot!" I screamed.

Frantic now, I tried to escape from the arms holding me back. My legs were weak, and they refused to hold me upright any longer. Lo's voice was in my ear.

"I know. I know, babe. They're going to take care of him. We just need to let them do their jobs now."

"No!" I kept struggling but was becoming weaker by the moment. None of this was right. None of this made any sense. This could not possibly be happening. My peripheral vision darkened. Everything else went fuzzy as dizziness overcame me. None of my muscles would respond to my mental commands, and I started to fall as darkness surrounded me.

A moment later, I was on the couch in the living room with a blanket pulled up to my chest. My feet were resting on top of a pillow, and there was a woman in green kneeling beside me.

"Chloe?"

"Is she awake?" Lo's face loomed above me.

"Can you tell me your full name?" the woman asked.

"Chloe Ellison," I replied automatically.

"What's your address, Chloe?"

I rattled it off as I tried to raise my head and look around the room.

"Where's Aiden?"

"He's on his way to the hospital," Lo said. "Listen to the nice lady, and then I'll take you there."

"He got shot," I whispered as tears began to fill my eyes. "Lo, she was shooting at me, and he got in the way!"

"Well, you must be someone pretty damn special then, don't you think?"

Four hours.

Aiden had been in surgery for four hours.

No one would tell me anything. Apparently, being the girlfriend meant nothing. The receptionist wouldn't tell us what was happening, and the police kept showing up and asking me all kinds of questions. I tried to answer them, but it all kept coming back to the same thing.

He took a bullet for me.

Eventually, they left. Redeye and Lance came in shortly afterward and spoke to Lo and Mo, heads bent together and glancing at me where I sat and waited in one of those hard, plastic chairs and stared at Aiden's red baseball cap as I held it tightly in my hands. I could hear their conversation, but the words weren't really registering in my head.

"What are they saying?" Redeye asked Lo.

"They're trying to reach his mother," Lo said as he glanced over at me. "They won't talk to any of us."

"Lance, why don't you help Chloe out?" Redeye said. "I'm gonna take care of this."

"I got her." Lance came over to my chair and reached for my hand. "Jennifer gave me some clothes she thought would fit you. Let's get you changed."

"But they haven't found his Mom yet," I protested. "They won't tell me how he is!"

"Leave it to me," Redeye said with a wink. He walked over to the receptionist and leaned against the counter as Lance coaxed me out of the chair and toward the nearby bathroom.

"Do you need help?" he asked.

I could only stare at him. Did I need help? Yes, I did. I needed someone to tell me what the hell was going on behind the large doors marked "SURGERY."

"Come on," Lance said quietly.

He pulled me inside and locked the bathroom door. He closed the toilet lid before sitting me down on it and then filled up the sink with warm water and soap from the dispenser. He took Aiden's cap from me and placed it on the back of the toilet, then pulled off my blood-stained T-shirt and shorts. He left them on the floor as he used some paper towels to wash the blood from my hand and legs.

I just sat there watching the red-stained towels multiply in the trashcan.

Lance pulled out a clean shirt and a pair of yoga pants from the bag and helped me get them on as he tried his best to stare at the floor.

"I'm just gonna put your clothes back in the bag," he said. "I'll make sure they get back to you, okay?"

"Okay," I replied mechanically.

Once I was cleaned up, Lance handed me the cap and led me back to the waiting room and sat me down next to Lo. Redeye was still at the receptionist's desk, but there was another hospital official with them now. I couldn't hear the words, but Redeye was speaking very animatedly.

Another hour passed.

At some point, Redeye came back to the group and sat on the other side of Lo. They talked quietly while I sat and watched the hands of the clock on the wall move incredibly slowly.

"Miss Ellison?" A man in green scrubs with a badge on his shirt walked over to us.

I stood up and took a step forward. Lo did the same.

"Yes?" I croaked.

"You're here for Aiden Hunter, correct?" he said quietly.

"Yes," I whispered.

"I'm Doctor Miller," he said as he shook my hand briefly. "I'm the surgeon who's been working on Aiden."

"How is he?" I couldn't stop the tears, but Lo was right there beside me, holding my hand.

"Well, he's out of surgery now," Doctor Miller said, "and since we haven't been able to locate any next of kin," he paused and glanced at Redeye, who raised an eyebrow, "we're going to let you go see him for a little while."

"Is he going to be all right?" I asked.

"He's not completely out of the woods yet," the doctor said. "The bullet was lodged next to his spine, but I didn't see any cord damage. We had to repair his intestine, and there was a lot of internal bleeding, but we got it all. I can't tell you anything for sure until he's awake, but it looks good right now."

If Lo hadn't been holding on to me, I probably would have fallen to the floor. Mo stepped up on my other side, and they both helped me back into the chair. Redeye crouched down beside me.

"That's good news, Chloe," Redeye said softly as he rubbed my shoulder. "Hunter's a tough one. He isn't going to let this stop him. It's good news—focus on that."

I nodded. Aiden was strong. He'd be okay. I had to believe that because anything else was too painful to think about.

"You can come see him now but just for a minute. He's still going to be out for a while, and we need to let him rest."

"Go ahead, Chloe," Lo said as he gave me a gentle push. "Tell him we're all out here rooting for him."

I followed Doctor Miller through several sets of double doors and down a long hallway. There were doctors and nurses everywhere, some behind desks and others rolling patients around on gurneys. The doctor led me to a glass-walled room, and I looked at a bed with lots of machines surrounding it. He opened the door and motioned me inside.

"I'll give you a couple of minutes alone with him," Doctor Miller said. "Don't try to wake him up or anything, but you can talk to him. You can hold his hand if you want. Just be careful of his IV."

I walked in slowly, fiddling with the cap in my hands. The doctor closed the door behind me partway, leaving just a crack still open. I bit down on my lip and looked at the bed.

Aiden was lying there, hooked up to all kinds of equipment. He had a big plastic mask taped over his mouth, a needle sticking out of his hand, with a tube leading up to an IV bottle. His entire torso was covered in a huge bandage, and there were wires attached to him all over, leading back to the machines around the bed.

I pulled up a chair and sat by his side, leaving the cap to rest in my lap.

"Oh, Aiden," I whispered. I took his hand in mine, but it was limp—lifeless. I swallowed down the sob in my throat and squeezed his fingers gently. "I'm here."

I wiped tears away from my cheek with the back of my hand.

"Everyone is here," I corrected myself. "Mo followed the ambulance, and Lo brought me to the hospital once the paramedics said I was okay. Lance and Redeye are here, too. I don't know how, but I think Redeye convinced them to let me see you."

The machines beeped rhythmically. Aiden remained motionless as scenes from his house flashed in my mind.

"Aiden...I don't even know what to say to you," I admitted. "You saved my life—I'm sure you did. You didn't have to do that, Aiden."

My throat was sore and my voice hoarse. I swallowed a few times before I tried to go on.

"Thank you," I whispered. "Thank you for that."

I tried to blink back more tears, but it didn't help.

"You taught me so much, Aiden. Everything you've done for me...I can't even comprehend this now. You have to hang in there so I can give you a proper thank you. You know that, right? You taught me how to live, but you have to stay with me, you hear that? You have to stay with me."

"Miss Ellison?"

I glanced up at Doctor Miller as I tightened my grip on Aiden's hand.

"Can I stay a little longer?"

"Not just yet," he said. "You aren't technically allowed back here at all, really, but we've made an exception. Right now, Aiden needs to sleep so he can recover. When he's awake and stable, you can come back again."

I nodded, understanding somewhere in my head that he was right, but I didn't like it. I gripped his cap in my free hand and stood up slowly, holding on to Aiden's fingers as long as I could. As I let go, I leaned over and kissed his forehead. I wanted to put the cap on his head just so he would have it with him, but I couldn't with all the equipment in the way.

"I'll be right out in the waiting room," I told him. "I'll see you again soon."

A nurse led me back out through the hospital maze while Doctor Miller checked on Aiden. All the guys stood up when I walked back out.

"How is he doing?" Lo asked.

I tried not to fall apart as I told them how he looked.

"He's gonna be fine," Redeye assured me with a hug. "I know him—he's gonna be just fine."

Lance handed me a tissue from one of the boxes on the tables, and I wiped tears away from my face. It didn't seem to matter—they wouldn't stop. After a few minutes, I managed to catch my breath and calm down a little.

"What did you say to them?" I asked Redeye.

"What do you mean?"

"They weren't going to let me see him. Why did they change their minds?"

"I can be very convincing." He grinned at me.

"I've noticed," I replied. I sniffed and wiped my nose. "So what did you say?"

"Well…" Redeye chuckled, "some people just don't quite understand the situation staring them in the face. They need someone to hold up a mirror just to let them know they're breathing. Once I explained that you were the one he took the bullet for, and that I'd be happy to call a press conference over the whole thing, they saw things my way."

"What happened to them?" I turned to Lo. "What happened to Chris and Corinne?"

"Mo and I kept them covered until the police could take them," Lo said. "I think he's talking to the station now."

Lo nodded toward the doors of the waiting room where Mo was on the phone.

"I don't think they're going anywhere anytime soon," Lance said.

"Fucked with the wrong people," Redeye said. "That's what they did."

"You said it," Lance agreed.

Mo walked back up to us.

"They're being held without bond," he said. "With all the other stuff they're wanted for, this is apparently just icing. Considering they were caught on the scene and everything, they're expected to plead guilty."

"Hunter will be glad to hear that," Lance said.

I tried to find some sense of joy that Chris Marc and Corinne Harper were behind bars and not going anywhere for a long time, but I just couldn't. I kept seeing the image of Aiden on the floor of the kitchen, covered in blood.

I didn't know how long we stayed there in the waiting room. Lance tried to talk me into going to the cafeteria for something, but I wouldn't budge. He ended up bringing me back a sandwich and some coffee, which I tried to consume out of politeness but just couldn't stomach. The sandwich got a little hard, and the coffee went cold before anyone came out to talk to us again.

"Chloe Ellison?" a nurse called from the doorway.

We all stood up.

"You can come back now. He's awake."

A collective sigh escaped us all. I handed Aiden's baseball cap to Lo before I was led down a different set of maze-like corridors to Aiden's room. The setup surrounding Aiden was similar to what I had seen earlier, minus the mask around his face. Instead, there was one of those oxygen tubes taped below his nose.

"Here we are," the nurse said pleasantly.

Aiden opened his eyes and looked over at the door.

"Hey, you," he said. He tried to smile, but it came out as a grimace.

I bit down on my lip, trying to hold back the tears. I would have thought they would dry up eventually, but the supply was apparently endless.

"Hey, yourself," I responded. I sat down in a chair that looked exactly like the one in the recovery room and picked up his hand, wrapping my fingers around his. I felt myself relax as he squeezed back.

The nurse checked his vital signs and then left us alone.

"You're okay?" he asked.

"I'm perfectly fine, thanks to you."

He closed his eyes for a moment and then looked back at me.

"I'm glad."

"I can't say that I agree," I told him. "That was a stupid thing to do, and I'll never be able to thank you enough for it."

"Any time," he said softly.

"You better not."

"If anyone ever points a gun at you again, you can bet your ass I'll be between you and the gun."

I brought his hand to my face and kissed each of his inked knuckles.

"I thought I was going to lose you," I whispered. "When you

were there in the kitchen…and there was so much blood…I couldn't even think."

"I'm okay," he said. "The doctor said so. All the tests were good —no spinal damage. I'm going to be fine."

I leaned my cheek on his hand and bit my lip as I looked down at the bandage.

"I'm okay," he said again. "The only thing that matters to me is that they didn't get *you*."

"She might have missed me,'" I said. "You jumped right in front of her."

"I wasn't going to risk it."

I shook my head at him and was about to say something else about how stupid he was when Redeye appeared in the doorway.

"Thanks, I got it from here," he said to the nurse. He walked over and leaned close to me. "If anyone asks, I'm your brother."

He winked and then looked over at Aiden.

"Well, Hunter," he said, "you look like absolute shit."

Aiden started to chuckle then cringed.

"Motherfucker." He hissed through his teeth and placed his hand over his stomach. "Don't do that."

"Well, someone around here has to be the one to tell ya," Redeye insisted. "I don't think you've looked this bad since that party last spring when you and Clutch decided to turn Disney movies into a drinking game!"

"Oh, don't bring that up," Aiden said. "I still have flashbacks of Clutch naked in the pool, pretending he was a mermaid."

Redeye snickered.

"I'm not going to keep ya," he said. "I just had to see for myself that you were all right. I'll make sure Chloe's taken care of while you're out of commission."

"Thanks," Aiden said. "I appreciate that."

"My pleasure."

Redeye moved to leave but looked back at us from the doorway. His eyes dropped to our linked hands, and he grinned.

"Nothing says love like taking a bullet to the stomach." He turned and sauntered out.

I bit down on my lip, not sure what Aiden's response to the

comment would be. He turned his mouth into a half smile and glanced at me but didn't say anything.

I held his hand and ran my thumb over his fingers. We didn't talk very much—Aiden kept going in and out of sleep as he lay there. We just looked at each other. Words didn't seem to be necessary.

"He was right, you know," Aiden finally said. He looked down at our hands.

"Who was?" I asked.

"Redeye."

"About what?"

He took a deep breath and tightened his hand around mine.

"Why I did it." He licked his lips and met my eyes. "I love you, Chloe. I don't know what I would do if I lost you."

All my blood seemed to pool to my feet. I wasn't expecting anything like this, certainly not given our situation. Despite the hours that had passed since we had been wrestling on the living room floor, it seemed like such a short time ago when we were together, laughing playfully and talking about our plans for the day.

Tragedy has a tendency to bring out strong emotions. It's easy to confuse a bond over a terrible situation for something more. Is that what Aiden was doing now?

No.

It wasn't.

I knew it wasn't, because I loved him, too.

Mare had been right. Despite all the alarms in my head, I had been drawn to Aiden's forthrightness, his willingness to pursue the unknown without fear, his desire to make me a better person, his bright smile, and the boyish twinkle in his eyes. My feelings for him had been growing every second I was with him.

It didn't matter that he didn't look like my usual type or that he drove a motorcycle and had giant muscles covered with tattoos. All of that superficial stuff was just that—superficial. It didn't define him. The real Aiden was underneath it all.

I reached up and ran my fingers over his sweet face.

"I love you, too, Aiden. More than anything."

And with that, our bond was complete.

TWENTY

The day after Aiden was transferred from the intensive care unit, a heavy-set man wearing shorts and a black concert T-shirt came into the hospital room and introduced himself as Justin Walters, one of the hospital's counselors. Aiden glanced at me, but I just shrugged. I didn't know anything about him.

"When injury accompanies tragic or violent circumstances, it's standard for me to come in and have a little chat with you to see how you are doing," Justin informed us. "I'm just here to see how Aiden's coping with everything that's happened."

"I'm fine," Aiden said bluntly.

"Aiden," I said softly, "this might be a great opportunity."

I didn't want to push too hard, but he needed to talk to someone, and I wasn't going to be intimidated by his glare.

"I don't care about being shot," he said. "I'd do it all again in a heartbeat."

"You know that's not what I mean."

Justin started to say something but then stopped and watched us instead. Aiden looked between us, then sighed and pulled his cap off his head. He stared down at it and ran his fingers along the rim before glancing back at me.

"Could we talk about other stuff, too?" Aiden asked.

"Of course," Justin said. "Whatever you would like."

"Okay," Aiden said with another sigh. "Let's talk."

I bit my lip to hide my smile, but Aiden noticed anyway, and responded by rolling his eyes. I leaned over and gave him a quick kiss on the cheek before leaving them alone to talk. I knew it would be difficult for him, but seeing him take the chance brought out a sense of pride in me.

I wondered if it compared to the times he'd pulled me out of my shell.

For the next week, Aiden recovered slowly but steadily. He talked to Justin every day while he was there and seemed to be making a little headway. After the sessions, Aiden would usually tell me a little something about Cayden I hadn't heard before. Sometimes there were tears in his eyes, but he mostly focused on the good memories of times with his son.

I stayed at the hospital as much as I was allowed and spent my nights at Aiden's house. Mo and Lo had found a service that specialized in crime-scene clean up, and most of the mess was gone before I returned. I was extremely grateful for it. If I had walked into a kitchen covered in blood, I probably would have had a meltdown. The patio door had to be boarded up, but Lo said someone would be by in a couple of days to replace the glass. During the cleanup, Lo had found my phone. I hadn't even thought about calling anyone all this time, but when I looked at it, I saw a dozen missed calls and texts —mostly from Mare and my mother.

I called Mare and told her what had happened. After I finally convinced her everyone was fine, I promised to call her again as soon as I was back in town. I called my mother as well. Instead of the freak-out I was expecting, she was surprisingly quiet about the whole thing. She said she was just glad I was all right.

Weird.

Her reaction probably should have set off alarms in my head, but they were surprisingly silent. The very next day, she was walking up to the hospital receptionist's desk as I was waiting for Aiden's session with Justin to end so I could sit with him.

"Mom?" I ran over to her.

Mom turned and gave me a giant hug without a word. Then she

pulled back and held my shoulders at arm's reach as she looked me over.

"You really are okay?" she asked.

"I am, Mom. I'm fine. What are you doing here?"

"Well, it doesn't sound like Thanksgiving is going to work out," Mom said, "and I had this plane ticket that was non-refundable, so I just had it changed to Miami."

I hugged her again as I tried to stop myself from crying. My emotions had been all over the place since the day Aiden was hurt, and I seemed to have no control over them at all.

"Stop that now," Mom said. She pulled tissues from her purse and dabbed at my cheeks before handing them to me. "I want to meet this man who is apparently willing to die for my daughter."

I sniffed and took her hand to lead her down the hallway to Aiden's room. Justin was just leaving, and I waved at him as we passed by. All of a sudden, I realized I hadn't prepared Mom for Aiden's appearance, but it was too late to say anything because we were already at the door to his room before the thought had struck me.

Aiden was sitting up in his bed, his favorite cap sitting backward on his head. He was wearing one of the hospital's gowns, open part way down the front and plainly showing all the tattoos on his arms, across his neck, and down his chest.

Mom stopped in the doorway and just stared.

Aiden looked up from the motorcycle magazine Redeye had brought for him and looked from me to my mother, obviously confused.

"Well," Mom said with a bit of a huff in her voice, "I can't say you were what I was expecting, but then again, I never expected anyone to have to save my daughter's life."

She dropped her purse on a chair and marched over to the side of the bed. Without hesitation, she leaned over and wrapped her arms around his shoulders. Aiden could only look at me, confused, as he reached up and returned her hug.

"Thank you," Mom said quietly. "From the bottom of my heart, thank you for keeping my daughter safe."

Aiden's eyes fluttered closed for a moment, and I saw him take a deep breath.

"Always," he replied.

She pulled back, and I could tell she was trying to subtly look over Aiden's tattoos. She pursed her lips and looked back to his face, glaring a little.

I put my hand over my mouth, terrified of what she was going to say to him as she straightened her shoulders and pointed her finger at his face.

"Now if you ever try to get her to go skydiving again, I will have your balls. You understand me, mister?"

Aiden coughed and sat up a little straighter.

"Uh…yes, ma'am."

"Good!" She pulled up the chair and sat down next to his bed. "Now tell me everything about yourself."

After an hour, it was clear they were hitting it off really well. I had to commend Aiden he hadn't dropped a single F-bomb, and he was definitely on his best behavior. Mom grilled him with questions, and I realized if I had done the same thing, a lot of our misunderstandings might have been avoided from the beginning.

Live and learn.

Despite my protests, Mom had a hotel room arranged. She wasn't comfortable staying at Aiden's house, and I guess I didn't blame her. She stayed near the hospital and visited Aiden every day while she was there. Strangely enough, she got him to open up quite a bit to her about Cayden. Maybe it was a parenting thing, and she just knew all the right things to say, but she even had him laughing as he talked about the first time Cayden puked all over him as a baby.

"I thought projectile vomiting was just in *The Exorcist*," Aiden said. "I had no idea it was a real thing before it was suddenly all over me. And it wasn't just once—he did it over and over again! Then the pediatrician said it was normal, and I'm screaming into the phone that there is no way it can possibly be normal at all, and the whole time, he's spewing down my back as I'm on the phone."

They were both laughing so hard, they had to wipe tears from their eyes.

"All the things no one ever warns you about," Mom mused as she dabbed at her eyes. "If we knew about all of it beforehand, we'd never have children at all."

"Yeah." Aiden cleared his throat and sat up a little. "And then you just wish you could have it all back again."

I ran my hand down his arm, and he looked over to me with a sad smile.

"I can't bring him back," Aiden said quietly. "Even with those shitbags in jail, he's still gone."

"I know," I said as I squeezed his hand.

"The memories of him will live with you forever," Mom replied. "It's hard at first, because your focus is on the loss. In time, you realize how important your relationship was and how much joy you gave to him. Even if it was far too short a time, you made every moment count."

"I wasn't there when he needed me the most," Aiden whispered. "I failed him."

"You did your best," Mom told him. "Success isn't defined by a single moment. Your success came from all of the moments you did have, all of the moments you spent loving him. No one can take that from you. It's yours."

Aiden pressed the heel of his hand against his eye as he tightened his hand around my fingers.

"At least I was there for you," he said under his breath. "I couldn't be there for him, but I was there for you."

I wrapped my arms around his neck and brought his head to my shoulder. Mom came up to the other side and joined in the hug.

The next day she had to head back to San Francisco, and I was sorry to see her go.

"I'm really glad you came," I told her as I gave her a big hug in the hospital waiting room.

"I'm glad I did, too." Mom hugged me back. "I'd tell you to be careful, but I have the feeling Aiden's going to keep a close eye on you as it is. No more crazy stuff."

"We'll see," I said with a smile. "I don't think he'll be up for much in the near future."

"We can make Christmas plans after I get home."

"Definitely."

"Hopefully, you will have found a job by then," she said with a shake of her head. "I still can't believe you did that."

"It's probably best I did," I said. "With all the time I'm spending down here, I might have been fired anyway."

"You might not have been here to get shot at," Mom pointed out.

"True." It wasn't the first time the thought had crossed my mind. "But then Aiden would have been alone, and he might not have come out as well as he did."

Mom nodded, hugged me again, and headed out with her suitcase trailing behind her. I watched her get into the cab and then went back to see Aiden again.

"Everything okay?" he asked as I walked in.

"Yes," I said. "I think she really likes you."

"What's not to like?" Aiden grinned his boyish grin, and I leaned over to kiss his cheek.

"Your cockiness?" I suggested, I sat at the edge of the bed, and Aiden grabbed my hand.

"I was trying to hide that from her."

"Hmm...we'll see if it worked. She's mostly worried about me finding a job at this point. I haven't exactly been searching. I need to get on that."

"You could look for a job down here," Aiden said. His eyes didn't leave our hands.

"What do you mean?"

"Don't get another job in Ohio," Aiden said. "Find a job around here. There has to be something in your field. Don't all companies have projects to manage?"

"Well, yeah, I guess so."

"So find something here."

"Aiden, that's a bit of a jump, don't you think?" I knew people in Ohio. I had contacts and references there. Finding a job in Florida hadn't even crossed my mind.

"Not for me," Aiden said quietly. "I want you to stay."

"Stay where?"

"Here," Aiden said. "Well, not here in the hospital, but here in Miami. I want you to move down here with me."

I considered his words for a moment, and the reality of what he was suggesting suddenly dawned on me.

"You mean, live with you?"

He nodded.

"You are asking me to move in with you?"

"Yeah," he said with a shrug. "Why not?"

"Isn't that a little…premature?"

"Is it?" he asked as he looked into my eyes. "By whose standards?"

"We've known each other just over a month," I said.

He smiled a sweet smile.

"It's enough for me," he stated.

As I looked into Aiden's eyes, I knew his sincerity couldn't be denied. Reclining in the hospital bed, wrapped in bandages, he'd already made it clear he would do anything for me. Having me live in the same house was a drop in the bucket by comparison.

"Well?" he prompted.

"Aiden, I don't know. It wasn't something I had considered, and it's just taken me a little by surprise."

He nodded and pulled my hand up to kiss it.

"Please tell me you'll think about it?"

"I'll think about it," I said.

"Promise?"

"Promise."

He pulled me down to lie next to him on the bed and wrapped his arm around my shoulder. I lay my head against him and tried to imagine what it would be like to live with Aiden all the time. I knew there would be pitfalls; living with someone was never easy. Even having a roommate could be tricky, and both Aiden and I were used to living alone.

What would he think about my superheroine dolls?

On the other hand, Aiden was also going to need someone to help him out when he came home from the hospital. The doctors had already told him that. He could be released in a few days, and I had been talking to Redeye about scheduling all of his friends in shifts. If I moved in with him, they wouldn't have to do that.

Still, it was a risk. What if we found out we didn't get along with each other on a more permanent basis? Would all of my things even fit in his house? He probably had bad habits he'd managed to keep from me when I was just visiting, but those would become apparent if we lived with each other. What if he left the cap off the toothpaste, used my expensive conditioner on his beard, or left toenail clippings on the floor? Worse yet, what if he rescinded his agreement to continue counseling? It was a big risk.

Then again, what was life without risk?

With Aiden back at home and Nate's recruiter calling me to set up interview appointments, I had to return to Ohio to figure out what my next move was going to be. All the flying back and forth was getting to me, not to mention carving into that nest egg I hoped would keep me going until I found a new job. Redeye kept trying to slip me additional money for flights, but I had been adamant about refusing his help.

I couldn't mooch off of Aiden's friends. I wanted to be with him as much as I could, and they were there for him when I couldn't be. Lo came up with a list, and everyone was planning to take turns helping Aiden out while I was in Ohio.

I still hadn't answered him about moving. As much as the idea intrigued me, at some point I had to leave excitement and adventure off to the side and think about real life. I needed a job—a job that would pay well enough for me to be able to afford all these flights.

At least I was racking up the frequent flier miles.

I spent some time at Thirsty's catching up with Mare and our friends. They'd all heard most of the story by now—Mare had spilled the beans right after I called her from the hospital. They all wanted to know everything about Aiden and why I hadn't told them what was going on. It felt strange to talk to them about him, and I realized I had hidden him from them on purpose because I was afraid of how they would react.

I still had a lot to learn.

The job hunt was in full force, and it seemed I had sent resumes and cover letters to every company with an opening. I'd had a couple of interviews, but nothing seemed to fit quite right. The money wasn't enough or the drive was too far. In the meantime, I found out my boss had been fired over the server upgrade fiasco, and I could apply for his position.

I didn't. It felt like moving backwards.

I did a few phone interviews the recruiter set up for me. Eventually, one of them called him back.

"It's the perfect opportunity," Brian said. "The salary is right in your range, and the job description practically matches your resume word for word. You impressed them over the phone, and they said they want you."

"Which one was this?" I paged through my interview notes as Brian gave me the company name. I remembered the woman I had spoken to but couldn't seem to find the company's address. I'd liked her when we spoke over the phone—I definitely recalled that. We'd laughed when we realized we were both into superheroines.

"There's only one catch," Brian said.

"What's that?" I braced myself, waiting to hear the worst. I wasn't sure it was going to matter—I needed the job. I couldn't go forever without a paycheck.

"The company is located in Fort Lauderdale," he said.

My heart began to race.

"Fort Lauderdale," I repeated, "as in Florida?"

"Sunny Florida, yes. You would have to relocate."

"Where is Fort Lauderdale?" I asked. I pulled up Google Maps on my laptop and started to search.

"Just north of Miami, on the eastern coast of Florida."

"You're kidding," I said. I stared at the map on my screen. I located Golden Beach, where Aiden lived, and found it was only a half hour drive to Fort Lauderdale from his house.

"Not at all," he replied. "They want you to start right away if you can. They'll pay all your moving expenses."

I started to laugh.

"Is that a good laugh?" he asked.

"Yes," I said. "Yes, it is. I'll take it. I'll definitely take it."

You never realize how much stuff you have until you try to move it into an already occupied house. Even though I'd sold a lot of my furniture before the move, I still had a ton of items that needed to find a new home in an already engaged space.

"Where do you want this?" one of the moving men asked as he hauled in my bookshelf.

I hadn't even thought about it, but as I glanced around the full living room, I knew there wasn't a place for it.

"I have no idea," I said.

Aiden maneuvered his way through boxes, holding on to his side as he went. He was supposed to be using a cane to get around, but he'd left it by the front door and refused to use it when there wasn't a doctor around to insist.

"Put it in the bedroom down the hall," he said. He pointed toward his weight room.

"Aiden, there's no room for it in there."

"There is now."

I went back to the room to see that it had been completely cleared out. All of the weights and training equipment were gone.

"Where's your workout stuff?" I asked.

"In the other room," Aiden replied with a shrug. "I figured you'd need some space, and this room is bigger than the other one, so I had Mo and Lo move the gym stuff. Besides, this room faces the ocean."

I peeked in and saw that it was true—everything had been moved into the smaller room. All of the boxes that had been in there before were gone.

I walked back into the living room as the moving guy started taking the bookshelf and boxes of books to the cleared-out space. I stood next to Aiden and looked up at his eyes.

"Where did you put the other things?" I asked quietly.

"In the garage," he said. "I was going to go through them, but... well..."

He licked his lips as he looked down the hall. I reached up and put my hand on the side of his face until he looked back at me.

"Maybe once I'm settled in, we can go through them together," I suggested.

"Maybe," Aiden said with a slight nod. He reached out and put his hand on my hip. "I don't know. Not yet."

"When you're ready," I said, "I'll be there to help."

He nodded.

"Thank you, Aiden."

"For what?"

"For giving me a place for my things." I reached up with my other hand and hugged him around his neck. "All of this has happened so quickly, I didn't think about everything."

"I want you to be happy here," he said simply. "Everyone needs some space."

I ran my hands over his shoulders and down his arms, gripping his hands lightly before I reach around his middle and gave him a big hug.

Aiden's muscles tightened up, and he grunted.

"Oh, crap!" I said, stepping back and pulling my hands away. "I was trying to stay away from the bandage!"

"It's not that," Aiden said. He gave me half a smile. "I was going to show you later."

"Show me what?"

Aiden grabbed the edge of his shirt and pulled it up as he turned around. The small spot on his lower back that had been devoid of ink was now covered with an elaborate tattoo of a conch shell with "Chloe" scripted over the center of the image.

I blinked a couple of times as I focused on the design. The skin around the tattoo was still red and looked sensitive.

"You…you got a new tattoo?"

"Yeah." Aiden chuckled.

"For…for me?"

"Yeah, for you. How many Chloes do you think I know?"

I was shocked and honestly didn't know how to respond.

"The kayak trip was our first real date," Aiden explained. "You liked that conch so much, and now whenever I see one, I think of you. I thought it fit."

I swallowed hard, but words wouldn't form.

"Do you like it?" he asked nervously.

I tore my eyes away from the design and looked up at his face.

"I love it," I whispered. "It's beautiful."

Aiden turned back around, letting his shirt drop before he brought his hand up and cupped the back of my neck. He leaned down close to me and whispered in my ear.

"*You* are beautiful."

I wrapped my arms around his neck and kissed him.

"I love you, Aiden Hunter."

"I love you, too, Chloe Ellison."

And with that, everything began to fall into place.

EPILOGUE

"Where do you keep the cheese grater?" I called to Aiden.

"In the top drawer, right side of the stove."

"Found it!"

Living with Aiden was fantastic. Trying to get around in his kitchen was not.

I had no idea how he originally organized the place, if it could be called organized at all, but I couldn't seem to find anything without asking Aiden where it was hidden. He had pans where I would have put dishes, towels where the silverware ought to be, and spices were apparently supposed to be kept in the garage on a rack near the door.

Moving into someone else's house was a bit of a challenge. As if there hadn't been enough boxes around before, now all of mine were added to the mix. At least the room Aiden had cleared for me was finally taking shape as a guest room. There was plenty of room for my bookshelf, and my superheroines now had a great view of the Atlantic. Mom was due for her visit in a couple of hours. Mo and Lo still came over when we needed to move furniture or heavy boxes around. Aiden still wasn't allowed to do anything strenuous, and the weight room had gone unused.

He claimed he was losing his gains, whatever the hell that meant.

"Okay, now where's the cheese?" I crammed my head further into the refrigerator, but no cheese was magically appearing. When

Aiden didn't respond, I clambered out and walked into the living room.

He was on the floor, leaning against the couch, with a large box to one side of him. It was full of toys Cayden had played with. Justin had set a goal for Aiden to go through one box a week, but he hadn't been doing very well with the task. The process didn't seem to upset him, but he had a memory for every item he came across. He usually decided he needed to keep it all and ended up just putting everything back in the box.

Still, it was a start.

"Aiden?" I said again. "Where's the cheese?"

He dropped a Teenaged Mutant Ninja Turtle action figure back into the box and looked up at me, his expression blank.

"What?" he asked.

I knelt down beside him.

"You doing okay?" I asked.

Aiden reached into the box and pulled out a plastic Batman figurine.

"I suppose," he said unconvincingly. "I was just thinking."

"About?"

"My Mom, actually." He glanced up at me. "She never met Cayden."

"Oh." I wasn't sure how to respond, so I sat down next to him and put my arms around his shoulders.

"I was…well, I was kind of thinking about calling her."

"You were?"

"Yeah, Justin and I talked about it yesterday. The thing is, I have no idea what to say to her."

"Maybe you could just start with hello," I suggested.

"Yeah, that's what he said." Aiden leaned his head against the top of mine. "It just doesn't seem like enough. I haven't talked to her in eight years."

"That does make it difficult," I agreed, "not impossible, though. I think dialing the number might be the hardest part."

"Yeah, it is." He lifted his head and placed the figurine back in the box. "What were you asking me before?"

"I was trying to find the cheese," I said, remembering.

"I think I used the last of it."

"Ugh!" I sighed stood back up. "I guess I'm heading to the store."

"Cool," Aiden said. "There are a few things we need, so I started a list. It's in the bathroom."

"In the *bathroom?*" I crossed my arms as I stared at Aiden.

"Yeah, it's a great place to think."

"About food?"

"Well…sure! I mean, it's the logical end, ya know?"

"You are not right in the head."

"Never claimed to be!" He grinned as I tossed my hands up and went to find the list.

With my purse in hand, I climbed into the jeep and headed to the supermarket. Driving the monster vehicle around had been a bit of a challenge at first, but I was getting the hang of it. It just didn't having the turning radius I was used to, and I kept hitting curbs.

After parking successfully for once, I headed inside. I looked over the list as the cart I had chosen wobbled down the aisle on a bad wheel. I probably should have taken it back and chosen another one, but I wanted to get back to Aiden as quickly as possible. He wasn't quite healed yet, and I didn't like leaving him alone for too long.

I gathered up zucchini, mushrooms, spinach for a salad, and more eggs. Damn, Aiden ate a lot of eggs. Toothpaste was on the list, so I headed over to the pharmacy section of the supermarket. There was a green toothbrush just like the one Aiden had for me that first day, and it made me smile.

I glanced around, wondering if we needed anything else. I wasn't even sure where Aiden kept extra toilet paper, but figured I should get some. Men just didn't seem to stock up on the same things women did.

Then I stopped.

Alarm!

I focused on the display in front of me and felt my heart rise into my throat. Silently, I counted. Had it been the fifth of the month? The sixth? It had been almost two weeks since I moved down here officially…what was the date today? No wait…that was last month, not this month. This month was…was…

Oh, shit.

Leaving the cart in the aisle, I walked up to the pharmacy desk and picked up a little blue and white box. I bought it and headed straight to the restroom.

By the time I returned from the restroom, my cart had disappeared, and I had to do all the shopping again.

I sat in the jeep in the driveway, gripping the wheel with my hands and trying to come to grips with the thoughts in my head.

It wasn't working. I couldn't even decide how I felt about it. Everything was still so new, so uncertain. Major life changes were also major stressors, and those would impact a relationship. I'd just moved, just changed jobs, and Aiden was still recovering from a bullet wound.

I rubbed my hand over my stomach.

Had he saved more than one life?

I opened the jeep's door and walked slowly over the driveway stones, staring at my feet as I went. I unlocked the front door and stepped inside. Aiden was on the couch, watching *The Avengers*. The box of toys was off to the side, apparently abandoned. He looked half asleep but glanced up as I came through the doorway.

"Hey, babe," Aiden said as his eyes met mine. "Where are the groceries?"

I glanced back at the front door as if I expected them to be walking in on their own.

"Uh, I left them in the car."

He narrowed his eyes and tilted his head as he looked at me.

"Do you need help with them? I'm allowed to lift stuff now if it's under twenty pounds."

"No, I can get them." I walked slowly into the room, still staring at my feet, and sat down on the couch. I motioned toward the television. "Um, can we turn that off a minute?"

"Sure," he said. He grabbed the remote from the floor and paused the movie. "What is it?"

I could hear my heart pounding. I found I was unable to look him in the eye as I tried to figure out what words I should use. While in the car, I'd played it over in my head so many times, so many scenarios, so many outcomes.

I really didn't know how he was going to respond. He was only now beginning to recover from losing his son, and there was no predicting how he would react to this. I wasn't entirely sure how I felt about it yet.

"Chloe?" Aiden prodded. He gripped my thigh with his hand. "What's going on in that head of yours?"

I licked my lips. There was no getting out of it now—he knew something was up.

"I have something I need to tell you," I said slowly.

Aiden stilled. His arms and legs tensed.

"When I was at the store, I, uh…" I trailed off, the words still not coming. Was it best to just blurt it out? Ease into it? Come up with some other topic altogether and try again in the morning?

No, I couldn't do that. I had to get this out.

"I thought something was a little…well, a little off."

"What do you mean, *off?*"

"I hadn't been paying attention," I said quickly. "With you in the hospital and everything, I just wasn't keeping track. I didn't realize what it was at first, but then I checked, and…"

I was babbling.

"Chloe, for Christ's sakes, spit it out!"

Deep breath. In. Out.

"I figured out I was late," I finally said, "like, really late. Over a month. So I took a test."

Aiden's eye's widened, and his face paled.

"Are you…?" He didn't complete the thought, but I saw him glance at my stomach.

"Yes," I whispered.

"How far?" he asked. "I mean, how far along?"

"I'm not sure. I think a couple of months, at least. I haven't gotten my period since…well, since I went back to Ohio that first time."

He watched me closely as his fingers wrapped a little tighter around my leg.

"How do you feel about it?" he asked quietly.

"I don't really know," I replied. "Terrified, more than anything else."

"Do you…do you want to…I mean, do you want to have it?"

"I wasn't sure if you would want to."

"Oh, Chloe," Aiden whispered as he sat up and took my face in his hands, "I can't think of anything I'd want more."

"Really?" The tears escaped and flowed down my cheeks.

"Don't you?" he asked, his voice serious.

I had spent more time worrying about Aiden's reaction than I had considering my own feelings. Every time we had sex, there was always that little twinge in the back of my head, telling me I'd never gotten on birth control. I knew I was taking a risk, but thoughts of the actual consequences hadn't really taken hold.

Now the risk was reality.

How did I feel about it? I didn't believe I was ready to be a parent, but what new parent did? The thought of a little child with Aiden's bright, playful eyes made me feel warm inside.

I remembered my mother's conversations with Aiden about babies and how happy he was talking about his son as an infant. Of all people, I would have expected him to be the most hesitant to try parenthood again, but he really wanted this.

I looked into his eyes as he awaited my answer, and I knew I wanted it too.

Ready or not, here I come!

"Yes," I said. "Yes, I do, Aiden. I really do."

He let out a sigh as a smile spread over his face.

"Good," he whispered under his breath. He reached over and pulled me against him, his grip tight around my shoulders. "You had me worried there for a second."

"I'm a little petrified," I admitted.

"Me, too," he said. "Mostly excited, though."

"Me, too." I snuggled against his bicep and closed my eyes.

"You realize what this means?" Aiden asked.

I raised my head and looked into his eyes.

"What?"

"I have a reason to call Mom."

Aiden brought his fingers up and stroked my cheek. I leaned against his hand and watched his face break out in that beautiful, boyish smile. His eyes twinkled, and he kissed me.

Yes, it was going to be difficult, but I couldn't spend my life thinking about all the things that could possibly go wrong. That wasn't life; that wasn't *living*. There were so many things to consider and so many tough times ahead, but we would learn from them and be stronger for having taken the risks. Aiden and I would face them head on. We would hold hands, lean forward, and take that jump together.

And with that, I accepted life's risks—the joys and the heartaches —everything that it meant to *live*.

THE END

OTHER TITLES BY SHAY SAVAGE

THE EVAN ARDEN TRILOGY

OTHERWISE ALONE - EVAN ARDEN #1
OTHERWISE OCCUPIED - EVAN ARDEN #2
OTHERWISE UNHARMED - EVAN ARDEN #3

SURVIVING RAINE SERIES

SURVIVING RAINE - SURVIVING RAINE #1
BASTIAN'S STORM - SURVIVING RAINE #2

STANDALONE TITLES

TRANSCENDENCE

WORTH

ABOUT THE AUTHOR

Always looking for a storyline and characters who fall outside the norm, Shay Savage's tales have a habit of evoking some extreme emotions from fans. She prides herself on plots that are unpredictable and loves to hear it when a story doesn't take the path assumed by her readers. With a strong interest in psychology, Shay loves to delve into the dark recesses of her character's brains–and there is definitely some darkness to be found! Though the journey is often bumpy, if you can hang on long enough you won't regret the ride. You may not always like the characters or the things they do, but you'll certainly understand them.

Shay Savage lives in Cincinnati, Ohio with her family and a variety of household pets.

She's an avid soccer fan, loves vacationing near the ocean, enjoys science fiction in all forms, and absolutely adores all of the encouragement she has received from those who have enjoyed her work.

18008584R00155

Made in the USA
San Bernardino, CA
23 December 2014